ALMOST *Beautiful*

Almost Beautiful
Beautiful Disaster Series (Book Five)
Jamie McGuire

Edited by Karin Enders
Formatted by Alyssa Garcia
Cover Design by Hang Le

First edition.

ALMOST *Beautiful*

JAMIE McGUIRE

#1 NEW YORK TIMES AND INTERNATIONAL BESTSELLER

Also by Jamie McGuire

Providence
Requiem
Eden
Sins of the Innocent
Sins of the Immortal

Beautiful Disaster
Walking Disaster
A Beautiful Wedding
Almost Beautiful

Something Beautiful: A Novella

Beautiful Oblivion
Beautiful Redemption
Beautiful Sacrifice
Beautiful Burn
A Beautiful Funeral

From Here to You
The Edge of Us

Red Hill
Among Monsters

Happenstance: A Novella Series (Parts 1-3)

Apolonia

To Jessica Landers
My right hand, my right brain, my therapist, my biggest cheerleader, my ride or die, my best friend. In a very literal sense, there would be no me without you.

CHAPTER *One*

NEWLYWEDS

Abby

FINALLY, WE WERE ALONE.

Travis towered over the bed and our luggage, quietly separating our dirty laundry.

We couldn't even call our quick trip to Las Vegas a whirlwind—it was a hurricane; one that had no end in sight. We'd run to elope, hunkered down for a family meeting with Shepley and America, and Trenton and Camille to go over the new story of our whereabouts, and now it was just the two of us in our apartment, waiting in the eye of the storm. Sure, it was quiet, but knowing what was coming was almost worse.

Travis had been silent for the most part since we'd gotten home from his dad's to break the news of our elopement.

Jim took it well. Better than well, he was ecstatic, but he could tell there was something else looming over us. Now that the whole nation knew about the fire, I could tell Jim didn't want to ask.

"Trav, you've been quiet. What are you thinking about?"

He held my wedding dress in front of him, and after several seconds he laid it carefully onto our comforter. "Nothing."

"Nothing?" I repeated, dubious.

"Mostly about the few hours between the wedding and leaving for the airport. It wasn't long enough."

I crawled across the bed, over the laundry, and clasped my fingers behind his neck. "Agreed. It felt like a different dimension. But on the bright side, we can have as many nights alone as we want."

Travis smiled, but it was strained. He looked over to my dress again. The satin and tulle were a bit wrinkled and ruffled, in part from travel but mostly from our wedding night.

Travis was right, it hadn't been enough time—those magical, perfect hours between our *I do*s and the plane ride home—but we'd made the most of them.

Even though Travis had kissed me, touched me, held me many times before, his excitement for the wedding and that he could call me his wife, those once-familiar things had all felt new. As we consummated our marriage over and over again, Travis convinced me he wanted nothing and no one else, that being my husband was the most important thing to him in the world.

I kissed his cheek and then returned to my spot on the bed, watching him resume sorting laundry. In truth, there wasn't much, but he made sure to turn each article of clothing right side out and laid it flat, something he'd never taken the time to do before, as evidenced by the four older piles on the floor.

Travis seemed determined to get lost in mundane chores, anything to keep his mind off the questions and worries swirling inside of him.

I held up my left hand, staring at my diamond ring the way Travis had revered my wedding dress just moments before. I wiggled my fingers, enjoying the way the diamond caught the light, and then noticed Travis staring at me as he came into focus just beyond my hand. One side of his mouth turned up into a half-smile and he laughed once.

"Still okay?" he asked for the third time since we'd arrived home.

"Still Mrs. Maddox," I said. "So… yes. But I wish we had more time before classes start up again."

"We can skip a few days," he said with a smirk.

At first, I thought he was joking, but when his gaze met mine, he dropped the clothes in his hand and walked around to the other side of the bed to sit next to me. He scanned my face with his warm, brown eyes, a day's worth of scruff on his jaw. He was still as breathtaking as the day I'd met him, his inked skin pulled tightly over his lean, cut muscles.

The tattoos covering his arms varied from artistic to tribal, but none were as precious to him as my nickname scrolled in delicate cursive across his wrist, or the phrase in Hebrew along his rib cage, spanning from under his arm to the crest of his hip. It read, *I belong to my beloved, and my beloved is mine*—and I was.

Officially.

I'd even gotten a new tattoo in Vegas: *Mrs. Maddox*. For someone who'd never considered getting a tattoo before, I couldn't stop staring at it ... or my new husband.

Husband. The word would forever give me butterflies, I was sure of it.

He nuzzled my neck, pressing tiny kisses on certain very lucky patches of skin. "I have never been so tempted in my life, but I have statistics this semester. Not a class I want to miss."

"You'll do fine," he said. "You solve problems the way I throw punches."

"Nothing is that beautiful."

He leaned back to catch my expression, a dozen emotions scanning across his face. His eyebrows pulled in, finally settling on adoration. "My wife is."

"I don't think hearing you call me that will ever get old."

"Good. Then I don't have to feel so stupid about how happy it makes me."

He turned my head and planted his lips on mine, forcing his other hand between my back side and the bed, making every inch of my skin beg to be touching some part of him.

"Do we have time for this?" he asked.

"We're newlyweds, we'll make time," I said, scooting further down on the mattress.

Travis reached back to grab his shirt and then pulled it up and over, tossing it to the pile of clothes on the other side of the bed. He slipped my black leggings off with ease, and then kissed me for a few moments more before reaching down and sliding his fingers beneath the cotton fabric of my panties.

I breathed out, a small whimper slipping with it. That tiny sound made Travis's movements less patient, and he yanked down his shorts and, without pause, thrust himself inside me.

Once he was fully seated, he forced himself to pause, his faltering breath hot against my ear.

"I should … slow down … I'm gonna …"

"Don't," I said, locking my ankles behind him. "Not this time."

He paused for just a few more seconds—long enough to kiss me—but once he moved again, slow wasn't something he could manage. He rocked into me over and over, his arms shaking, so lost in the feeling that he ignored the performance of it all and allowed every nerve to be overwhelmed with the way his skin felt surrounded and caressed by mine.

"Pidge …"

"Don't stop," I whispered.

He felt as different as he did familiar, letting go of his control as he finished.

"God, you feel good … God da—" He groaned through his climax, trembling, holding himself inside me as he came.

We were both breathing hard, but then he inhaled, deep and slow, and then sighed. "Damn, I'm sorry."

"Sorry for what?" I asked, smiling as I kissed his cheek.

"I got a little carried away."

“And that’s a bad thing?” I asked, keeping my leg hooked over him as he lay next to me.

He stared at the ceiling. “That wasn’t making love to you, that was blowing off steam.”

“I’m not mad about it.”

He looked over at me. “Why do you love me so much? I think I’m a fuck up and you just … understand me. You already know before I ever explain.”

“I don’t know,” I said, running my fingers over his whiskers.

“Probably not a good sign,” he said, only half kidding.

“Well, I don’t love you because of the way you look, that’s infatuation. I don’t love you because of our sexual chemistry, that’s lust. I don’t love you because you love me, that’s empathy. I don’t love you because of what you can give me or what you can do for me, that’s transactional. I don’t love you because of the way you treat me, that’s gratitude. I don’t love you because you keep me safe, that’s security. I don’t know why I love you, babe. That’s how I know it’s real.”

Travis pressed his lips together and shook his head, touching his nose to mine.

I closed one eye tight. “We should probably …”

He turned onto his back with a groan. “I know … I know. How about this weekend we just take a day?”

“I’m on board.”

Travis stood, reaching for my hand and pulling me upright. We couldn’t help but smile as we dressed, and then I took a look around our bedroom and perched my hands on my hips, blowing an errant strand of hair from my face.

"It's not that much, Pidge. We can knock it all out this evening."

"I know, it's just … nothing. Never mind. You know," I said, taking another long, hard look, "it just hit me how different your room looks from when we met."

Travis scanned the paint between each corner. Just a few months before, a lone sombrero hung from his wall, now frames holding black and white photographs hung in its place and everywhere else. Moments of us from every stage of our relationship: friends, enemies, and lovers. It wasn't surprising that in every shot we were smiling or that Travis was touching me in some way.

I'd missed our bedroom, but the last time we were in it I was proposing to Travis, his face smeared with soot from the fire not long before.

A hint of smoke still hung in the air.

"What's that look?" Travis asked, his body stiffening.

"Nothing," I said.

"It's not nothing. I'm going to make you happy; I want you to know that. To believe that. It won't be that different, except we come home to each other every night. Doesn't sound that bad …"

I tilted my head. "*That bad*? Travis, stop. You act as if I'm going to change my mind at any moment."

"Are you?"

I frowned.

His shoulders sagged. "I'm sorry. I can't help it."

I took a few steps until I was just a couple of inches from him. "Look at me. Right here," I said, using my index and middle fingers to point to my own eyes. "I won't change my mind, Trav. I am so, *so* happy. I promise."

His muscles relaxed. "I keep trying to push the thought out of my head, but it won't go away."

"It's been a rollercoaster. I don't blame you for feeling that way, no one would."

He nodded and offered a contrived smile. "Okay. I won't mention it again."

"Yes, you will. Because if you don't, I can't reassure you. And I will, a million times if I have to."

"God, I love you, Pidge."

I pushed up on the balls of my feet and kissed the tip of his nose. "I love you. We'd better get this laundry started so we can relax tonight."

Travis took an empty basket to the end of the hall. The dryer door opened and then the washer, then Travis returned with warm, fresh and dry clothes to fold.

I reached for a towel and began folding it. "Shep and Mare seem to be on board."

He nodded, and as quickly as he'd relaxed, he seemed to retreat back into his shell.

"Your dad is happy. And no matter what America says, she's happy, too. Shepley scored a room at Helms Hall. It's like it was all meant to be."

"That was … tough," Travis said.

"Which part?"

"Asking Shep and Mare to lie. Not telling Dad the truth."

"They weren't there. They're not lying … they're just … forgetting the phone conversation we had before we left. Emotions were high. They don't remember."

"I don't want anyone to get in trouble for me. Least of all you."

"No one's getting in trouble. It's handled."

Travis met my gaze. "Handled, huh?"

"You know what I mean." I gathered one of the piles into my arms and turned for the door, wondering if Travis felt as content and yet displaced in our new marriage as I did.

"Where you going?" Travis asked, tense.

I motioned with a tiny twist of my upper body toward the hall. "Laundry." He made a face, and I laughed. "I'll be just down the hall, baby."

He nodded, but I could tell he was still worried about our marriage being erased somehow, as if it hadn't really happened. That the moment I was out of his sight, he would wake up in bed alone.

I passed the doorway to the living room, stopping less than two feet later to push the folding door aside, revealing the stacked washer and dryer. The unit was loud, yellow tinged, and older than I was, but it worked well enough. I only put in half the load I was holding, knowing the tiny drum couldn't handle more than that. Just after I poured in the detergent, twisted the knob and closed the lid, someone knocked on the door.

I let the rest of the clothes fall to the floor and stepped over them to hurry across the living room. I peeked out of the peephole and swallowed, taking a moment to gather my thoughts before opening the door.

"Hi," I said, trying to seem surprised.

The police officers were in plain clothes—meaning they were detectives—and they didn't seem at all surprised to see me.

"Miss Abernathy?" the one on the left asked. He was round, his belly bulging over his belt buckle, and his worn tweed blazer was a bit small. The badge just over his jacket pocket read *Gable*.

His partner, Williams, was smartly dressed in a purple button-down and matching tie. He crossed his arms, his smooth, dark complexion the opposite of Gable's rosy skin and freckles.

"I was. I'm Mrs. Maddox now," I said, knowing Gable was confirming, not asking.

"Oh? We're looking for Travis Maddox. Your… husband?"

"Yes. He's here. He's in the restroom," I said, hoping Travis couldn't hear us over the sound of the washer. It would be much easier to cover for him if he stayed hidden in the bedroom. I needed to prepare him. He wasn't as good of a liar as I was because he hadn't needed to be. I couldn't remember him ever telling a lie in the seven months since we'd met.

"Can we step in for a moment? We need to speak with him," Williams said.

"Is this about the fire?" I asked.

The detectives traded glances, already feeling like they were a step ahead. "Yes," Gable said. "What can you tell me about it?"

"I saw it on the news. As soon as we unpack, we're going to his fraternity house. He lost some of his brothers. He's heartbroken," I said, knowing that part wasn't a lie.

"You said you're his wife," Gable prompted. "That's new?"

"We eloped this weekend. To Vegas. We came home early because of the fire."

Gable narrowed his eyes. "We have a few eyewitnesses who said Travis might've been in the building at the time of the fire. They've made statements that he was a regular opponent in the, uh"—he looked at his notepad—"floating fight ring." He enunciated each word as if he were speaking a foreign language.

"I mean ... I guess it's illegal to lie to you," I said, hanging on to the edge of the door. The men leaned in, eager to hear my confession. "We've been to a few. There's not a lot to do in Eakins." I snorted, and then pretended to be uncomfortable and awkward when they didn't find my joke funny.

Gable leaned over, noticing something behind me. "Mr. Maddox?"

I turned, seeing Travis frozen in the hallway.

"Hi, baby," I said. "These officers were told you were at the fight this weekend. They're asking questions."

"May we come in?" Williams asked.

"Sure," Travis said, stepping over the pile of clothes I'd left on the floor. He wiped his hands on his pants and offered a firm handshake to Williams first, then Gable as they introduced themselves as detectives. "Travis Maddox."

"Nice to meet you, sir," Gable said, flicking his hand in reaction to the pressure Travis had used during their handshake. Gable stepped in, past me, noticeably wary of the man he was confronting.

"You've met my wife," Travis said as I closed the door behind the detectives.

The men nodded. Williams sniffed. "Did you drive or fly to Vegas?"

"Fly," we said in unison, then smiled at each other. Travis took my hand as we sat on the couch.

Williams chose the recliner. Gable took up most of the loveseat.

"They're really saying he was there?" I asked.

"That you were both there, actually," Gable said, writing something down in his notebook. "Do you still have your boarding passes?"

"Yes," I said, standing. I made my way to the bedroom, digging into my purse for the passes and the hotel receipt. I wanted to keep them handy for when the investigators arrived to question Travis on his whereabouts. I grabbed my wedding dress on the way out. I didn't want to leave Travis alone with the detectives any longer than I needed to.

"That was quick," Williams said, suspicious.

"We just got back a couple hours ago," I said. "It was all in my purse. Here," I said, handing him the passes and the hotel receipt.

"That's your, uh ..." Gable began, gesturing to the dress draped over my arm.

"Yes," I said, holding it up with a proud smile.

"Oh!" I said, startling Travis. I hurried down the hall again, tossing my dress onto the bed and returning to the living room with a DVD case in my hand. "Would you like to see the ceremony?"

Before either of them could answer, I popped it into the player and grabbed the remote. I sat next to Travis, snuggling next to him while we watched him stand next to the officiant, fidgeting. I kissed his cheek, then he turned to me and pressed his lips against mine.

"Okay," Williams said, standing. His phone chimed, and he held it to his ear. "Williams. What? When? That's bullshit, and you know it."

Travis shot me a quick glance, but I squeezed his hand while keeping a smile on my face. I stared at the television. The recording made it easy to pretend I wasn't focused on Williams's every word.

Gable mouthed *What*? to his partner.

Williams shook his head. "Yes, sir. We're here now. I understand, sir. Yes, sir." He sighed and put his phone away, looking to Travis with an annoyed expression. "The Federal Bureau of Investigation is taking over the case. I'm sure they'll have more questions for you."

"The FBI?" Travis asked.

Williams frowned at his stunned partner. "Looks that way. Have a nice day, Mr. Maddox. Congratulations and good luck."

Travis stood, bringing me with him. We watched the detectives leave, and then Travis paced.

"Trav," I said, reaching for him. He didn't stop to let me catch him. "Travis, stop. It's going to be okay. I promise."

He sat down on the couch, resting his elbows on his knees and covering his nose and mouth with his hand. His knees were bouncing, and he was breathing hard.

I was bracing myself for an outburst.

I sat next to him, touching his bulging shoulder. “We were in Vegas getting married. That’s what happened, and that’s what we’ll keep saying. You didn’t do anything wrong, Travis. It was an awful thing that happened, but I’m not going to let you go down for this.”

“Abby,” Travis said through his hands. He closed his eyes and took a deep breath. “Did you know this was going to happen?”

I kissed his shoulder. “What do you mean?”

“That I’d need an alibi.”

My heart began to thump in my chest, banging against my ribcage. “What are you talking about?”

He turned to me with subdued fear in his eyes, already regretting the question he was about to ask. “Tell me the truth.”

I shrugged. “Okay ...”

“Did you marry me to keep me out of jail?”

I swallowed. For the first time, I was afraid my famous poker face couldn’t save me. If I admitted to creating his alibi, he wouldn’t believe me that I also married him because I loved him and wanted to be his wife. He wouldn’t believe that the only reason I would agree to be his wife as a freshman in college—at just nineteen—was because of that love. I couldn’t tell him the truth, and I didn’t want to start off our marriage with such an enormous lie.

I opened my mouth to speak, not knowing which I would choose until the words came out.

CHAPTER *two*

LIGHT

Travis

NOT LONG BEFORE MY MOM DIED, I remember hanging onto her leg while she was washing dishes. Soft white sun beams cascaded into the kitchen window, creating a soft glow that tightly hugged her profile and clothes. The light highlighted the dust motes that fell around us.

Mom was taking her time, making sure the plates and pots didn't clink together, humming a song that's forever stuck in my head. The house was quiet, the only sounds were the water and suds gently sloshing against the dishes and her sweet song.

I'd tried my entire life to figure out the tune she'd always hummed around the house, but she must've just made it up because I've never heard anything like it since. The only place it existed now was in my memories. The most vivid from that day, the day I realized much later was the beginning of a sweet, slow goodbye.

All of my older brothers were at school since Trenton had started kindergarten. Being alone with Mom was the best part of my day.

I loved my brothers but having her all to myself was a luxury each of us only got to experience for a short time. I wasn't sure if I had a feeling about what was coming, but I was acutely aware that time with her was fleeting.

Mom chuckled at how clingy I was, more than any of the other boys had been, not that she minded. It would be wishful thinking to believe her endless patience was because I was the baby and she knew that I was her last. Mom knew she was sick, and she was enjoying every moment of her life for as long as she had it.

Being loved by Abby reminded me of both of those things: feeling so calm, soft, and quiet, like when I was leaning against Mom in the kitchen, listening to her hum that beautiful song. And the unshakeable, unexplainable feeling—one I didn't understand—that my time with her could end at any moment.

I knew Abby loved me. She'd said it countless times, but more importantly she showed me with her actions. Hell, even when she was pissed off at me it was for my own good. Only two women in my life had made me feel that way.

I couldn't lose Abby. If that meant lying to the police, lying to my friends and family and the world, I would do it. I wasn't the same person without her. With her, I was different … better.

My wife gave me purpose, finding new ways to love her and make her happy gave me something to look forward to. There was nothing and no one that made me feel more joy.

In that moment, waiting for her to answer why she'd really married me, my brain flipped through thousands of scenarios. If she said marrying me was to keep me out of jail, it wouldn't change anything. I would still want to be her husband and still hold out hope that even though the situation moved the goal post, I would eventually make her believe that she'd made the right decision.

Some people might call me a selfish asshole, but she wouldn't have done it if she didn't love me. Timing was the issue, social constructs, but not love. If she alleviated my fears and said that yes, she'd wanted to marry me within the hour of the fire, would I believe her? Was I so sure of my suspicion that I'd consider it a lie? If she was lying, did that mean I couldn't trust her?

The wheels were obviously spinning in Abby's head, too, and she shifted in her seat next to me on the couch trying to maintain her rock-solid poker face.

When her features were smooth in a tense moment, she was hiding something. A part of me had a real problem starting out with secrets.

I was her husband; I'd changed to be better for both of us. My whole life was different because of her. I wanted her to trust me with the truth. But, at the end of the day, if the shoe were on the other foot and I was afraid she wouldn't let me save her …? You bet your ass I'd lie. In a heartbeat. I'd lie through my fuckin' teeth. Suddenly, I was angry at myself for asking the question. *Do I really want to know?*

Before I could take it back, she began to speak.

CHAPTER Three

WHITE LIE

Abby

"TRAVIS," I BEGAN, TOUCHING HIS knee. "I married you because I'm in love with you."

He hesitated. He didn't want to be asking these questions, and I wished that he wouldn't. Still, he couldn't seem to stop himself.

"Is that the only reason?" As soon as the words came from his mouth, I watched him brace for whatever excruciating pain my answer would cause.

"No."

His chest heaved as if all the air had been knocked out of him. An hour before, he was just beginning to accept that our weekend wasn't a dream. A month before he would have trashed the apartment, unable to decipher hurt from rage.

I could see him fighting the urge to lash out at the closest inanimate object, even under the immense pain he was feeling. Seeing that conflict in every tiny twitch of his expression made me love him even more.

Travis stared at the floor as he spoke. “Abby, when I say I love you ... I didn’t know until this moment that I would want something more than for you to be my wife.” His breath faltered, and he cleared the trembling from his voice. “The truth is … what is more important to me than anything, is for you to be happy. You didn’t have to do this if it’s not what you truly wanted.”

“I *am* happy. Today, I’m the happiest I’ve ever been. Tomorrow, I’ll be even happier. But your happiness is just as important to me, Travis, and,” I hesitated.

No matter how many ways I tried to explain, Travis wouldn’t understand. Eloping to Vegas to save him from prison meant more to me than deciding on a whim to be married at nineteen. Maybe it wasn’t as romantic as the random, impulsive proposal Travis thought it to be, but I had put action behind my feelings. To me, it was proof that my love for him transcended all else, but I couldn’t be sure Travis would see it that way.

“Just say it, Pidge. I need to hear you say it. I just … need to know the truth,” he said, defeated.

I cupped his jaw in my hands and skimmed his ear with my lips. “When I thought you were trapped in that fire, I knew. I knew I would never love anyone else, that you were it for me. That I wanted to spend the rest of my life with you, and I thought it was too late. I am your beloved,” I whispered. My eyebrows pulled in. “And you’re mine. Getting married … I don’t know, it feels real. Unbreakable. Being your wife is what I want. It’s all I want.”

He turned, touching my cheek with his fingertips, and watched my eyes for the tiniest hint that I wasn't being completely honest.

I offered a small smile, keeping my worries hidden deep inside. The words passing my lips were the truth, but I felt the need to protect them as if they were lies.

Travis didn't need to know that I wanted to save him. He only needed to know why.

He nodded, exhaling as his muscles relaxed. "Have you ever wanted something so much, something so out of reach, that once it happened you were almost too afraid to believe it?"

"Yes," I whispered, kissing his lips. "We are one, now. *Nothing* will ever change that."

"I don't know," he said, shaking his head. "A twenty-year prison sentence could change that."

"How can you think you have no control over what happens to us? You made me fall so hard that I proposed to you at nineteen."

He laughed once.

I raised an eyebrow. "Have you stopped to think that I asked you to marry me because I'm the one afraid of losing you?"

That surprised him, and then he seemed exasperated. "Where am I gonna go?" he asked, pulling me onto his lap. "You're my anchor. There's not a thing out there I would want if it took me away from you."

The corners of Travis's mouth curled up, but only for a second. "I'm being investigated by the FBI, Pidge. What if I get arrested? What if I'm gone for a long time?"

I shook my head. "Won't happen. You weren't there. We were in Vegas getting married." I held up my hand, wiggling my fingers so the light reflected off the facets of my diamond.

His expression made my eyes gloss over, and I threw my arms around him, holding him tight, digging my chin in the crook of his neck. I didn't have to hide that I was afraid. "I won't let them take you from me."

"Someone's gotta pay for what happened."

My eyes danced around our apartment, at the tiny candles I'd bought from the Eakins Strip Mall, and the ash tray Travis kept by the door to grab before he went outside to smoke. I thought about his favorite spatula next to my favorite serving spoon in the kitchen drawer, his shot glasses next to my coffee mugs, his smelly gym socks mixed with my Victoria's Secret lace.

I thought about Eastern State's campus and feeling giddy when Travis somehow found me in a sea of students, and the time half the cafeteria broke out into song just because he wanted to help take the attention off me.

I had moved from Kansas to Illinois to escape my past and landed face-first into the last person I'd wanted to get mixed up with—who happened to be the one person who would love me more intensely and unconditionally than anyone ever had.

Travis Maddox made me smile, made me look forward to every day. There was no Abby without Travis.

"Not you," I said. "You didn't choose the building. You didn't hang the lanterns. The fire was an accident, Trav. An awful, terrible accident, but if it's anyone's fault, it's not yours."

"One of these days I'm going to have to come clean, Pidge. How do I explain this to Dad? How do I tell my brothers that I had a part in it? Some of our fraternity brothers are gone forever. Fuck," he said, running his hand over his short hair. "Trenton almost died in that fire."

"But he didn't. Travis?" I shook my head. "You can't tell them. You can't tell anyone. Because if you do and they don't turn you in, they'll be in trouble, too."

He thought about that for a moment, and then nodded. "But ... what if they arrest Adam?"

I looked down. "He's already been arrested."

"What? Where did you hear that?"

"On the news, while we were in Vegas."

"And you didn't tell me? Pidge!"

"I know! I know. But I didn't want to ruin anything. What could we have done about it? What would it have changed had I told you?"

"If I'd known I was going to jail—"

"You're not going to jail!"

"If I'd known, I wouldn't have dragged you down with me!" Travis realized what he'd said, then rubbed the back of his neck.

I grew quiet. "Maybe it's you having second thoughts."

"No," he said, shaking his head. "No, I swear to God that's not it."

"Wow," I said, feeling a sinking in my gut. "How has that never crossed my mind before?"

He took my chin gently in his strong hands. "Because it's never crossed mine."

I stared into his worried, russet irises. "We're going to take this one step at a time. The first step is our marriage. We come first, every time," I said, touching his chest with my finger. "It's us, our family, then the world. Adam is a lot of things, but he's no snitch."

In truth, I was unsure how I would handle the variable of Adam. Even the strongest people did things out of character when afraid. If even one person in that basement during the fight was willing to testify, our alibi might not matter.

Travis nodded, then kissed me. His lips lingered, and I could feel them trembling against mine before he finally pulled away just enough to speak his next words against my mouth. "I fucking love you," he whispered.

The doorknob jiggled, and then Shepley and America burst through, both holding bulging brown sacks and chatting about jalapeno cilantro hummus. They stopped just behind the couch, staring at us while we were in a frozen embrace.

"The fuck, Shep? Knock!" Travis said.

Shepley shrugged, the sacks moving up, too. "I live here!"

"Lived. You lived here. I'm married. You're a third wheel. Third wheels knock," Travis said.

America snatched the keys from Shepley's hand and held them up for Travis to see. "Not if the third wheel has a key," she snapped. "By the way, Shep got Brazil to lend us his truck to get Abby moved the rest of the way in. You're welcome."

She turned for the kitchen in a huff, signaling for Shepley to follow. She was still angry about our elopement, ignoring that sneaking away in the night without telling anyone was the only way it could be.

They opened all the cabinets and began unloading the sacks, filling the nearly empty shelves with cans and bags and boxes.

"I'll help," I said, beginning to push off Travis's lap.

He pulled me back down, nuzzling my neck.

"Oh," America snarled. "You're married now. Let the third wheels put away the two-hundred dollars in groceries they just bought."

"Whoa! Nice, Shep!" Travis said, turning to look into the kitchen long enough for Shepley to shoot him a wink.

"I buy, you cook. That hasn't changed, right, Trav?" Shepley said.

"Right," Travis said, lifting his thumb into the air. "Who wants to eat at the cafeteria three times a day?"

"You're going to have to teach me, babe," I said sheepishly.

"To cook?" Travis asked.

I nodded.

"But if I teach you, I won't get to cook for you as often."

"Exactly," I said, patting his knee. "I want to help."

He grinned, his dimple sinking into his cheek. "Then the answer is no."

I playfully pinched an inch of skin just beneath his arm, giggling when he yelped.

America passed by the couch to the loveseat where the remote was barely poking out between the cushions. I thought about warning her that the large detective had kept it warm like a hen sitting on her nest, but before I could, America tugged on the remote until it was finally free. She pointed it at the television, watching as the screen flashed on, instantly displaying the local news. They were still covering the fire, the reporter standing in front of the Keaton building, black stains above the windows while yellow words scrolled across the bottom of the screen.

I touched my throat and swallowed, remembering choking from the smoke and how terrifying it was to see the flames coming closer. I was confused, lost, and terrified, feeling death could come at any moment—until I heard Travis's voice amid the screams and crying from the main room.

America slowly sat down on the loveseat, letting her hands and the remote sag between her legs. "Emily Heathington died in that basement. She was in my water aerobics class," America said, laughing without humor. "She hated the water. She said the thought of going under and having anything between her and a deep breath made her feel claustrophobic. She took the class to try and face her fear. For her to die like that ... it's almost a sick joke."

"Mare," I warned, noticing Travis's expression.

"I'm so glad you got out," America said, wiping her cheek. "I don't know what we would have done if something had happened to either of you." She stood, tossing the remote to Travis. "Yes. Even you, asshole."

Travis caught the slender black rectangle with one hand, turning back toward the kitchen. "Should we go to Sig Tau?"

"I just went," Shepley said. "It's pretty quiet over there. A lot of guys sitting around staring at the floor."

"They were talking about holding a fundraiser," America said.

Travis nodded. "Yes. We should definitely do that."

"Travis," Shepley said. "How are you going to pay the rent now? Any money Adam had on him from the fight was confiscated so we're out what we would've been paid. That would've taken us through the summer, and we have no more money coming in."

"I get a fuckin' job," Travis said, leaning back.

America wrinkled her nose. "Doing what? All you've ever done for money is throw punches."

I frowned at her, but she just shrugged.

"We'll figure out something," I said. "I saw an ad for a Calculus tutor on the cork board by the door in class before break. I'm going to look into that."

"Good for you," Shepley grumbled. "I suck at math."

Travis made a face. "Your parents pay your bills. Not sure what you're crying about."

"It was nice not to have to ask," Shepley said.

"We won't find anything that pays that good, I guaran-fucking-tee you that." Two lines formed between Travis's brows. He exhaled, shaking his head.

"Like you said," I rubbed his back, "we've got two incomes. It's okay that you'll make less. Even by half."

"I'm going to miss that money," Travis said, staring off. "I had a lot of plans for us."

"Like a car?" I asked.

He stifled a smile. "Don't you worry about that."

I playfully smacked him. "What do you mean?"

"I mean I've got that covered."

"Did you buy us a car?" I asked, sitting up. I'd never owned a car before.

Travis's only mode of transportation was his Harley Night Rod. Although he looked incredibly sexy riding it, it wasn't practical, more than a bit drafty in the winter, and impossible in the rain.

We'd been relying on Shepley to either give us a ride or let us borrow his car, but now that we were married, that would change. Everything would change. We were no longer college kids who could depend on others for a ride, we were a married couple and there was a certain expectation—mostly on ourselves—to be responsible and self-sufficient.

Marriage was so much more than a ceremony and promises. I had never thought twice about Travis having a roommate when I was just his girlfriend, but marriage made that feel different, too. Just like not having a vehicle was different, or jobs, or ... The reality of it all began to weigh on me, and I sunk back into the couch.

Travis frowned, concerned with my reaction. "What, baby?"

Shepley chuckled. "Now you're really broke."

"I still have some cash left. I did save, ya know. And, on the bright side, with a car, we definitely don't need you here all the time," Travis grumbled.

Shepley made a face, looking like he suddenly smelled something revolting. "Well, that's fuckin' rude."

Travis moved me off his lap and then scrambled over the couch, tackling his cousin to the tile floor in the kitchen.

Shepley grunted when his knee hit the lower cabinet door, and then he yelped as Travis grabbed for his crotch. "Quit fighting dirty, douche balloon!" Shepley cried.

America leapt back, narrowly missing Travis's quickly moving legs.

I moved to stand next to her, hooking my arm around hers.

"Are you sure you know what you've gotten yourself into?" she asked. "You're in this now, you know. This is yours."

"You're next," I said, tugging on her arm.

"Oh, no. Just because you got married as a freshman doesn't mean the rest of us are crazy." She looked at me, confused. "Which is just … weird. Explain this to me, you have a near-death experience and decide to run off to Vegas and get married?"

"We're not talking about this, remember?" I said.

She shrugged. "I just … I need to know."

I took a few steps away from her and then turned around, crossing my arms. "No, you don't Mare. Just leave it alone."

The boys stopped fighting, and Shepley stood, breathing hard. "Mare," he warned. "You promised."

"I just … I still can't understand why you did it. We

all know you love him, but marriage wasn't even on your radar, Abby. The fire breaks out, and you two just happened to decide to elope ..." Recognition flickered in her eyes. "There's more you're not telling us, isn't there? Abby …?" America began, suspicious.

"You're ridiculous, just stop," I said.

"But, I'm right, aren't I?" she asked. "You did it for an alibi. I mean, that would make sense, I don't blame you, but—"

"There is no but!" I pointed to Travis, who looked like he was about to throw up. "I love him! I've loved him since the moment I saw him. I almost lost him, Mare!" I said, my voice breaking. "I saw him across the room in that basement and he couldn't get to me. He couldn't get to me! He was screaming at Trent to get me to safety, and that might've been the last time I saw him. What might've been his last moments on this earth, he was only thinking of me, and even then, if he hadn't stayed behind, if he hadn't risked a horrible death to find me and break the window so we could get out, I wouldn't be here. He saved my life! So, I'm sure what you're asking is if the fire made me realize I will never love anyone else the way I love him, that he loves me more than his own life, and I don't want to spend another second without him. Because the answer is yes!"

Tears flooded America's eyes. "Abby …"

"Don't cry," I said, forcing myself to calm down. I didn't get angry with America often but seeing the expression on Travis's face made me desperate to protect him. "Stop crying, Mare. It's okay. We're not going to talk about this again. We weren't there, remember?"

"We know," Shepley said. He hugged his girlfriend to his side, still trying to catch his breath. His cheeks were flushed from unsuccessfully grappling with his much larger cousin. "We know, right, Mare?"

America's bottom lip quivered. "I'm sorry."

I turned to hug her, then Shepley joined in. I reached for Travis, and he held all of us in his arms.

CHAPTER *Four*

SILVER

Abby

PLATES, POTS, AND SILVERWARE CLINKED and banged together, muffled by the running water pouring out of the tap. Steam floated from the sink basin as America and I rinsed the few remnants of Travis's trademark Cajun Chicken Pasta from the dishes and placed them into the dishwasher.

Shepley was wiping down the stove and countertops. No one had said much during dinner, in part because Travis was an amazing cook, but mostly because we weren't sure how to talk about the truth without incriminating everyone in the room.

Shepley finished up and then patted America's backside. "Want me to take over?"

"We've got it," America said. Once Shepley joined Travis in the living room, she paused, leaving the water running over the plate in her hands.

"Mare?"

She sniffed. "I'm such an idiot, Abby. I don't know what I was thinking," she whispered. "Should I apologize to him?"

"No," I said, keeping my voice low. "I know you're worried about me. I know that. But Travis ... You can't say things like that in front of him. He's still worried this isn't real or that I'm going to change my mind. I'm just as surprised as you are, Mare, but I really am so happy. I promise."

"That's all I needed to know. I won't ask again. About any of it."

"That's why you're the *best* best friend ever."

"That's true. I am. You're so lucky."

I grinned.

America pressed a few buttons, and the dishwasher began to buzz and hum. She dried her hands and stood behind me, cupping my shoulders to pull my back against her chest. Her chin gently pressed into the crook of my neck, and then she kissed my cheek. "The investigation will be over soon. Everything's going to be fine."

"I know," I said, still looking down at the sink.

I dumped a small pool of blue dish soap into my palm, scrubbing my already pruning skin. As serious as I had perceived our problems in the past, we were in real trouble—both of us—because if Travis went down, we both would.

I had just lied to police detectives, obstructed justice, aided and abetted, not to mention been a willing accessory before, during, and after-the-fact. But I was willing to accept the consequences, whatever they were, if it meant Travis had even a chance of avoiding prison. I glanced over my shoulder at my husband.

He was standing with his bulky, inked arms crossed over his middle, chatting with his cousin. He turned his red baseball cap backward, shifting his weight from one leg to the other like he couldn't stand still.

Shepley had a calming effect on Travis, and he was talking him down from whatever ledge Travis was on.

I smiled and looked down at the water running over my hands, washing the suds away, wishing my hands were truly clean.

"Okay, Shep, we're all done," America said.

She walked over to Travis, giving him a big hug, and long after it would've been natural for her to let go, she held on.

Travis looked to me, and I smiled. He playfully hooked his arm around her neck and kissed her hair. "We good?"

She let go and looked up and him. "Are we?"

Travis turned somber. "We're family, Mare. No matter what, at the end of the day, we'll always be good."

She hugged him one more time, then Shepley did, too, and they waved at me before heading for the Charger parked outside.

Travis walked into the kitchen, leaning his backside against the counter and crossing his arms. "She feels bad, huh?"

"She does. Sometimes her mouth works faster than her brain. She didn't realize how it sounded when she said it."

"I'm glad she said it."

"You are?"

"You haven't really talked about it … the fire. I wouldn't have known you felt all that had she not."

I sighed. "I just feel like if I keep it all in, it's not so … terrifying." I turned to face the sink. "You're right, though. I need to communicate better. I can't keep saying we're in this together if you didn't even know how I felt during the fire."

He walked up behind me, wrapping his arms around my middle. "I mean, I knew a little. I didn't know that part. I'm glad you know, and you have proof. I do love you more than my own life. I'll always protect you."

"It goes both ways, baby. You have to let me protect you sometimes, too."

The sun was beginning to set, casting a warm glow through the windowpane that sat over the sink. My view consisted of the parking lot, the apartment units farther down, and the tops of the campus buildings peeking just over the trees a couple of miles away.

The sky was still hazy from the smoke that had bellowed from Keaton Hall just a few days before. The fire was one of the most frightening experiences of my life, but I had lived. The fear that was just a memory for me had consumed the final moments of so many of our classmates.

"Can you still hear it?" I asked. "The screaming?"

"Every night."

I closed my eyes and squeezed his arms tighter around me. "It'll get easier, right?"

"I don't know, Pidge. I hope so."

I dried my hands and turned, making my way to the hall. I changed over the laundry, adding more and taking the basket to the bedroom and setting it on the bed. *Busy is good.*

Travis came in, making the basket bounce when he fell face first onto the bed. He took a few deep breaths and then turned onto his back, crossing his arms behind his head. He stared at the ceiling while I walked around our bed to hang my wedding dress on the curtain rod.

The bare branches of the tree outside quivered in the wind. I'd watched almost every season change that tree from Travis's bedroom window, and now that window was ours.

"Remind me to take this to the cleaners and have it preserved," I said, smoothing the skirt.

"Preserved? What the hell does that even mean?" he asked with a grin.

"To keep it from yellowing. To keep it fresh."

"For what?"

"Forever," I said, returning to the bed. "Like us."

Travis held my gaze for a moment, watching me walk back to him with an appreciative smile.

I resumed the tedious but welcomed task of folding our clothes from Vegas and the towels we'd used after we washed off the smoke and soot from the fire. I wished there was a way to make it all go away so easily.

Travis sighed. "I'm not afraid to go to prison, Pidge. I've felt, pretty much from the first time I saw you, that ... I dunno. It sounds perfectly normal in my head, but I know if I say it out loud ..."

"Just say it."

"I've never thought I'd get to keep you, but now ... What do I do if I never get to see you again? Or get to touch your hair? See the way your eyes look in the sunlight? Feel your wet hair against my arm when I fall asleep at night? The thought of not seeing you every day scares me to death."

I lined up his socks and folded them into each other. That was Travis and me, one big, knotted bundle.

"You see these socks? They're a pair. Even when one gets lost, the other has to wait for it to come back, because they'll always be a match. Even when apart, we're still a *we*. It's just geography. It doesn't change anything. And it doesn't matter anyway, because you're not going anywhere."

"You can't fix this, Abby," he said. "I'm not going to lie. If I was wrong, I deserve to—"

"Stop," I said, throwing the folded socks at his face.

He caught them just before they hit their mark.

"I'm your wife. Your duty is to be here with me, to protect me, to love me. You promised. We've always fought one battle at a time. This is no different."

He nodded, looking back up at the ceiling. After a few restless minutes, he jerked up, planting his feet on the ground. "I can't hang around here. It's making me crazy. Let's go."

"Where?" I asked.

"Pinkerton's."

"The car dealership? Shouldn't we save our money?"

Travis smirked. "It's already paid for. Just pick a color."

I arched an eyebrow. "Don't mess with me, Maddox."

He changed into a long-sleeved T-shirt and a clean pair of jeans, then bent over to slide on and lace up his boots. "We're going."

I didn't budge from my basket of clothes, but Travis strolled over, bumping me with his hip before pulling out one of my shirts and grabbing a hanger. In less than a minute, we had finished and put away the clothes. I stared at the closet with my arms crossed, pretending to be unimpressed with my choices.

"Just a sweater and jeans, baby. You're beautiful. You don't even have to try."

My cheeks flushed red, and I looked down. "They close soon, don't they?"

"What? You don't want a car? *Vamos*! Get your ass in gear, Mrs. Maddox!"

I giggled, grabbing the first pair of jeans and sweater that I touched, dressing quickly and meeting Travis in the living room.

He had Shepley's keys in his hand, his face lighting up when he saw me. He opened the door, gesturing for me to go first.

"You just do that so you can stare at my ass, don't you?" I asked.

"You're damn right I do," Travis said, closing the door behind him.

We walked down the steps holding hands, and I took a deep breath. "Smells like rain."

"Good thing I called an Uber, then," he said, walking to a red Volkswagen Jetta waiting in the parking lot.

He opened the back passenger side door and waited for me to slide in before jogging around the front to sit behind the driver. Once he settled in, he put his hand on my thigh and shook his head.

"What?" I asked. "Forget something?"

"Every five minutes or so it hits me, and I can't believe it." He leaned over, cupping my cheek in his hand before planting a quick kiss on my lips. He pulled away just as the driver put the gear into drive, making a face when a country song came over the radio. "Is there another station we can listen to?"

"Of course!" The man said, fiddling with the buttons. "Are you warm enough?"

"I am," Travis said, "my wife's a little chilly."

"Easy fix," the driver said.

"Wait, this one," Travis said as Dexy's Midnight Runners came over the speakers. He bobbed his head, and I laughed at him as he mouthed the words, *C'mon Eileen*.

Travis seemed relaxed and happy. His hand rested on my knee, still singing and bobbing his head to the music. He knew every word. It was sort of impressive. Once in a while, he would look at me and mouth the words with such enthusiasm, I couldn't help but sing with him.

I was glad he insisted we leave the apartment. I hadn't realized how trapped I'd felt, or how much I needed to laugh.

The driver parked the car and Travis stepped out.

When I closed the passenger door, he walked ahead of me, reaching behind him with both hands until I intertwined my fingers in his.

He wrapped my arms around him, his steps coming to a halt at the end of a short line of Toyota Camrys.

An older gentleman walked out, smoothing his tie and silver hair, preparing his spiel by clearing his throat and offering his most charming smile.

Travis's was better.

To my surprise, the salesman greeted Travis by name. Travis released me to shake his hand.

"I was wondering when you'd be out. Is this Abby?" He shook my hand. "Richard. Nice to finally meet you."

I craned my neck at Travis.

Travis shrugged. "I told you. Pick a color."

I choked out a single laugh. "Are you for real?"

He held out his hands and let them fall to his thighs. "Have I ever lied to you?"

I slowly reached around his neck, feeling his muscles relax from my touch. I pushed up on the balls of my feet and gave him a quick peck, seeing Richard in my peripheral trying not to watch.

"Never." I looked down the line of Camrys.

Richard pointed. "Attitude Black, Barcelona Red, Classic Silver, Clearwater Blue, Cosmic Gray, and Sandy Beach Metallic. We don't have the Pearl or Magnetic Gray in stock."

"But he can get it," Travis added.

"Yes, of course," Richard responded.

Travis led me down the line. "Open them up and look inside. They all have different interiors."

I walked over to the silver car, opening the driver's side door. "What is that? A television?"

Richard stepped closer. "That's a, uh ... the navigation system and radio." He continued to ramble off the various features as Travis encouraged me to sit inside.

The interior was light gray, and the buttons around the large display screen and on the steering wheel made me think of a NASA control panel. I couldn't imagine ever being familiar with them all.

"I can't believe you did this for me," I said, running my fingers over the steering wheel. "I've never had my own car."

Travis squatted next to me, resting his hand on the ledge inside the open door. "I'd do anything for you, Pidge. I'm going to give you everything you've ever wanted."

I touched his cheek. "You already have."

Travis leaned against my touch, and then pecked my palm, suddenly excited. "What do you think?"

"This one."

"The silver?" he asked.

"The silver," I answered. "It matches my ring."

Travis moved his head to the side, keeping his gaze on me. "You heard my wife, Richard. She wants this one."

"Done," Richard said. "I'll get it ready."

I lunged at Travis, pushing him back onto his backside.

He laughed, and then cradled me on the asphalt,

kissing my lips just as thunder echoed in the distance and rain began to fall from the sky.

"You happy, Pidge?" he asked.

"The happiest," I whispered against his smiling lips.

Travis had already negotiated a price and paid before we got there, so at least I didn't have to listen to them go back and forth in addition to the mind-numbing offers of extended warranties and what felt like dozens of signatures.

The car was listed under both of our names. The first thing, besides Toto, that Travis and I owned together, and for some reason that made me feel oddly affectionate toward an inanimate object.

Travis held my hand as he drove the Camry back to the apartment, and it seemed surreal as he parked our car in the spot next to Shepley's Charger. "I guess they're back. Did she text you?"

"Mare? No. They probably forgot something." I stared at the car and then back at Travis, unable to contain the ridiculous grin on my face.

"That makes sense. It's stopped raining for the moment so America would chance getting her hair wet."

I grinned. "She's not that bad."

He laughed, nodded, and we both said, "*Yes she is*" simultaneously. Neither one of us could contain ourselves then, and I was wiping away tears by the time our laughter died down.

I didn't realize I was staring at Travis until he said something.

"What?" Travis asked, holding my hand to his lips.

"I don't know. It's stupid," I said, waving him away.

"Tell me."

"Owning this car together kind of makes it feel real, you know?"

He smiled, rubbing my upper arms. "I was thinking the same thing."

"Yeah?" I said, leaning in.

My eyes were closed, waiting for a kiss, but when Travis's lips never touch mine, they popped open. Travis was glaring in the direction of our apartment, and I turned to see exactly what he was unhappy about.

"You've gotta be fucking kidding me," Travis said.

I closed the passenger door and wrapping my arms across my middle.

Jesse, America, and Shepley were standing at the bottom of our steps. Jesse walked over to me, America right behind him.

"I tried to tell him to leave," America said.

"Hey, Abby," Jesse said, ignoring her. His eyes were bright, the fact that Travis had just arrived next to me didn't faze him.

"What are you doing here, Jesse?" I asked.

He looked down at my left hand, grabbed it, and lifted the evidence. "Had to see this for myself."

I pulled my hand away.

Travis's anger was radiating off him, and Shep put a hand on his chest when he took the smallest step forward.

I stepped in front of my husband. "Yes, I'm married. You came all the way here to see my ring? You couldn't have just called?"

He shrugged. "I don't have your number. Neither does Mick."

"There's always Instagram," America said, unimpressed.

"Does Mick know, too?" I asked.

"That you're married?" Jesse said with a chuckle. "Yeah. So does your mom."

I swallowed. "How?"

He smirked. "What happens in Vegas that Benny Carlisi doesn't know about?"

I looked around. This many people standing in a tight group would draw attention, and that was the last thing we needed. "Why did you really come all the way here, Jesse?"

"He knows about the fire, too. He sent me to tell you personally that he'd be happy to help."

"Help with what?" America asked.

I narrowed my eyes. "You're running errands for Benny, now? Are you insane, Jesse?"

Jesse flashed me his trademark captivating smile. The smile that made me fall for him years ago, in what felt like another life.

When we were kids, he'd wanted to be a Baptist preacher. He'd ended up as a Vegas pit boss, and now he was clearly neck-deep with the mafia. Benny didn't send just anyone to deliver messages.

Raindrops began to fall again, the first touching my lip, and then the rest saturating my hair and shirt. America looked around in a panic and then jogged to the stairs, making a racket in her chunky wedge sandals as she made her way up to stand on the stoop, out of the rain.

Shepley stayed behind, presumably to make sure Travis didn't kill Jesse.

"We respectfully decline the offer," I said.

"It's not your offer," Jesse said, looking to Travis. "It's just one more thing he can do for you, Maddox. He can make you rich, make your problems go away …"

"Who are you right now?" I asked, disgusted.

"You're not fighting anymore," Jesse continued, ignoring my jab. "You're a married man. You have bills to pay. Benny can make all of it go away, Maddox. All you have to do is what you do best."

"It's not what I do anymore," Travis said. His rage was boiling just beneath the surface, and it bled through to his tone.

"Well," Jesse said, handing him his card. "Let me know if you change your mind, but you should probably decide quickly. Our ears at the FBI say you don't have much time." He looked to me, for the first time his confidence waned, replaced by a tinge of sadness. "You, too."

"Her?" Travis asked. "Why her?"

Jesse returned his attention to Travis, all sympathy disappearing from his eyes. "Decide soon. Benny won't get involved once charges are filed." Jesse walked a few steps backward, then looked up at America. "And head's up. They bugged your whole place."

"Since when?" I asked.

"I got the call on my way here. You were at the

dealership."

"They were just here?" I asked, pointing to the apartment. "Inside, installing surveillance equipment in just the last hour and a half?"

"It's what they do. Doesn't take long for suits."

"We can work around that," I said, looking to Travis. "And we have plans for income. We don't need Benny's help." I turned back to Jesse. "We don't."

"He's not doing this out of the goodness of his heart, Abby. You have something he wants. Both of you. But he's willing to help you with just what Travis has to offer. Abby," he said, moving toward me. Travis took a step, his chest touching my back.

"If you touch her …" Travis began.

Jesse held up his hands. "I care about her, too, Travis, and have for a lot longer. We're wasting time. You're both in a lot of trouble. Abby"—he looked to me again—"no matter how you feel about Benny or your dad, I'd take him up on it. This might be your only chance."

He turned and walked away, stopping at a slick, black McLaren.

"Holy shit, that's a three-hundred-thousand-dollar car," Shepley said, unable to hide his excitement. As Jesse backed away and drove off, Shepley snapped out of it. "Wait. You're in trouble with the Feds? Because of the fire? Trav, are you going to prison over this?"

Travis ran his hand over his wet hair and face, and then looked down at me.

"No," I said. "We'll find another way."

Travis nodded and turned his attention to his cousin. "Not another word, Shep. Never discuss this again."

"Are you going to be okay, though?"

"Shep, listen to me. I'm scared, too, but you have to stay out of this. You don't know anything. Don't ask me anything again. You don't want to get involved."

"You're family, Trav. I can't just stay out of this!"

"Damn it, Shep! You can't help me!" he yelled, calming himself before he spoke again. "Do for America what I didn't do for Abby. Keep her safe."

I took his hand and squeezed, hating that he felt that way.

After a long pause, Shepley nodded, worry darkening his face.

CHAPTER *Five*

WHAT'S LEFT OF RIGHT

Travis

ABBY'S HAND FELT SMALL BUT RELAXED in mine as we walked down the wet sidewalk, past the yellow tape surrounding Keaton Hall.

I kept my thumb on the band of her wedding ring; the doubts in my head were relentless. It was stupid as fuck, but touching her ring was the most discreet way to quiet my fears.

The building and the muddy ground bordering the four corners of brick and stone were now a crime scene. The FBI had gotten involved, investigating the death of a hundred and thirty-two college students, most of them not old enough to buy a beer.

I'd been wondering for days when or if I should tell Dad, how he would take the news that his youngest son had been involved in the most tragic event in Eastern State's history, and what he would say.

I imagined the disappointment in his eyes, the worry and stress that would plague him, even after the Feds carted me off to prison.

Dad had promised Mom, on her death bed, that he'd quit the police department and never let any of us go into law enforcement of any kind. His years of late nights and close calls had been hard on her, their marriage, and she didn't want that for her boys.

When I'd declared my Criminal Justice major I thought he'd blow a gasket, but he'd only gently reminded me of his promise with the hope I'd find something in the field that would help him keep it. I closed my eyes.

I wasn't going to be able to take the expression on his face when he found out, the only thing that would feel as shameful as going against her only dying wish.

The bricks over each window of the building where Adam had staged my last fight were stained black from smoke. The horrified screams from just a few nights before still rang in my ears, and I recalled the terror I felt when I was desperately looking in the basement through the dark maze of halls for Abby. The overwhelming dread that came over me when I realized Trenton wasn't outside with the rest of the survivors was still fresh.

The shrill, audible fear and desperation to escape was exactly what I imagined Hell would sound like. The hairs on the back of my neck stood on end just thinking about it.

Still, none of that touched the heartbreak so many parents had been feeling since the story of the fire had broken on the news. Even though Abby never missed an opportunity to say that what happened wasn't my fault, I still felt responsible.

I paused in front of a makeshift memorial for the victims: a pile of notes, ribbons, flowers, photos, and stuffed animals.

Abby tugged on my hand, pulling me forward without saying a word. She knew I was beating myself up about it, but she didn't know I was struggling with the urge to turn myself in. The only thing stopping me was the thought of spending even a day apart from my wife.

"Trav?" Abby said.

"Yeah, baby?"

"We shouldn't talk about any of this at the apartment anymore."

"I know."

"It's not just the apartment. It's our phones. The car. We can only discuss anything to do with the fire away from the apartment, outside, and never on the phone. Definitely no texts."

"That's Hollywood shit, Pidge."

"Where do you think Hollywood got its inspiration? Just, trust me, okay?"

"Okay, but—"

"Hey, kids," Finch said from behind us. He hooked his arm around Abby and me. "How're you holding up?"

Abby turned to hug him. He held her tight, winking to me with a half-smile.

I wondered if he knew anyone that belonged to any of the memorials, and if he knew I'd had a part in it. If he did, he wasn't angry.

"It's so good to see you," Abby said, wiping her eyes. "I'm glad you weren't there."

"Me? In a dusty basement with all those cavemen frat boys? Actually, that sounds exactly where I'd be, but no. It was my dad's fifty-ninth birthday dinner."

"Oh, that's right, how was it?" Abby asked, her expression changing within seconds to a surprised smile.

Finch helped her with some smeared mascara under her eyes. "I'll tell you what, biscuit. I have to get to class and so do you, so let's get coffee soon and I'll catch you up on Dad's boring ass birthday and my new tall, dark and handsome, and you can catch me up on"—his eyes scanned me from boots to hairline—"what it's like to be married to a mad dog." Finch spoke the words, his eyes playfully alluring.

I shook my head and led Abby away by the hand.

"Wait. You have a new guy? Who?" she called after him.

"Later, darling. Later."

"Always good to see you, Finch," I said, waving with my free hand.

I walked Abby to the building where she had her first class, and after kissing her in a way that would let anyone who saw know she was my wife, I watched her walk up the stairs and disappear behind glass double doors.

Shepley slapped me on the shoulder. "They grow up so fast."

I shrugged away from his grip. "Fuck off, shit sack."

Shepley chuckled. "One of the sisters from Sig Cap already asked America if the rumor was true."

I frowned. "What rumor?"

Shepley stared at me as if I were an imbecile. "That you're off the market."

"I've been off the market since I met Abby," I grumbled.

Shepley had framed the information he was passing on as forlorn coeds seeking confirmation, but something told me most people couldn't believe Abby had taken such a huge risk by marrying me.

I'd pretty much had my pick of females on campus, sure, but I wasn't stupid enough to think any of them saw me as husband material. I'd never admit it, but it was embarrassing that everyone knew I didn't deserve my wife, and even though I couldn't deny the truth, I also couldn't help but feel butthurt about it.

I lit a cigarette, adjusted my backpack and began to walk under a gray sky, feeling the cool morning air infiltrate my long-sleeved T-shirt.

Shepley struggled to match my pace, every so often breaking into a short jog. We didn't speak until we reached the liberal arts building where we both had a class.

I took two steps at a time, finally prompting Shepley to complain.

"For fuck's sake, Trav. Where's the fire?"

I turned to face my cousin, clenching my teeth. "What is wrong with you?" I said, under my breath.

Shepley paled. "Sorry, man. Poor choice of words. We're not late. Class doesn't start for another fifteen minutes. Why are you rushing?"

"I've got a lot on my mind," I said, yanking open the door.

The hall was flooded with students coming and going, flowing past one another until they parted long enough to bypass an obstacle in the center of the walkway: a glass box sitting on top of a podium. Encased inside was a bust of Gerald P. Stymie, the former president of Eastern State, and former member of Sig Tau.

Dr. Stymie rushed Sig Tau with my dad and Uncle Jack, and I had many memories of him dropping by our house often during my formative years. He attended our holiday parties and my mother's funeral.

He'd died four years after he retired, which was six years before my freshman year of college. I wondered if he would be more disappointed that I had helped orchestrate Eastern's biggest tragedy or that I wasn't owning up to my involvement.

The energy was so different from the week before spring break, when everyone was smiling and walked with a bounce in their step. Now the halls were quiet, the air heavy and somber. The girls were wiping away tears, the guys holding them close, all recognizing their own mortality—some for the first time.

"A lot on your mind?" Shepley asked, slipping inside the building behind me. "Like what? Oh. You mean the thing I don't know about? Or did you just realize marriage is forever?"

I grabbed Shepley's collar in both fists, shoving him against the nearest wall.

The breath was knocked out of him, and he stared

at me, wide-eyed, with his hands up. "Hey!" he said, glowering at me. "I'm on your side!"

I slowly loosened my grip, aware of the curious eyes of passersby. I straightened Shepley's shirt and patted his shoulder to apologize, and then took a deep breath. "This isn't funny, Shepley. Any of it. And I'm hanging by a thread, here. Cut me some fuckin' slack, would ya?"

Shepley took a quick glance around, and then leaned in, keeping his voice low. "You're right. I'm sorry. Just trying to lighten your mood. But you need to keep a low profile, Travis. Now is not the time to draw attention to yourself."

I looked over my shoulder at fellow students. Kids, young and stupid like me but without a wife or bills or detectives knocking on their door. Their biggest worries were grades and explaining the credit card bill to their parents.

Abby and I had those silly worries just a few days ago. The wedding had helped me pretend the fire hadn't happened, but now the aftermath was staring me in the face. The worries of losing Abby to Parker seemed like a lifetime ago. Now, I could lose her for real ... forever.

"You're right," I said. I smoothed his shirt, and then patted his cheek, forcing a smile. "You're right, buddy. I'm sorry."

"Get to class, dick head," Shepley said, readjusting his backpack before turning the corner to climb the stairs.

I walked to the end of the hall and ducked into class, nodding to my humanities professor before taking a seat. A couple of students from the previous lecture were still hanging around his desk, asking questions about the mid-term.

I glanced at my watch and then pulled out my phone, smiling when the display lit up. Abby's gorgeous smile graced the screen, laughing at something from a simpler time. But my stomach did somersaults when I saw she'd texted me.

Hey <3

I smiled, tapping out a reply. **WTF. How can I miss you already?**

Three dots appeared—the manifestation of anticipation. *Same.*

I chuckled to myself. Abby was an enigma. I knew she loved me. Hell, she'd married me. But her short answers and refusal to get too emotional, other than to express frustration or anger, had me guessing most of the time. I loved that about her.

I loved how stubborn and even how petty she was. I loved how insane she made me feel, how unsure, how afraid. Surely that wasn't healthy, but I didn't fucking care. No one had dared make me feel those things before—at least, not on purpose.

I just wrote Abby Maddox on my notebook. With hearts. How lame am I?

A huge grin spread across my face. **Finally.**

Was that weird for you?

Nope. Gotta go. <3 you.

Professor Halsey stood from his seat and walked around to the front of his desk, leaning his ass against the wooden edge. He was a gangly thing. All arms, legs, and nose, his black, greasy hair styled over to one side to poorly hide the bald spot on the crown of his head. He fanned out his fingers and pressed the tips together, touching his pointers to his lips.

"As I'm sure you're all aware, the school has suffered a terrible loss this past weekend."

An uncomfortable silence filled the room, and students shifted in their seats. I sunk into my desk.

Halsey continued. "We've been instructed to inform you about the free on-campus counseling services provided for every student by Eastern State. Based on the numbers, I'm sure we have at least one person in this very classroom who knew someone who was injured, survived, or became a victim in the basement of Keaton. This can be a frightening, overwhelming time for anyone, whether you were close with one of the victims or not. So please ... don't ignore any feelings you're having trouble processing. We're here to help." He paused just long enough to let his words sink in, and then he continued with the lesson.

A girl or two sniffled a few times, but other than that, we proceeded as normal, taking notes and asking questions.

The moment he dismissed class, I bolted for the door, quickly making my way outside, and then breaking into a jog all the way to where Abby would be leaving class. She'd just stepped out of the doors, stopping when she saw me. I crashed into her, and she hooked her arm around my middle, guiding me down the steps and around the side of the building.

"What happened?" she said, keeping her voice quiet and calm.

My chest heaved as I gasped for breath. I shook my head, unable to answer.

"Travis, look at me," she said, grabbing my jaw and lifting my head until my gaze met hers. "Talk."

"They're all dead. So many people are walking around without their friends, roommates ... family members." I pointed at my chest. "I did that."

"No. You didn't." She peeked over her shoulder, and then back at me. "It's not your fault. We all made choices that night. It was an accident. A horrendous, nauseating accident. But—" She grabbed my jaw to face her. "Look at me. You need to get it together, Maddox. If people see you like this and tell the cops—"

"Maybe they should. Maybe I should turn myself in," I said. No breath I took was deep enough. The more air I pulled in, the less satisfying it felt.

"What the hell are you talking about?" she asked. For the first time, she was struggling to retain her poker face. "You better listen to me." She gripped the bottom hem of my shirt. "I'm not going to let them take you, and you're not going to leave me willingly, do you hear me?"

"You think I want to?" I spat, flustered.

"They died, yes, and it is awful, yes, but you don't get to leave me. You are going to pick your wife and your marriage over everything else from now on. You choose us over your guilt, over your goddamn morals, and you choose us even over the right thing to do! If that makes me selfish or a bad person, I accept that. I'll take it, damn it! But they won't understand that you didn't mean for any of it to happen. They won't care that you didn't choose the building or put up the lanterns. They'll arrest you, Travis. They'll arrest you, and cuff you, and take you away from me, and ..." Her bottom lip began to quiver.

I pulled her into my chest, holding her as she trembled in my arms. "Baby," I said, surprised. I'd never seen her so rattled.

She pushed me away, keeping hold of my T-shirt in her fist, pulling as she spoke. "Don't do anything stupid, Travis. Don't you fucking dare." Frustrated, she tightened her free hand into a fist and hit my chest.

It didn't hurt, but it was just hard enough to make a point.

Her eyes glossed over. "You're the *only* family I've got. Do you hear me? If I lose you, I lose *everything*."

"You always have Dad and my brothers, and Shep and America. Mark and Pam. Finch. You're not alone, Pidge."

"*You*, Travis"—she pointed to my chest—"I need *you*. You are the most important person in my life." She shook her head and shrugged as she spoke. "I don't want to do this without you. Don't you ever talk like this again, do you hear me? You can't turn yourself in. You can't do that to me."

"Okay," I said, blinking. I pulled her in again, swaying a bit, trying to comfort her the best I could. I kissed her temple, cursing myself.

I knew I couldn't leave her, even if it was to do the right thing. I'd just wanted her to tell me not to. Unloading something on her that I knew wasn't going to happen was a dick thing to do. "You're right. I wasn't ... I don't want to get arrested. I just needed to hear you say it, I guess."

"Fine. I'll say it as many times as you need me to. I'll say it ten times a day. I will take the blame, guilt trip you, beg you, whatever it takes, but you can't leave me."

I sighed, rubbing the back of my neck. "Jesus, I can't believe I just did that to you, I'm so sorry, I panicked."

She lifted her chin, a tear escaping down her cheek. "I get it. It's a lot. I don't blame you for having weak moments. I just need you to promise me you will never stop fighting to stay with me. That you'll never stop fighting for us."

I choked down my emotions, clenching my teeth. She loved me as much as I loved her. I didn't know that was possible. "Okay, Pidge. Okay ... I promise."

She pressed her forehead against my chest, took in a deep breath, and then nodded. After taking a moment to gather herself, her eyes peered at the ground as she made the choice to trust me not to ruin her life. She wiped her eyes, turned on her heels, and walked away in the direction of her next class.

The smell of smoke still lingered in the air as she walked out of sight, leaving the ashes of my conscience in her wake.

CHAPTER *Six*

TRUTH

Travis

THE SOLES OF MY BOOTS squished against the wet steps that led to my apartment. The sky had been pissing on me off and on all day between classes. I was glad.

The grounds around Keaton Hall were still soaked from the deluge of water the fire hoses had poured into the building. The rain made the rest of the campus blend in with Keaton's charred, saturated grass and sidewalks.

My keys jingled in my hand as I pulled them out to unlock the door. As soon as I touched the knob, I heard tiny scratching on the other side. I smiled and pushed, immediately leaning over to greet Toto.

His wiry dark fur brushed against my face as he covered me with puppy kisses. He'd already grown so much, but he squirmed, yelped, and bounced around like he did his first day in the apartment. He wouldn't settle down, so I finally picked him up, holding him against my chest while he soaked my face with dog slobber. I lifted my chin so I didn't end up with puppy tongue in my mouth.

I took him outside and down the steps, setting him on the grass and then crossing my arms while I waited for him to do his business.

Brazil used the spare key to pick up Toto after we'd already left for the airport, and even though he'd agreed with no notice and no questions, Abby was more than just unhappy when we'd picked Toto up.

She'd given him a bath the moment we got home to wash away the stench of cigarettes and dirty socks. After she'd dried him off and made up for lost snuggle time, he'd curled up in a ball on his bed in the corner of our bedroom and slept the rest of the night. She'd reminded me that morning that I'd promised to talk to Brazil about it.

I tapped out the message on my phone.

> **Dude. I appreciate you picking up my dog, but if you didn't want to take care of him, you should have just said so.**
>
> It didn't take long for Brazil to respond. **What do u mean?**
>
> **He smelled like shit. You were smoking around him? I don't even smoke around him. And he was comatose for 24 hrs**

after we got him home.

Sorry, man. I had a party. There was a fight in the front yard. I had to break it up. When I came back in, Jenks had let him out of my room and was trying to feed him beer. I made Jenks leave, but Toto wasn't hurt or anything, I swear.

Remind me not to ask you for any more favors.

Won't happen again, Travis. Sorry.

I called Toto inside, his nails clicking against the linoleum in the kitchen while I opened a can of his favorite food. I scrunched my face at the rancid smell, wondering how in God's name any creature could eat something so revolting. The irony wasn't lost on me that I was talking about Toto, who enjoyed licking his own asshole.

I poured the food into the orange ceramic bowl Abby had found online with Toto's name on it, and added to his water bowl before returning my attention to my phone. I scrolled through my contacts until Brandon Kyle's name appeared. My thumb hovered over the phone icon.

One of my frat brothers had given me Brandon's contact information. He was the owner of Iron E, one of three off-campus gyms in Eakins. Two of those gyms were Brandon's, and Iron E was his pride and joy: a newer gym on the eastside that was significantly more popular than the others because of the high number of coed memberships.

Every time I'd lifted there, Brandon had approached me with some kind of offer to hang out. Concert tickets, trips to watch a myriad of professional sports teams. He'd even invited me to Dubai. He was nice enough, in an annoying, superficial way, but he had a pregnant wife and more than one side chick—not someone I could stomach calling a friend.

I pressed the button and held the phone to my ear. It rang a few times, but then I heard a click followed by the screeching, banging, and intermittent yelling I'd expect if Brandon was still at the gym—and he always was.

"Brandon Kyle," he answered. Pompous prick.

I couldn't stand the kind of people who used their name instead of a greeting.

"Hey. It's Travis Maddox. I heard you were looking for a part-time trainer."

"Maddox! It's about time you called. I've only given you my number a half dozen times. I was just at the Nickelback concert with Ty and Chuck. They told me you were thinking about the position. It's not what you know but who you know, am I right? Man ... we'd love to have you on the team. Especially Chuck. He's been watching you and says you know your shit. I agree. And holy God, would you bring in the ladies. Come get an application and I'll show you around. We'll discuss details and then we can decide if it's something we both still wanna do."

"Uh ..." I wasn't expecting his response. "When do you want me to come in? Today is my early day from classes, but I have to go pick up my wife and ..."

"Wife?" Brandon laughed. "Since when?"

"Since last weekend."

"Oh!" he said, his voice muffled. He was likely holding his fist over his mouth the way I'd seen him do before when he made fun of people. "Damn. Did you knock her up?"

"What did you just say?" I asked, feeling my blood boil. I turned on my heels, realizing I was pacing with my free hand balled into a fist.

"Nothin' ... Nothin'. Just fuckin' with ya, man! Is it that the Abigail chick I saw you with at The Red?"

"Abby Maddox."

"Really?" He paused. "I saw you with her but hey, you're always surrounded by pussy. You were all over her on the dance floor one night. She's hot as fuck. I'm glad I didn't approach her like I was going to. I didn't know you two were that serious. But, yeah! Come on in! I'll see you then."

I stretched my neck before answering, trying to calm down instead of threatening his life before I asked him for a job. "So," I blew out a breath. "Just whenever?"

"This is a pretty slow week. All the fatties have given up on their New Year's resolutions. My schedule is open until Thursday. Weekends are too busy for administrative bullshit. You know how it is up here."

I told him thanks through clenched teeth, and then hung up. There was no way I could work for that tweedle dick. I'd assault him on my first day.

Toto finished his lunch, and I put him in the green plaid sweater Abby had bought him. He pawed at the door, wanting out again. With some effort, I hooked his leash on his collar while he tried to lick my hand, and then led him outside.

We walked to the far end of the complex, and then began to walk back. His little legs trotted three to four steps to my one, and he was panting by the time we reached the bottom of the apartment steps.

Just as I turned to go in, a shiny Porsche rolled up, parking parallel behind my Harley. The window rolled down, revealing Parker's smug smile.

"Maddox! Heard you're in some trouble with the local authorities. And the non-local authorities."

"Lick my nuts, Hayes."

Parker's expression turned serious. "Is it also true ... about Abby and you?"

"Didn't she kick you to the curb for me? Twice?"

Parker frowned. "Is it true or not?"

"Of course it's true. You didn't think you really had a chance with her, did you?"

He waited a beat before speaking, his jaw tensing beneath the skin. He was a spoiled, entitled, rich, little fuck who wasn't used to not getting what he wanted. He was subduing a full-blown tantrum. "You don't deserve her, Maddox. You have to know that."

"Abby thinks I do, and her opinion is the only one I care about. So you can eat shit and die, Parker, because no one here cares what you think. You were a distraction. A commercial. She was never going to end up with you. It's fucking pathetic that you tried."

"I didn't try that hard. If I had, you wouldn't be married."

I tilted my chin down, glowering. "Get out of your pussy car and come say that to my face."

Parker swallowed, and then rolled up the window halfway. "Pussy car? How about your pussy dog?! Nice sweater!"

"This dog takes shits bigger than you."

"She's going to leave you, Travis. Abby's going to realize what she's done, the new is going to wear off, and she's going to leave you, and I want to see that arrogant smile wiped right off your face when she does."

I took a step forward, my muscles tensed and ready like they were just before a fight in The Circle. I knew if I threw one punch I wouldn't stop, but in that moment killing Parker was the only thing that was going to make me feel better.

"Get out of your fucking car. Right now."

Parker hid himself behind the dark tint of the window, and then drove away.

I stood with my hands in fists, my entire body trembling with anger. Toto nuzzled his nose against my jeans, and I looked down. Adrenaline absorbed back into my system as my gaze fell to his expectant eyes.

He was cold before we began our walk; now he was shivering like I was. He sniffed and kicked back a few tufts of grass like he owned the place.

I smiled. "Yeah. You woulda destroyed those skinny ankles. Pussy dog, my ass."

I scooped him up and took him inside. The second

I set him down, he trotted off to my bedroom, probably curling up on his bed for his afternoon nap.

I grabbed my wallet, phone, and keys, and headed out the door and down the stairs, sliding behind the wheel of the Camry. Even though I inhaled to breathe in the new car smell as deeply as I could, anxiety washed over me. My knuckles turned white under the pressure of my grip on the steering wheel.

Abby's last class wasn't over for another hour, and I was itching to vent about Brandon and Parker. Something white caught my eye, and I looked down between the seats. I reached down, fishing out the envelope that contained my mom's letter to my future wife; to Abby. I gently set it on the passenger seat, and put the gear into reverse and backed out, driving toward Dad's.

The streets on the way to the home where I grew up were filled with potholes and lined with dilapidated houses with broken down vehicles sitting in the yards. Dad's placed wore chipped paint and broken porch boards and shutters, but it was where I threw my first punch and caught my first fist in the mouth.

That overgrown grass was where Thomas used to hold me back so my brothers wouldn't beat my ass because I wouldn't give up. And where Trenton would try to mow down anything standing between him and me—even Thomas.

I smiled as I turned into the drive, the gravel crunching beneath the tires.

Dad pushed open the screen door and rested his hands on his round middle, watching me approach the porch with an appreciative smile on his face. "Well,

well," he said. "I didn't think I'd see you around here for a while."

"I'm three miles away," I said, climbing the steps to the weather worn wooden slats that made up the porch.

Dad patted me on the shoulder, and I brought him in for a hug.

"Your mom and I didn't leave the house for three weeks after the wedding."

"Dad," I scolded. My face twisted into disgust, and I stepped past him into the living room to the couch.

Dad chuckled, closing the door behind us. "This weather is a son-of-a-bitch," he grumbled. He took a peek outside the small glass square near the top of the front door, and then shook his head, waddling to his recliner.

He sat on the edge, leaning forward with his elbows resting on his knees. "Whatcha got there?" He gestured to the white envelope in my hand.

I lifted it a few inches, surprised at how nervous I felt.

Dad didn't talk about Mom a lot. Not that he tried not to, but I could still see the emptiness in his eyes—the same way I would feel if I ever lost Abby.

"It's a letter."

"The, uh, the one Mom left you?"

I nodded. "I gave it to Abby before the wedding."

"I'd hoped you'd remember."

"I did."

"Good," he said, clearing his throat. "Good."

"Do you want to read it?"

He shook his head. "It wasn't for me."

I pulled out the thin paper from the envelope, my eyes tracing Mom's delicate handwriting. "I know. It's kind of like hearing from her again. It reads just the way I remember her."

He looked surprised. "You remember her?"

I nodded. "It's fuzzy, but yeah. Bits and pieces."

Dad thought about it for a moment, and then nodded, waving his hand toward him. "Okay, then. Bring it over."

I jumped up, handed the paper to Dad, and then returned to my seat on the couch.

Dad blinked a few times, trying to focus, and then, seeing her words on paper, his bottom lip began to tremble. He rested his chin on his hand to try to mask his emotion, but then he blinked several times, and his eyes began to gloss over. A smile touched his mouth, he shook his head and chuckled once.

Dad lowered the letter with one hand, and then wiped his eyes with the other. After a full minute, he cleared his throat and then looked up at me.

"It's been a long time. It was good to hear her voice again. Even if it was just in my head. Thank you, son."

I nodded. "I miss her, too. All the time."

He laughed again, wiping another escaped tear. "I miss her every moment of every day. For damn near seventeen years. And the way you look at Abby"—he sighed—"that's the way I looked at your mother. My God, did I love that woman. I'd never felt anything like that before ... and never since."

My eyebrows pulled in. "Do you think I'm going to lose her, Dad?"

"Abby?"

I nodded.

Dad touched his lips with his fingers, and then looked down at the floor.

I couldn't move or breath while I waited for the answer.

He finally leaned forward again and looked me straight in the eyes. "Travis, I hate to break this to you son ... but your wife? She's stronger than you. You'd leave her before she'll leave you."

His words knocked the wind out of me, and after I couldn't keep my expression straight or my eyes dry, I covered my face, letting the relief wash over me in waves.

Dad was never wrong, and I trusted him with my life.

I looked up at him. Because I loved my wife, I was going keep the truth from him. And because of the love he'd felt for my mom, I knew Dad would understand.

CHAPTER *Seven*

FIRST BREATH

Abby

ADVERTISEMENTS CLUTTERED THE CORK BOARD next to the exit of Reiger Hall, all with headers like For Sale, In Search Of, and Help Wanted, and at the bottom, numbers cut into strips. An ad near the top had official school letterhead and a list of subjects.

I narrowed my eyes, read the fine print, and then ripped off a tab and put the phone number in my pocket. The school was looking for tutors and Calculus was one of the subjects.

Halfway into second semester, and the books and supplies in my backpack were weighing me down, cutting into my shoulders. I didn't realize I'd be married and looking for a job when choosing my classes before winter break. I hopped a bit as I took my first step toward the exit, trying to shift the straps to give the indentions next to my neck a break.

The early spring air hit my face the moment I stepped onto the concrete steps outside. Coats in every style and color peppered the sidewalks, a patchwork setting students apart from our gray surroundings. I looked up at the sky, feeling mist instantly cover my face. It had either poured or spat rain all day. The morning fog was just beginning to move on.

"Hey!" America yelled, jogging toward me. She waved, her bright smile the only sunshine. She stopped in front of me, holding the loose straps of her backpack at her chest, breathing hard. "The sorority girls are going nuts. I love it."

"What do you mean?"

"About Travis and you. Everyone's talking about it. I got to tell Alexis she was a jealous twat. To her face. It was amazing."

I felt my cheeks flush. "Great."

I continued down the sidewalk and America followed, beaming with pride.

"Not even half believe it."

I stopped abruptly. "Believe what? That we're married? Or that he married me?"

She shrugged. "Both." When she realized I was offended, she back peddled. "But, c'mon. Look at you. Of course he did. I mean, it's Travis. No one thought he'd ever get married. To anyone."

I looked down at my less-than-special plaid flannel shirt and olive-green vest, skinny jeans and tall, brown boots. My hair was damp and in a high, messy bun. I couldn't remember if I'd bothered to put on makeup before leaving the apartment or not. I looked around, noticing people's lingering, curious stares.

Someone whistled, and I turned, watching the sea of students part to reveal Travis walking toward me.

He was strutting down the center of the walkway, his hands in his jean's pockets, wearing a gray beanie, a black and white Ramones T-shirt under an open red and black flannel button down. His black leather boots added just that extra *Don't fuck with me, I'll end you* to the look.

Even with a wedding ring on his finger, the coeds stopped to stare. His perfect jawline, the dimple, his flawless stride—Travis was beautiful. An overabundance of sex and charm radiated from him without effort.

It wouldn't surprise me if he started walking in slow motion with Sweetie's *My Type* playing from somewhere.

"Look at that," I said. "That's why people don't believe it."

"You'll have beautiful children, I'll give you that," America said. "And look. So cute. Y'all married with matching flannels."

I frowned. "They're different colors."

One side of Travis's mouth turned up, his right brow lifted the tiniest bit, and I swallowed, feeling butterflies in my stomach.

He stopped a couple feet away, staring at me with the same look on his face as when the officiant in Vegas said *man and wife*. Travis didn't even have to say he loved me, I could see it in the way he looked at me, the way he moved, hear it in the way he spoke, even if what he was saying had nothing to do with me.

He breathed out a laugh, noticing my expression. “What is going on in that head of yours?”

I shook my head and threw my arms around his neck. “I’m good,” I said softly, pressing my cheek against his. Feeling his whiskers against my face was comforting, as was the smell of his cologne. “I just ...” I let him go and shrugged. “I love you.”

He stared at me for a moment, a wide grin spreading across his face. “That’s all I need.” He slid my backpack off my shoulders and swung it over one of his, took my hand, and then led me to the parking lot.

If people weren’t staring, they were pretending not to stare until we passed.

I could feel curious eyes ogling the back of my head. I wondered if Travis could also hear the whispers about the fire, the wedding, and just the fact that he and I were walking together after the big scandalous breakup only a tiny campus like Eastern would bother to care about.

“You gonna talk to me, Mare?” Travis asked, nudging her with his elbow.

“Maybe once I stop hating you.”

“You don’t hate me,” he said with a grin.

She frowned. “Well, when you do things like carry her backpack without her even asking, it does make it harder. You’re good to her. Can’t deny that.”

“And that won’t change.”

“It better not,” she said, hugging me goodbye.

Travis held my hand as he cut across the grass, his

boots squishing in the wet mud. I hopped over puddles and ruts, glad when my husband finally swooped me up into his arms and carried me.

I laced my fingers behind his neck, unable to stop smiling at the sight of Travis being unable to stop smiling.

"What are you so happy about?" I asked.

"You."

"No. It's something else. What have you been up to today? Did you get good news or something?"

"Kind of. Parker stopped by the apartment today to ask if the rumor was true."

"Parker?" I said, wrinkling my nose.

Travis laughed. "That's the reaction I hoped you'd have. He wasn't happy when I confirmed."

"Ugh, who cares?"

Travis's smile grew even wider. "He said the new was going to wear off and you were going to leave me. But that look on your face when you saw me a few minutes ago? Just blew his theory out of the water."

He lowered me to the asphalt next to our car and dug into his pocket for the keys.

"America heard the same today. That no one believed you would marry me."

He looked appalled. "I'm not calling America a liar but there is zero chance anyone thinks that. No one thinks I deserve you, Pidge. And they're not wrong."

"The sorority girls, do, apparently."

"The sorority girls voted Lexi as their Chapter President and she can't get past remedial math."

I burst into laughter for a moment before frowning.

"How do you know that?"

"They were talking about it in class. Here," he said, handing me the keys.

"What do you want me to do with these?"

"Your turn to drive."

"Me? No," I said, shaking my head.

He snorted. "Pigeon. You've gotta learn some time."

"I know how to drive. I just don't like to."

"What if I'm at work and you need to get somewhere?" He opened the driver's side door and gestured for me to get in.

I pushed the door closed. "Then I'll drive. But you're not at work, you're ... Hey, did you find a job?"

"Not yet. I called a guy. I don't think it's going to work out, though."

The mist turned into droplets that grew louder with every passing second.

"Why not?" I asked.

Travis opened the door again. "Get in the car, Pidge. It's going to start pouring any second." My brow arched, and he sighed. "They're hiring at Iron E."

"Don't you work out there? You like that place."

"Baby, get in the fucking car. You're getting soaked."

I started to walk toward the front, but he reached for my arm to stop me.

"I'm not driving in the rain, Trav. C'mon. I'll drive tomorrow."

He frowned. "Fine."

He slid in behind the wheel and leaned over, pulling on the lever and pushing open my door while I jogged around, ducking into the passenger's seat.

I scrambled to turn the heater on high, and then Travis took both of my hands, simultaneously rubbing and breathing on them. An errant, wavy strand of darkened caramel hair hung in front of my eyes, dripping wet.

Travis was unhappy, two lines forming between his brows.

"What's wrong with Iron E?" I asked.

"I like the gym. I just don't like the owner."

"That Chuck guy we met at the Pizza Shack that one time?"

"No, Chuck runs everything. Brandon Kyle is the owner, and he's a real piece of shit."

"How so?"

"His wife is pregnant ... like ready-to-pop pregnant. He's fucking the receptionist, two of the trainers, the clients."

"So?"

"So? He's human garbage, Pidge. I don't wanna work for him. He brags about it all the time. He's talking like he wants to pimp me out to the female clientele. He'll earn a throat punch the first hour."

I frowned. I didn't like the idea of the owner encouraging other women to try to seduce my husband, but I also trusted Travis implicitly. "Do you have any other prospects? We have rent, baby."

Travis sighed and looked out his rain-streaked window. "No. And he made it sound like all I have to do is apply and I have the job."

"Then what are you waiting for?" I said with a surprised laugh.

Travis turned to me, serious. "I just told you, Pidge. He's not the kind of people I like to be around."

I shrugged. "You won't be around him all the time. It's just until you find something else, right?"

"There's girls. Lots and lots of college girls. And bored housewives. And—"

"I trust you. Do you not trust yourself?"

"It's not that, it's just something I don't want to deal with. Brandon even said it himself... It's a meat market. He's not my pimp. And the women at that gym are used to the way he runs things."

I laughed out loud.

"It's not funny," Travis grumbled. "I'd rather trade punches than deal with the cougars that come through that gym."

"It's something else. Something you're not telling me."

"He also made a comment about you on the phone today. Said he saw you at The Red with me and thought about approaching you. Said he didn't know we were serious."

"Well, we know how that would've turned out."

"The crazy thing is … I mean, yeah, the thought of you being with anyone else makes me want to break things, but even worse is thinking how he would treat you. If you'd ran into him while we were broken up, or worse, if it was him instead of Parker that you were talking to …" he sighed. "I woulda fucking killed him if he hurt you."

I touched his face. "Is that what you're so pissed off about?"

"I know, it's stupid," he said, scowling. "It's just the way my brain works."

"Well, I've never spoken to him, and even if it had been him instead of Parker, you and I would still be sitting right here in this car together with rings on our fingers. Take the job, baby. You've got this. It's easy money." I dug into my pocket and pulled out the damp white rectangle. "I think I've found something, too. They're looking for Calculus tutors."

Travis wasn't impressed. "If I fought for Benny, we'd—"

"Not be together."

Travis looked down, defeated. "I wanted more for you, Pidge."

"More than what? Don't you dare wish away this part! The tiny apartment and clipping coupons and living on ramen until payday? Balancing the checkbook together and talking about our weekly budget, picking up a sweater in the store just to hang it back on the rack because holding your hand with our rings touching is way better than carrying a bag full of clothes.

"I want to feel giddy to be with you at the movie theater once every two months because it's something special instead of expected. I want to build our castle one block at a time ... just you and me. No easy outs."

His half smile reappeared, and he held my hand against his cheek. "Yeah?"

"Absolutely."

He took in my words and then nodded, already feeling better. "Speaking of being broke ... it's coin beer night at The Red. If we're both going to start working every night, let's get it out of our system."

I grinned. "I'm in." I tapped out a group text to Shepley and America, and immediately got a response. Excited, I shrugged my shoulders. "Shep and Mare will meet us there at eight-thirty."

Travis backed out of the parking spot and navigated his way to the street, turning up the radio and serenading me all the way home.

I looked out the window and sighed. We were going to be okay. Everything was going to be okay. I could feel it.

CHAPTER *Eight*

THE NEW NORMAL

Abby

STEPPING THROUGH THE FRONT DOOR of our favorite bar felt like a trip in a time machine.

My heels clicking against the sticky floor and holding tight onto Travis's hand as he weaved through the crowded club made me feel like we'd gone back in time, before the investigation, before the wedding, before the fire.

Coeds were barely covered in their metallic rompers and micro minis, twirling their hair as they talked to whatever silly boy was going to buy them a drink.

Sure, The Red was a meat market. Everyone was voluntarily on display to catch the eye of someone—anyone—or for couples to announce or reestablish their claim to one another.

The occasional patron was present who just loved to dance, or drink, or play pool, but humans needed other humans, and The Red was just crowded and dark and loud enough to see and be seen without judgment.

The speakers vibrated with music, beating like blood through a heart. With my free hand, I pressed my fingertips against my chest to try to lessen the pounding through my ribcage.

Mouths were moving, but the only sound was the music, everyone speaking the same language, singing the same song. Connection. Acceptance. A way to leave the stresses of college behind.

As we approached the bar, Travis waved to Raegan, and she shooed a couple of guys from the stools directly in front of her. She grinned as we sat down, wiping down the wooden bar in front of us. "I was wondering if you two would be back here."

"Why wouldn't we be?" I asked, watching her pop the top off two domestic beers and then place them in front of Travis and me.

Raegan crossed her arms. "I dunno. You're married now. I figured that would magically change you somehow, I guess."

"We still like to drink and see our friends," Travis said, clicking the neck of his beer bottle to mine. He kissed the corner of my mouth before taking a quick swig and surveying the room. "Where's Trent and Cami?"

Raegan answered as she walked away to tend to other customers. "She's pretty much working full-time at Skin Deep now."

"With Trent? That should be interesting," I said with a smirk.

"Oh, it's always interesting with those two."

"That's no shit," Travis said, amused.

I watched Raegan and Jorie work the line, taking two or three orders at a time. Making the drinks with precision and speed, taking payment, tapping furiously on the cash register, and then starting over.

Raegan's side was crowded—three rows deep. If we didn't know the bartenders through Camille, and Travis wasn't—well, Travis—we would have waited for a seat all night. The tables were full, too, just like the pool tables and the dance floor.

I hadn't seen it that busy in a while, and I wondered if it was because the fire made everyone want even more to be around friends and experience life and laughter.

Two cold hands cupped my shoulders, and I turned into a hug from America. Gigantic earrings dangled from her ears, her hair up in a messy bun. Her top exposed one shoulder. She had the *effortlessly glamorous* look down pat.

"Hey, betch," a voice said from behind me.

I flipped around. "Finch! You made it!"

He shrugged, the collar of his white button down grazing his ears as he did so. "I almost didn't come, but I refuse to sit around and wait for you to text me from Married-land. It apparently doesn't have great service."

I covered my eyes. "I meant to, I just … Okay, I'm a terrible friend." I grabbed him by the upper arms. "Let's grab lunch this week and I'll catch you up on everything."

"No need, America already did."

America grinned.

I wrinkled my nose. "Lunch, anyway?"

"Hell, yes. And you're paying." He looked behind him, scanning the crowd.

Jorie appeared with a smile. "You guys want a table? I can have Raegan clear one for you." She winked. "She loves being a bitch."

"Nah, we're good," Shepley said, sharing a single handshake and side hug with his cousin. He kissed my temple. "You doing okay?"

I nodded.

America and Finch wasted no time dragging me onto the dance floor.

I locked eyes with my husband a few times, watching him watching me, noticing the four women purposefully ignoring his wedding ring as they shamelessly flirted with him.

Unfortunately, that was something that hadn't changed.

Travis, though, wasn't as patient as usual, and dismissed them with a few effective words I wished I could've heard.

The sorority sisters left in a huff.

When I returned to my stool, Travis ran his finger down my arm, enjoying the slickness of the sweat on my skin. He leaned over to kiss my shoulder, flicking his tongue with each peck.

I stood up and leaned into him. "We're not going to stay long if you keep that up."

Travis looked up at me with a wry smile. "Promise?"

I kissed the top of his cheek, and he slid his hand around me, cupping my ass.

"You're people watching again," I said.

"It's just funny to me, the games people are playing, the assessment, the flirting, the push and pull and harmless manipulation ... Everything we've been doing all year right up until our wedding."

I smiled, and then kissed him again.

"For fuck's sake, you two, get a room," Finch teased.

Travis patted my backside and stood. "Heading to the john. Need anything?"

I arched an eyebrow. "From the men's room? No."

Travis chuckled and set his empty beer bottle on the bar. "Would you mind ordering me another one?"

"Not at all," I said, pressing my lips against his when he leaned down for a quick peck.

Shepley handed America his beer.

She shook her head. "I don't know why everyone makes a big deal that girls go to the bathroom in groups. Guys are just as guilty."

Shepley shrugged. "I'm just making sure he doesn't get into a fight while he's in there."

"He doesn't need babysat," America said.

Shepley made a face, as if America should know better. "He kinda does. The guy he just followed in there acted like he was going to slap Abby's ass on the dance floor. Y'all didn't see it but, unfortunately, Travis did."

"What are you waiting for, Shep? Go!" I said, playfully pushing him toward the men's room.

Shepley followed Travis, disappearing behind the crowd.

Finch crossed his arms, watching the spot where Shepley had squeezed through. "Whoever Travis was following can't be from Eastern State. Few men had enough courage to flirt with you when it was just common knowledge Travis Maddox was in love with you. No one would be stupid enough to do that now that you're his wife."

"He won't do anything. He said he was done with all that."

Finch squinted his eyes. "Oh, sweetheart. He will try like hell to keep his word, too. I have no doubt. Just remember he's human when he fucks up, okay?"

I nodded, looking in the direction of the bathroom.

America turned to me. "When he said he was done fighting, he meant The Circle, Abby. And they'll be fine! So," she said, fussing with her bun. "Does this place feel different now?"

"Why does everyone keep asking me that? I got married, not a lobotomy."

America laughed out loud and then took a sip of her cocktail, blinking when she noticed two college kids approaching. "Oh, shit."

"What?" I asked.

"They're not gone five fucking seconds and we already have to fend someone off," she complained.

"They're not coming over here."

America stared at me, unimpressed and unconvinced, then turned to watch the men approach with the same expression on her face.

"You're both stupid. They want me. Hi, boys," Finch said to the first one to reach us.

"Hey," he said. His hair was thick and brushed over, similar to Parker's. He was taller than me and lanky, but still fit, like the physique of a golfer.

If he'd seen me with Travis, I couldn't imagine why he'd think he was my type.

The shorter one opened his mouth to speak. "You look—"

"We don't, actually. We're not thirsty, don't want to dance, and definitely not lonely," America said, interrupting. "I have a boyfriend and she's married." She pointed to me.

The maybe-golfer smirked, looking up at his much taller friend and then back at us. Great. He was one of those guys who thought taken women were a challenge.

"Hi married, I'm Ricky."

Finch snarled at him. "Hilarious. Are you also from nineteen eighty-four? Who names their kid Ricky anymore?"

"Finch!" I hissed.

Ricky wasn't fazed. "This is Justin. Nice to meet you."

Justin was taller, his hair a lighter shade of brown, but he didn't look much different than Ricky. He was trying not to fidget. Something about both of them was … off.

"We haven't given you our names, so technically we haven't met," I said.

"I'm sorry," Justin said. "Have we offended you somehow?"

I looked down, ashamed. "Sorry. No, you haven't. We're just trying to help you out. Our boyfrien—my husband and her boyfriend are here, and they'll be back in a minute."

"So?" Ricky said. His cockiness was manufactured, forced. Red flags were shooting up all over the place, and not the Travis kind.

I sighed. "My husband doesn't appreciate strange men talking to me."

"Oh, he's jealous?" Justin said. "That must get old."

"Not really," I said. "Thanks for saying hi, but you should get going."

"I'm good," Ricky said with a smirk.

I rolled my eyes. America was right. The moment Travis got back, there would be a confrontation and our fun night out would be over. Neither of these guys seemed like they'd be smart enough to walk away if Travis warned them to move along.

Ricky put one hand in his pocket, glancing around while he sipped his seltzer.

I quickly recognized that he wasn't really trying to flirt with us, or even trying to talk to us.

He seemed to be waiting for Travis and Shepley to return.

I watched him intently, growing more suspicious with every passing second.

"Are you a cop?" I asked.

Both men turned to face me, surprised.

"What?" Ricky asked.

"Are you a cop? Because if you are, by law you have to tell me," I said.

America craned her neck at me, confusion on her face.

Justin chuckled. "No. Not a cop.""

"What about you?" I asked, lowering my chin and glaring at Ricky.

Ricky gave me a once over, from my eyes to my knees, and then back up. He wasn't interested in me at all. He was assessing me, trying to decide out how a nineteen-year-old girl could figure him out. He was there for Travis.

He didn't answer, so I took a step toward him. "Get the fuck outta here. If you want to talk to him, you're going to have to arrest him."

Ricky stood taller, but he took a step back. "Which could be arranged. He's not even twenty yet, drinking in a bar. I bet you all have fake IDs."

I narrowed my eyes and leaned closer. "Then what are you waiting for?"

"What's going on?" America asked, alarmed.

Justin looked around, a bit nervous. He wasn't a cop, and if he was, he was likely a rookie, maybe even an informant, young-looking enough to be assigned to try to fool us.

A strong arm hooked around my neck, and Travis kissed my temple. "Hey, baby." As predicted, he glared at the two men standing in front of us. "Who's this?"

"Who?" America asked, playing dumb.

Travis wasn't amused. He pointed to Justin and

Ricky—if those were even their names. "These clowns."

Ricky laughed once, getting back into character but clearly over doing it. "Clowns? We're not after your bitches. Calm down."

"Oh, you're fucking brilliant," Shepley said, already pulling off his jacket.

Before I could yell stop, Travis had already let me go and lunged for Ricky, taking him to the ground.

As usual, the rest of the bar joined in. Any drunken idiots who were walking around looking for a fight had just found one.

Finch held me back from the growing mountain of swinging fists, a wide grin on his face.

As I tried to find my husband, I couldn't help but wonder what the purpose would be for goading him into a fight. Ricky had already admitted that they could have arrested him for being underage.

As the brawl spread, America and I were pinned against the bar. Raegan reached for us, trying to help us over before we were crushed.

"Shep!" America yelled as I pushed her over the barrier while Raegan pulled. "Shepley!"

Once America was over and standing safely next to Raegan, I hopped over, too.

Travis was nowhere, and the longer he was out of my line of sight, the more I worried. I wasn't sure what the men wanted. They could be cops, or FBI, or worse, sent from Vegas. Benny was still unhappy about Travis turning him down, and no one ever really got away with turning down a mob boss.

I yelled for my husband again.

The bouncers pushed through the crowd, pulling apart the numerous humans who were acting like animals—Travis included.

"Travis Maddox!" I yelled.

Travis stood up, wiping blood from his lip with the back of his hand, smiling down at the men still on the floor. His face was smug, his eyes bright. He'd missed fighting.

Shepley tugged on his shirt and Travis walked backward, and then turned at the bar, reaching for me. He helped me over, and then set me down on my feet.

"You okay?" Travis asked.

I frowned at him, but he wasn't sorry.

Travis's love for throwing punches would always simmer just beneath the surface, hoping and waiting to be unleashed on someone. People kept asking me if I felt different, and it was then that I realized that was the one thing that I'd hoped would change.

The crowd jostled and Travis turned away from me, holding a protective stance as if the men writhing in pain on the floor were still a threat. The bouncers led them out, signaling to Travis and Shepley that they had to leave, too.

Raegan came over, leaning in to speak to Travis. "You keep this shit up, Trav, and Jorie will ban you from this place for good."

"She says that every time," Travis said with a grin, wiping his mouth again.

"Are you ... Are you bleeding?" I said, turning him to face me.

Travis didn't get hit unless he allowed it. That was sort of his thing.

I wasn't used to seeing him bloody, and that made my paranoia even worse.

"Yeah," Shepley said. "I might have elbowed him on accident."

I raised an eyebrow. "Didn't see that coming, huh?"

Travis made a face. "I did, but I was in a great position and mid-punch at that little maggot who called you and Mare bitches ... so I didn't bother to dodge."

"Come on, guys. Don't make the bouncers escort you out," Raegan said, patting Travis on the shoulder.

"I'm staying," Finch said, pretending to tuck hair behind his ear. "I didn't do shit and I just got my night started."

"You sure?" I asked, already knowing the answer.

Finch kissed my cheek and waved, leaving us for the dance floor.

I sighed as we began walking toward the exit. I couldn't blame Travis, but I was also disappointed. It was our last hoorah, and we'd barely been out for an hour.

We walked out with Shepley and America, our vehicles parked side-by-side in the parking lot.

"Did you figure it out?" America asked.

I shook my head. "No, but I will."

"What are you talking about?" Shepley asked, straightening his shirt.

"Those guys were weird," America said.

"They came over to talk to us," I said. "But after we told them you were coming back, they hung around.

They didn't talk to us, try to buy us drinks, anything. Almost like they were waiting for you."

Travis and Shepley traded glances.

"Have you seen them before?" I asked.

Travis made a face. "No. And I better not see them again."

"What he said about us being bitches," America said. "He knew it would set Travis off. The whole thing is just sketch. Something is up."

"You two need to stop watching those crime shows on Netflix. You're getting paranoid as fuck," Travis said, looking at me.

I frowned. "Those guys were half your size. You didn't need to swing on them."

Shepley shrugged. "I just roughed him up. If I'd thrown a real punch, I might've killed him."

"Same," Travis said, monotone.

I tugged on Travis's hand. "I'm telling you guys, something's up with them. Mare's right. We need to find out what it is."

Travis looked to Shepley, who shrugged. "One of them had a Parkland College keyring with an Eastern State one on the same chain. They're just a couple of cock suckers from Champagne, Illinois who've never met a Maddox."

I arched my eyebrow at Shepley. I thought I was the observant one.

Travis took off his jacket and draped it over my shoulders.

I hadn't noticed until that moment that I was shivering.

"You know what we need to do?" he asked, kissing my cheek. "We need to move on. I'm not going to spend my life looking over my shoulder, Pidge. I don't want you to, either. I'm going to call on that job next week, and you're going to start tutoring. They'll finish the investigation, and it will all be over."

I nodded, waving to America when Travis opened the passenger door. I slid in, annoyed that I was still shivering. I wasn't cold, I was nervous.

Justin and Ricky had come to pick a fight with Travis.

I needed to know why.

Travis stood outside my door and lit a cigarette, holding his other hand flat against my window.

I pressed my palm against his, and he winked at me, blowing out a puff of smoke.

He took a few puffs and then pinched off the cherry, mashing the lit ash into the gravel with his boot. He stuffed the butt into his pocket, and just as he walked around the back of the car, Justin and Ricky came into view.

They were standing in the far shadows of the parking lot, staring at the Camry. Ricky and I locked eyes, and he spoke something to Justin, but didn't look away.

I lowered my chin and lifted my hand, prominently displaying my middle finger.

Travis opened the door and I put my *fuck you* away, smiling at him as he turned the ignition and then placed his hand on my knee while he drove to the road.

The men stepped back into the darkness, out of Travis's eyesight, but I knew they were there, watching.

"Everything okay, baby?" Travis said. "I'm sorry. I know you were looking forward to tonight."

"I'm not upset," I said, letting the suspicion and concern fall from my face as I turned to face my husband. "I'm fine. Really."

"You still think those guys with their tiny noodle arms are rogue FBI or something?" he teased.

Travis's birthday was in a few days, and I knew he was already teetering on turning himself in. There were plenty of reasons to lie.

I looked out the window to the side mirror, noting that a pair of headlights were hanging back almost a mile behind us. "No. I don't think they're anyone. False alarm."

Travis patted my knee and drove toward the apartment, smiling like everything hadn't changed—and I smiled with him.

CHAPTER *Nine*

WRECKED

Travis

"BABY! I WANTED A LATE snack. Stir fry in five!" Abby called from the kitchen.

"Awesome, I don't know why but I've been hungry since about an hour after dinner," I said, staring into the bathroom mirror.

I walked into the kitchen and kissed her cheek.

She looked at me, a concerned expression on her face. "You okay? It was the first day back to classes, the first time to see Keaton after the fire. Maybe we should've skipped The Red tonight and gone to bed early."

"I haven't been sleeping great. I think I hit a wall. I feel like I can barely keep my eyes open."

Her eyebrows pulled in. "You look exhausted. Take a shower and go to bed. We'll eat in there."

"In bed?"

"Yep, I'll get the trays out and we'll have a quick picnic and hit the sack."

"You are an angel," I said, giving her a peck before trudging to the shower.

The water ran over me, but where it usually woke me up, I just felt more tired. Wasting no time, I scrubbed and stepped out, wrapping a towel around my waist and padded in my still damp feet to the bedroom.

Abby handed me a pair of shorts and once I got them on, I climbed in bed. She sat a tray over my lap, and I leaned back.

"Swear to God, babe. I don't deserve you."

She sat next to me, grabbing a fork and shoveling food into my mouth. "If you didn't, I wouldn't be hand-feeding you stir fry in bed. You absolutely deserve it."

I chewed and then leaned my head back again.

There were so many things I loved about Abby, and I hadn't even seen this side of her yet. She'd always been a little aloof, just beyond reach, and now she'd settled in, gotten comfortable, and—though I'd never say this out loud—seemed to be enjoying being a doting wife.

"Don't expect it every night," she winked, standing.

"There she is," I said with a smile. I stabbed some veggies with my fork and shoved a huge bite into my mouth.

Abby turned for the hallway and I mumbled for her to stop before I could swallow.

"What?" she asked.

"Where are you going?"

She pointed to the hallway. "Dishes."

"No fuckin' way. You cooked."

"Tonight I'm doing both. There's not much. One of these days I'll be sick, and you'll have to carry more of the load. That's how this works."

"It can't be this easy. People get divorced every day. Is this really how easy marriage is?"

"It's not easy. This is the easy part."

I pointed the fork at her. "Well, I'm going to enjoy it."

I finished my food and tried to stay awake for her to come back to bed, but I must've passed out before she came back for my tray, because I woke up, the tray was gone, and the room was dark. Abby was curled up behind me, her arm over my middle.

"Shit," I whispered, looking around.

"What?" Abby asked, stirring.

"What time is it?" I sat up, looking at the glowing numbers on the clock.

"You were tired, babe," she said, squeezing me after I laid back down.

My phone pinged.

"What the hell?" I said. "Who would be texting me at this hour?"

It pinged again.

"I'm not moving," I said. I felt a little better than I had earlier, but I was warm, comfortable, and cuddled up to my wife. I wasn't going anywhere.

Ping!

"Reminds me of fight night," Abby said, her voice muffled against my back.

Then, her phone chimed.

"Must be Shep and Mare," she said, sitting up. She grabbed her phone and opened her messages. "Oh, God. Trav?"

"What?"

"It's your dad."

"What?" I said again, this time sitting up and reaching for my phone. "Why is he up this late? Is he okay?"

"I'm calling him," she said, holding the phone to her ear.

I flipped on the lamp and waited.

"Jim? What happened? *What*? When?" Abby asked.

"Is he okay?" I asked. I could hear Dad's voice. He was worried.

She nodded to me, then continued to listen. "We'll be right there, Jim. We're coming." She hung up and then turned to me.

"Is it Dad?"

She shook her head. "Trent's been in an accident," she blurted out. "With Cami."

"Tonight?"

She nodded, her eyes filling with tears. "They were T-boned by a drunk driver after work. Your dad's at the hospital, waiting to hear from the doctors. Thomas is on a plane home."

"So it must be bad," I said, instantly feeling sick. I stood, going straight for the closet and pulling on the first hoodie I found.

Abby got up to get dressed, too.

"He's stable," she said as we rushed out to the car.

"Cami's in pretty bad shape. I guess they were arguing, and Cami was driving and not paying attention. He carried her to the closest house. That's all he said before he passed out in the ambulance. He hasn't been awake since."

We slammed our doors and looked at each other. Abby must've seen the panic on my face, because she put her hand on my knee. "They're going be okay."

I backed out and then rushed out of the parking lot, turning the wheel and taking the corner a little fast, instinctively reaching over to make sure Abby's seat belt was fastened tight.

"Baby, be careful. You've been drinking. Don't drive too fast in the rain."

My hands shook as I twisted the steering wheel under my grip and lifted my foot off the gas. "Goddammit, Trent."

The hospital's emergency room doors swept open with a rush of air, and I squeezed Abby's hand, pulling her through the threshold.

Exhausted mothers holding sick babies were sitting alongside frail old men, and a group of skateboarders were sitting around a friend who was holding his wrist against his chest. Moaning, whimpering, babies crying, cell phones ringing, kids playing on their tablets, and iPhones with the volume way too high layered with announcements over the PA system. It made me want to bail, but I had to find my family.

Beyond the borders of the waiting room, behind secured, double doors each with small, rectangular windows, came a muffled ruckus—a man swearing and yelling.

"Trent," I said under my breath.

I approached the receptionist's desk, but she didn't even look up. "Hi," I said, glancing down at the name-plate, "Gladys. I'm looking for Trenton Maddox."

"Are you family?" Gladys asked with her nasally voice, unimpressed with my obvious urgency.

Twin beaded chains hung from her oval glasses. Her thin lips pursed and wrinkled between responses. She'd probably worked around ten years more than what her empathy could survive and didn't give two fucks that my brother was hurt or that my dad was beyond those doors where I couldn't get to him, worried.

"He's my brother," I said. "He was in an accident."

"Oh, the drunk driver," Gladys said.

It took everything in me to keep my voice calm. "No. He was hit by a drunk driver."

"I know," Gladys said with a sigh. "He refuses to go to his own exam room."

"Can I see him? I can convince him to go where he needs to be."

She stared at her computer, unaffected. "I'll let them know you're here. Have a seat."

I balled my hands into fists, but before I could lose my shit, I turned on my heels and walked with Abby to a row of chairs not yet filled with the sick or injured. I sat, not realizing that my knee was furiously bobbing until I saw a kid staring at my leg. I propped my elbow on the armrest, and then pinched the bridge of my nose.

Abby was rubbing my back, but the wait was agony.

Trenton had already been in an accident with someone he cared about. Even though he'd survived, I thought losing Kenzie would kill him. If he survived this one, too, and Cami didn't ... I wasn't sure he could come back from that.

"He's going to be okay, babe. I have a good feeling," Abby said. "Trav," she said, patting my knee. "Your dad …"

"Travis?" Dad was standing in the doorway, the double doors wide open.

I jumped up and hurried across the room, pulling him in for a hug. "How is he? How's Cami?"

"Trenton's awake. He passed out for a bit, but he'll okay. He'll be hobblin' around for a while. Broke his arm in two places. His ankle's swollen, but the X-Rays came back okay. I think he rolled it when he was running."

"How are you holding up?" Abby asked, hugging Dad.

"Oh, you know. It's past my bedtime but my boy's hurt. Got up here as quick as I could."

"He's lucky to have you," Abby said, squeezing him again.

"Trent's on back there. I told him to wait while I came and got ya. That receptionist isn't the most helpful." He hooked his arm around mine, and then I felt him lean on me.

On the outside, he was keeping it together, but his hands were clammy, and his red-rimmed eyes were tired.

"Dad, you sure you're alright?"

"Me? Fine ... fine." He looked to the receptionist. She buzzed us in, where a nurse stood. "This is my son and his wife."

"You have a few boys it seems, Mr. Maddox."

"Sure do. I've got another one on the way. Flying in from California. My oldest."

"You've got a great family," she said.

"Sure do. I'll just take them on back."

"Sounds good. Let me know if you need anything," she said.

Dad led us to Camille's exam room but stopped just outside the door, keeping his voice low. "Camille's having a CAT scan. Trenton's with her. When he comes back … he's worried sick, son. Just be gentle with him. I know you boys jab at each other, but he just needs some reassurance. I've never seen him like this."

"Yeah, yeah, of course, Dad. What happened?" I asked. "Abby told me part of it, but she didn't know much."

Dad rested a hand on his belly, his gaze falling to the floor. "Camille left work upset. Trenton jumped into the passenger seat. It was raining, and they were arguing. Never saw that little bastard run the stop sign. Her Jeep flipped four and-a-half times. When Trenton came to, he pulled her out. When he couldn't get her to wake up, he picked her up and carried her over a mile to the nearest house."

"Christ," I breathed. "With a broken arm? In two places?"

"*Chyeah*, he did," he said, unable to hide his pride.

Dad put his hand on the door. "When they get back,

they're going to"—Dad choked, and then cleared his throat—"they're going to set his bones, and then cast his arm. They warned him that it's already started to heal and if he waited it would be harder to set, but he won't leave her."

I squeezed him to my side. "He's tough, Dad. He'll be okay. What are they saying about Cami?"

Dad's brow furrowed. "She's still unconscious. She has a decent gash on her head and some swelling. The window shattered and cut 'em both pretty bad."

I looked down the hall, trying to organize the thoughts in my head. I needed to say something, anything to make him feel better.

He couldn't lose anyone else.

I nodded. "Trent's too fuckin' mean to die, and Cami's tougher than he is."

Dad smiled and wiped his eyes with the back of his hand. "Well that's good odds, then, eh?" He pushed open the door.

Abby ushered Dad to the only chair in the room, and I popped into the hall looking for another. The nurse that greeted us was already bringing us one. "Thank you," I said, nodding.

Other than the two chairs and the three of us, it was an empty room. No bed or IV pumps, just the mess the ER staff left behind.

I looked down at a spatter of blood on the floor, and dozens of bloody blue rags. "Jesus," I said, placing the new chair next to Dad's.

"Have a seat, sis," Dad said, getting settled in his chair. "They should be back soon."

"What's the look for?" I asked Abby, noting the sour expression on her face.

"Nothing," she snapped.

I stood behind her, gently pressing my thumbs into her neck, kneading her tense muscles in small circles.

She let out a breath and relaxed.

"Baby," I said. "Tell me."

She glanced at Dad, who seemed to already know what she was about to say. "Trenton hasn't let a girl drive since Mackenzie. The first time he ... What she did was selfish. And Thomas coming here—" She caught herself. "Never mind."

"Yeah," I said, looking to Dad. "Tommy's flying in?"

Dad just nodded.

"What about the twins?"

"They were on standby for work, can't get coverage in time. They're coming next week."

"Because he's going to be okay," I said, thinking aloud. My eyebrows pulled together as I continued to work on Abby's neck. "But Tommy didn't wait? That's not like him."

Dad didn't offer anything more, but he couldn't hide whatever he knew from his expression.

A man with a shaved head and baby blue scrubs pushed through the door while pulling the end of a gurney. A woman pushed from behind with one hand, pulling Trenton's wheelchair with the other.

My brother's eyes lit up for half a second when he saw Abby and me, but then the light dimmed.

I took over for the woman, her blond hair was

pulled back tight into a no-nonsense, low ponytail. Her badge read *Stacy Z.*, and beneath that, *Radiographer*.

"Thanks for the help," the man said.

"No problem, Julian. Want me to help with telemetry?" she asked.

He shook his head.

"Let me know if you need anything else," she said with a bright smile.

Julian scowled at Trenton. "Only if he insists on tagging along again."

Stacy breathed out a laugh as she headed for the door, her blue eyes sparkling when she turned to wave good-bye. "I think it's sweet."

Trenton's jaw muscles danced beneath his skin, but he kept his eyes forward, a permanent frown on his face. His right arm was propped on his lap, a white hospital blanket used as a makeshift splint. A large ice pack peeked out beneath the thick cotton.

I grabbed the handles of his wheelchair, moving him out of the way while Julian positioned Camille's bed, locking it into place.

Abby knelt in front of Trenton. "Hey," she said, looking him over.

Bright red blood had seeped into the white of his right eye, and his face, neck, and arms were speckled with varying degrees of lacerations from the broken glass bouncing around in the Jeep.

I sat down in Abby's chair, planting my elbows on my thighs.

Trenton looked away, his eyes glossing over.

Julian pressed the last button of Camille's telemetry wires into an adhesive patch on her chest, nodding to us as he quietly exited the room.

"Trent," I began.

"Not now," he choked.

"I know what you're thinkin'," I said, letting my empathy seep through to my tone.

"No, you don't."

I paused, trying to think of what words would help me if I were in the same position—if it were Abby lying in that bed instead of Camille. I thought about searching for her in the fire, and the sheer pain and fear that came with even the thought of losing her.

There was nothing. Nothing could make me feel better in that situation other than knowing Abby was okay.

I scanned Camille's face. She was strangely serene for being so bloody, beat up and pale.

"You're right. I don't. This fucking sucks, brother, and I'm sorry."

Trenton's eyes returned to mine. His bottom lip quivered. "I tried to stop her."

I gently cupped the back of his neck, leaning my forehead close to his. "We know. She knows."

"She …" He sniffed and cleared his throat a few times before he could continue. "The guy from before. He's in town. Came to see her and Bishop saw them."

"Bishop?" I asked.

"He works with us at Skin Deep. Anyway, Bishop said the piece of shit tried to kiss her. I told Cami I was done. I didn't mean *us*, I meant done waiting around for him to decide to leave her alone. He knows about me."

Abby sighed and covered her eyes with her hand.

"She thought I meant I was done with her, and it upset her. Bad. So, she took off in her car. I jumped in and was trying to get her to pull over. I begged her. She was upset and it was all my fault. She was getting ready to stop, though, when we got hit. And now," he looked over at her, his bottom lip trembling. He lifted his good arm to gesture in her direction. "She's lying in that bed, lost in her head somewhere, and I can't get to her."

Dad stared at the floor.

I felt like the only one in the room that didn't know the full story.

"Dad …" I said. "What aren't you saying?"

He hesitated, saved just before he spoke by the nurse who entered the room.

Deep, double dimples bordered her wide smile. She was chewing a wad of gum the same color as her bright scrubs. "Hi all," she whispered. "I'm Katie. I hear you have someone on the way. Someone will be bringing more chairs soon. In the meantime, I'll be setting Trenton's arm. I hear he doesn't want to go to the casting room, so Rosh will be in momentarily with equipment."

Trenton was unfazed.

"Shouldn't the, uh, the doctor set his arm?" I asked.

Katie slapped the X-rays on the viewer and flipped on the light.

Abby's face scrunched at the images, and I inwardly cringed.

Katie turned to us, her dirty-blond hair bouncing. "I'm a PA ... and I'm all you've got. After Trenton's recent outburst, all the doctors offered me as sacrifice."

"Pussies," Trenton said with a huff.

A man wearing black scrubs pushed through the door, wheeling in equipment, a tray full of supplies, and a bowl of water.

"Hi, Rosh," Katie said, chipper even when whispering.

Rosh held up a roll of lime green casting tape. "I brought the best color we have."

"Thank you," Katie said. She lowered her chin. "Just waiting on the extra bed and the anesthesiologist."

Trenton shook his head. "No. I gotta be ready when she wakes up."

Katie hesitated, then took a glimpse at each person in the room. "She has family here. And, you'll be here, just not *here* here."

Trenton pushed his shoulders back, righting his posture. "I can do it."

Empathy weighed down Katie's expression. "If you yell ..."

"I won't make a fucking peep," Trenton said, meeting her gaze. "I swear."

Katie watched him for a moment, and then nodded. "I believe that. Okay, Rosh, let's do this."

She washed her hands, dried them, and then put on a pair of blue gloves while Rosh set a chair in front of Trenton, checking his wheelchair to make sure his locks were secure.

Trenton braced himself while Katie removed the blanket splint and ice pack. She palpated his arm, and then nodded to Rosh.

Abby held her breath, and Dad stood and walked a few steps away.

"Here, Dad. Sit," I said.

He shook his head, waving me away.

Katie looked up at Trenton from under her brow. "Ready? We're going to start with your wrist first."

He nodded, and Katie pressed and pulled, manipulating his wrist and hand.

Trenton's face turned red, and his jaw was taut.

I grabbed his left hand, and he dug his fingers into my skin.

"Don't hold your breath," Katie said softly. "Don't want you passing out on me if you're not prone in a bed. Almost finished."

Trenton breathed in through his nose.

"That's right. Concentrate on your breathing. You're doing great." She pressed and moved his hand around.

I disagreed with her. I was hoping to God he'd pass out. But Trenton withstood the pain, determined to be awake and alert for Camille.

Focused, Katie moved on to the second break.

Just when I thought Trenton couldn't take another second, his arm straightened, and Katie signaled to Rosh.

"Okay, the worst is over," she said. She placed the material while holding his arm in place, Rosh wetted something else, and then began wrapping his arm.

"Beautiful," Rosh said, grinning as he wrapped the lime green tape around the cast.

"As soon as that disaster dries, I get first dibs to sign it," I said. "I already know what I'm gonna say."

"It's not a disaster," Katie said. "That's one beautiful cast."

Dad quietly stood in the corner, letting me take my turn pacing.

"Camille's family was contacted. Why haven't they shown up?" I asked.

"Her family's … complicated," Trenton said.

"Nothing's complicated enough that you don't show up for something like this," I said.

"Inexcusable," Jim muttered. "Well, we're her family now. We'll just make sure we're all she needs."

Trent sat in his wheelchair next to her bed, still as a statue and only once in a while whispering something to her that I couldn't decipher.

Abby's stomach growled, and she looked to me, apologetic. "Anyone up for some all-night fast food?"

We all raised our hand, even Trenton.

"Okay, I'll go grab some dinner." She kissed me once.

"Be careful, baby."

"What are the odds of two people in our family getting in an accident in the same night?" she asked.

Dad frowned. "Unfortunately, sis, with us, the odds aren't in your favor. Wear your seatbelt. Stay alert. You're not too tired, are ya?"

Abby shook her head. "I'm fine. Text me what you want from In-and-Out." She pointed at my dad. "I won't check it until I get there."

Waiting for her to get back seemed to take an eternity. I paced, and paced some more, checking my phone even though I knew she wasn't supposed to text while driving.

"She's okay, bro," Trenton said.

"I know. I know she is."

The room was somehow quieter without her there even though she'd barely made a peep before. I tried not to look at Camille, because every time I did, it sent a wave of panic through my body.

My phone pinged, I read it and sighed. "She made it there. Waiting on food."

Dad smiled, tired but relieved. "She'll be back in no time, son."

Within twenty minutes, she was back, divvying out our food. We ate in silence, cleaned up in silence, and the time seemed to pass from one nurse or doctor's visit at a time.

After another hour and a few more tests, the staff informed us they'd be moving Camille upstairs.

"Why isn't she waking up?" Trenton asked.

The doctor took a breath and shook her head. "The brain is complicated. The swelling is going down, and her brain function is great, so that's good news. She's healing. Her brain is likely keeping everything shut down while she does—also good news. We got her a room in four-fourteen. It's a corner suite. Really nice, and more room for your brother and dad to pace." She winked and nodded once before leaving the room.

I gently patted Trenton's good shoulder for encouragement, and then nurses arrived to gather Camille's monitoring devices and IV poles.

They worked fast, unlocking her gurney in preparation for the trip upstairs before we realized they were ready.

We followed the nurses out, waving to Katie and Rosh as we passed the ER staff's station. When we reached the elevator, everyone immediately saw a problem. Camille's gurney and Trenton's wheelchair wouldn't fit in the same elevator.

"We'll see you up there," the nurse said, her strawberry blond hair grazing her shoulders.

Trenton used his good hand to push up.

I rushed to lock his wheels, and the nurse's eyes grew wide.

"Please don't!" she said.

Trenton hobbled into the elevator, steadying himself with the railing on the gurney. He nodded to me. "See you up top."

The elevator doors swept closed, and I waited three seconds before pushing the button again.

Abby huffed.

"You're still angry?" I asked.

"Yes. I'm sorry, but yes. I can't help but think she doesn't deserve all the fuss he's making over her. And then Thomas …"

"Tommy? What about him?" I asked.

"He should be here by now. That's all I'm going to say," she grumbled.

The other elevator opened, revealing an empty space. Abby guided Dad on, and I pushed Trenton's wheelchair in after them.

"I don't mean to talk bad about her while she's practically in a coma … God, I'm an awful person. It's just … Never mind."

"Tommy's flying here, Pidge. It's going to take him awhile. He's probably sick with worry."

"Sure he is." She said it under her breath, but I still caught it.

I started to defend him again, but Dad spoke up.

"I understand, sis," Dad said. "It's an emotional day. Sometimes it just feels better to blame someone. It's the only way we can make sense of it all."

When the elevator opened, we stepped out to see Thomas standing at the fourth-floor nurses' station.

"Hey!" I said.

He flipped around and came at me with open arms. "Have you heard anything?"

"Trent is awake."

"And Camille?" Thomas asked.

I shoved my hands in my pockets and shrugged. "She's not."

I noticed Thomas's shoulders sag.

"Trenton's arm is broken in two places," I said. "Carried her over a mile to the closest house."

Thomas shook his head, the deep wrinkle between his brow softening. "That's what the nurses said. Holy hell. He's been here one night and is already a legend."

"It's *so* great that you came, and that you got here so quickly." Abby shrugged with an innocent smile on her face, but I knew her. Something was up.

Thomas hugged Dad and then nodded, his head

swirling with thoughts. He glanced at all of us. "Can we go see them?"

"Yeah," Dad said. "They put her at the end of the hall ... four-fourteen."

Thomas was in a hurry to get to the room, and Abby shot me a glance just before he pushed through the door.

Once he saw Camille, he froze, covering his mouth. His hand left his lips and ran over the top of his short dirty-blond hair. "You ... you okay, little brother?" he whispered, his eyes never leaving Camille.

"I'll live," Trenton said. He sounded exhausted.

Abby closed the door behind the nurses as they left, and we watched Thomas approach Camille's bed.

He touched her fingers tenderly. Trenton watched, too, confusion darkening his face.

"What the fuck are you doing, Tommy?" Trenton asked, suddenly alert.

"I should have come sooner," he said, his face crumpling. "I'm sorry, Trent."

Trenton wrinkled his nose. "What are you talkin' about?"

"I ... didn't fly in. I've been sitting in my car waiting just long enough to make you believe that I was."

"What?" I asked.

Thomas loosened his tie.

"What the fuck is going on?" I asked.

Thomas's lips pressed together. "I don't … I don't fucking know. I sat out there … feeling stupid, feeling worried sick, drowning in guilt. It was fucking agony, and I'm so tired of ... I'm sorry," Thomas said again, this time to Camille.

"Tommy," I said, taking a step. "You all right, man?"

Thomas turned to face us, hesitating when he looked to Dad. "I've been in town. I came because of the fire, but then I stayed ..."

"Because of the fire," Abby said, unconvinced.

She lifted her chin. She studied Thomas the way she did cards in her hand. Her expression smoothed, as if she were relieved by a freeing truth. She sighed. "Just tell them."

"Tommy," Dad said quickly. "Maybe you should wait until everything settles down."

"Tell us what?" Trenton asked.

Thomas looked a little desperate and a lot guilty. "I can't." He gestured to Abby. "Go ahead."

Abby hesitated.

I turned to her. "Tell us what?"

She swallowed, seeming to try to choke down the elephant in the room. "Thomas James," she whispered.

I frowned, irritated that I hadn't caught on. But Trenton had.

He paled. "No."

"Trent," Thomas begged.

"No!" Trenton said, louder than we'd been speaking for hours. His breath became labored, and then he struggled for every lungful of air. He looked at our oldest brother, hurt and disappointed. "Tommy!" he said, his voice begging. "Tell me I'm wrong!"

Abby leaned in to whisper in my ear. "The guy from California Cami was dating ... T.J."

I felt the blood drain from my face. "*Oh, fuck.*"

Thomas stood in the middle of the room like a sitting duck, ashamed and more alone than I'd ever seen him.

I walked over to him, and then paused, my gaze falling on Trenton. I didn't know what to do. We'd never experienced this before.

"It's okay," Trenton said finally. "It's okay, Tommy. I get it."

Thomas was overwhelmed with Trenton's forgiveness, barely able to say his next words. "But you loved her first."

"And she was your first love," Trenton said. He chuckled, an awkward way to discharge his discomfort. "She tried to warn me. I wouldn't listen."

"Because I made her lie to you. Don't make excuses for me, Trent."

Trenton raised his good arm and let it fall back to the arm of his wheelchair. "What do you want me to say, Tommy? You want me to hate you? Yell at you? Throw a punch? You're my brother. I love you no matter what. And Cami … Cami loves you, too."

Thomas slowly shook his head. "Not like she loves you."

A small, appreciative smile touched Trenton's lips, and he looked at Camille. "I know."

"We're, uh ..." Abby said, waiting for me. I nodded, and she continued. "It's late," she said, hooking her arm around mine. "We're going to go home. We'll be back in the morning. Need us to do anything before we go?"

Trenton shook his head.

"You need a ride, Dad?" I asked. He shook his head, too.

I hugged him and Thomas, and then carefully curled my arm around Trenton, waved good-bye, and then led my wife by the hand to the elevator.

We didn't speak until we reached the car. I opened her door, jogged around to mine, and slid behind the wheel. As soon as my fingers curled around the top of the steering wheel, I puffed out a breath.

"You knew?" I asked. "How did you know?"

She opened her mouth to speak, then couldn't.

"*How*, Pigeon? How did you know?"

"I didn't. Not until I heard he was flying in. I tried to tell myself that maybe I was wrong, considering the twins couldn't come, but… then I thought about what they could be fighting about and T.J. came to mind. Then … Thomas. It just clicked." She reached out to me and intertwined her fingers with mine. "You okay?"

"I don't know. That was intense," I said. I backed the car out of its parking spot and headed toward the apartment.

The clock in the dashboard read 3:47 a.m. Our headlamps were one of the only pairs illuminating the backroads of Eakins.

We pulled into the apartment, and we both sighed, then trudged to the apartment. We greeted Toto, and then undressed and crawled into bed.

Abby lay her head on my chest, nuzzling my neck.

"It's been a long day," I said.

"Sure has."

"Do me a favor, Pigeon."

"Now?"

"Just … for future reference."

"Okay …?"

"Don't fall in love with Tommy. I won't take it as well as Trent."

"Deal," she said, sleepy, and then her breathing evened out.

CHAPTER *Ten*

COMPROMISE

Abby

IT ONLY TOOK ME THREE days to find the two men who'd approached America and me at The Red—and who'd subsequently had their asses handed to them by Travis and Shepley.

I caught a glimpse of them as they made their way to a doorway at the end of the hall from my English Lit class. I paused to make sure it was them, and then carefully followed, being sure to remain unseen.

Once I reached the end of the hall, I peeked around the corner, watching Justin sit down behind a computer.

Ricky stood nearby, a stack of papers in his hand. He seemed to be dictating to Justin.

The room they were in was abuzz. Some students were hopping from one desk to the next, the others tapping away from behind their computer screens.

I leaned back to see if any signage was on the door

just to make sure it wasn't a small, out-of-the-way library I didn't know about.

As I leaned in to try to hear what Ricky was saying, a girl I recognized from my statistics class shouldered past me.

"Excuse me," she said, in a hurry.

"Wait!" I said.

She turned around, her expression a combination of aggravation and confusion. "What? I'm late."

"I'm sorry," I said. "I just switched classes, and I'm lost. Is this Ancient Greek Philosophy?"

"Switched classes? This late in the semester?" Thankfully, she didn't wait for me to answer her question. "No," she blurted out, annoyed. "This is *The Eastern Star*." When she saw that I didn't understand, she sighed. "The college newspaper."

My eyebrows shot up, and I mouthed, *Oh* as she turned on her heels to rush to her desk. I observed them for a few minutes, and then retreated down the hall to the exit.

Ricky and Justin were at The Red for information, that's why they'd been waiting for Travis to come back. It was fortunate one of them was stupid enough to insult me before they could question him. They could be doing a story about The Circle. Or worse, Travis's involvement in the fire.

I clenched my teeth, trying to figure out how I was going to stop them from running a story. Even speculation could get students talking when they'd originally declined.

College students might be hesitant to speak to the

police, but a curious fellow student could potentially jar a survivor's memory.

I stopped in the middle of the hall, walked a few steps backward until my ass touched the wall, and then slid down to the floor. My elbows pressed into my knees as I perched my forehead on my arms. *Would it ever end? Would Travis ever be safe?*

Two pairs of shoes began walking toward me, stopping just inches from the toes of my Chuck Taylors.

"Abby?" a familiar voice finally said. "Are you all right?"

I looked up, into Ricky's eyes.

Justin stood next to him. His cheek was still purple from Travis's left hook.

"That depends," I said.

Justin and Ricky traded glances. "On what?" Justin asked, nervous.

"Where are you guys headed?" I asked.

"To ... To, uh," Ricky stuttered. "Why?"

I narrowed my eyes, but before I could speak, Justin stiffened. "Are you following us? Why are you following us?"

Ricky snorted, smug. "We caught you. You thought you could sit here in the middle of the hall, and we'd just pass by and not notice? We're journalists. We notice *everything*."

I didn't give away my confusion, I just watched them become more paranoid with every new speculation.

"So I guess Travis knows we write for the *Star*?" Ricky asked. "He heard we've been asking questions?"

He swallowed. "What's he … What's he going to do?"

I stood up, allowing the tiniest hint of a smile on my face. "You'll see," I said, turning slowly before walking away. I pushed through the glass doors and jogged down the steps, inwardly panicking. Of course, I was bluffing.

They were doing a story on Travis. They were heading out to ask more people more questions. If they kept digging, someone might crack.

I touched my jacket pocket, feeling for the car keys. My mind was racing, wondering how to head this off. How to stop Ricky and Justin without implicating Travis and without anything short of blackmail, threats, or bribes. After all, what is the most important thing to college student? The one thing I didn't have: money.

A deep voice said, "Whoa!" just as I ran head-first into someone's chest.

"Oh, God, I'm sorry. I—" My stomach instantly sank.

"Hey, Abs. I was hoping I'd run into you. Maybe not so literally."

"Parker," I said, accusation in my voice. I took a step to walk around him, but he gently took my arm in his hand.

"C'mon. Don't be like that." He released my arm and smiled brightly, as if the last three months hadn't happened. "Can't we just ... talk?"

"No."

"Abby. What do you want me to do? Beg? I'll do anything to make things right. What about lunch?" I made a face. "Or just coffee. Can we just discuss over coffee?"

"Coffee?" I asked.

He nodded.

I looked over my shoulder to the building I'd left behind. I felt nauseous with just the thought. "You'll do anything?" I asked, returning my gaze to Parker.

"Name it."

I swallowed back my bile. I was about to sell my soul to the devil.

"You okay?" he asked, genuine concern on his face.

I looked down to my watch. "Did you just get out of class?"

"Yeah?"

"What are you doing now?"

Parker offered his most charming grin.

It was pitiful next to my husband's. My husband. My throat felt tight.

"Are you saying you're free for coffee now? Somewhere off campus?"

I nodded. "Yeah, that's probably best."

The triumphant grin on his face made me want to punch him, but he was the only person I knew who had access to enough money to appeal to Justin and Ricky.

"My car's this way."

I looked around, hoping no one noticed. I followed a few steps behind, and Parker seemed to be getting a kick out of my attempt at secrecy.

When we got to his Porsche, he opened my door as always. I hesitated, nearly telling him not to do that, that it wasn't a date, but it's easier to attract flies with honey, and Parker Hayes was most definitely a maggot.

Parker took us to a boutique coffee shop far away from campus, full of hipsters and moms fresh from yoga class.

We sat down, and I looked over the absurd menu, trying to ignore Parker's stare.

"I just want a fucking cappuccino," I muttered.

"Done. But … wow … you're spending too much time with Travis. You didn't used to talk like that."

I closed the menu and glared at him. "I did, you just never knew that side of me. And yes, I spend quite a bit of my time with my husband."

His face screwed into disgust. "I don't get it. To be frank, I'm at a loss for why you would marry someone like him."

I crossed my arms and perched my elbows on the table. "You said you wanted to talk. Is Travis really what you wanted to talk about?"

"Don't you?"

"More about the elopement."

He sighed, relieved. "That's what I thought. I've heard via mutual friends how different you've been. It occurred to me that you might be feeling some regret. My parents have very good attorneys at an even better law firm. I could help arrange a quick annulment."

I choked on my spit, holding my fist to my mouth while I tried to breathe again. "You … What?"

"You must feel trapped, and I hate that for you. An annulment looks far better than a divorce. It'll be like it never happened."

"Look better for who?"

He hesitated. "For you, of course."

I stared at the table, speechless over the audacity. "Parker, I agreed to talk to you today because of the elopement, yes, but not for that."

"No?"

"We were in Vegas the night of the fire."

"Debatable."

I frowned. "Parker, we were. I promise you, we were. Now the campus paper is planning an exposé. You said you'd do anything."

"That's what you're worried about? Why? If you weren't there?"

"Hi," the server said with a smile. His thick-rimmed, rectangular glasses, five o'clock shadow, and dark, wiry goatee must've been part of the uniform. Several of his co-workers sported the same.

"Just a cappuccino," I said.

"Just a cappuccino?" the server asked, confused.

"Yes?" I replied.

"I'll have a matcha latte with soy and one pump of hazelnut," Parker said.

His order was significantly more acceptable to the server. "Great choice."

I leaned in. "Everyone knows Travis fights. No one really believes he wasn't there."

"I heard he *was* there. He's always there, he's Adam's main fighter."

"Not that night. That night there was something more important."

"Trapping you into marriage."

I glared at him. "It was my idea."

Parker's mouth fell open. "I don't believe that for a

second, Abby. I have to say, if you'd stop lying, I'd be more inclined to help with whatever it is you need, if it's not an attorney."

"Justin and Ricky from *The Eastern Star* are a problem."

"Those idiots? Why on earth would you be worried about them?" His expression turned to disgust for the umpteenth time during our conversation. "They can't find their way out of a card game. I took them for nearly eight hundred dollars last week."

"You what?"

"They write half the term papers and essays on campus because they're both obsessed with gambling. They must've been at the fights that night and saw for themselves whether Travis was there or not. Oh … that's right. Adam banned them for non-payment."

"What card game?" I asked.

"Poker night at the Sig Tau house. Every Thursday night. I was actually planning to invite you sometime. Normally women aren't present, but once in a while we bring them for entertainment."

I raised an eyebrow.

Parker chuckled and held up his hands, palms out. "A joke, of course."

"Sure." I picked up my phone and began tapping. "Thanks for the coffee, Parker, but this ran longer than I thought. I have to tutor a student in fifteen minutes. I'm sorry but I have to go."

I stood, and Parker gestured for me to wait. "You need me to drive you?"

"I just ordered a ride."

"Wait! Just ... wait a moment. What was it you needed from me?"

"Nothing. I need nothing from you. Take care, Parker."

Not two blocks from the coffee shop, Travis's face lit up my cell phone.

I touched my phone, trying to psych myself up to sound normal while choking on guilt. "Hi baby!"

"I just got out of class. Want to meet for lunch before I head to Mrs. Pennington's?"

"Who?"

"Dad's neighbor. She offered me a shit ton of money to clean out her garage."

"Oh. That's... that's great, Trav. I wish I could, but I promised coffee with Finch."

"No worries. I just miss you. I'll see you after this job okay? She said it'll probably be six or so hours."

"Yes, you will. I miss you, too, babe."

I hung up the phone, tapped out a text to Finch and waited. As soon as Finch replied, I tapped the Uber driver on the shoulder. "I need to change the destination, is that okay?"

"Sure, sure," he said, looking at his navigation. "Do you know how to do it?"

"Yes," I said, tapping the buttons.

Within fifteen minutes we were at Finch's apartment, and I sat on the stoop until he pulled up in his white G-Wagon.

He lifted his oversized glasses and shook his head at me. "Why you always messy? Stand up, we're not peasants."

"I don't have time to go in, Finch, I just need to … confess."

"Oh, yes, you came to the right place. Spill it."

"I can't give context, but … I just met with Parker for coffee and then lied to Travis about it."

He wrinkled his nose. "Ew. Hashtag fuck Parker."

"I know, I know, but there was a good reason for it. I was going to ask him for money to help me with something, but then got a better idea. I left but if Travis knew, he'd be pissed."

"He would. That was stupid. How much do you need?"

"I don't need it anymore. Like I said, I got a better idea."

"Such as?" he asked, looking at his nails as if he were bored. He wasn't. He was enjoying every word.

"Um … so … bribery? I guess it's more blackmail. But also like a tradeoff for debt."

"Prostitution …" he said, nodding.

"What? No! Nothing like that. I'm going to get them to owe me money, a lot of it, so they stay in their own lane. Basically."

"Them who?"

"I can't say."

"Thanks for wasting my time," Finch said, walking up the stairs.

"Finch!" I called after him.

He stopped but didn't turn around.

"Should I tell Travis about Parker?"

Finch looked over his shoulder at me. "Meeting up with your ex whatever and lying to your husband about it is cheating. I don't care what any bitch tells me, it is." He turned around. "And you're no cheater."

I sighed and nodded.

Finch went inside and I ordered another Uber, heading back to campus to grab the car and then home. I kept myself busy, putting away dishes, vacuuming, starting dinner in the crockpot, finishing an essay and chatting with a tutoring client about her homework.

Dusting, laundry, and reorganizing the closet took up the rest of my time before Travis finally got home.

"Where's my girl?" he called from the front door.

"I'm here," I said, rounding the corner from the hall. "How was your day?"

He leaned me back and kissed me. "Long." He stood me upright and then sighed. "I missed you all fucking day. It was torture! But I made a shit ton of money, so I hung in there."

"I'm proud of you. Dinner's ready. Are you hungry?"

"Best wife ever! I'm fucking starving!"

I led him into the kitchen, and Travis spooned out the beef stew into two bowls. "Dear God, this smells amazing."

"I added mushrooms this time, hope that's okay."

"It's perfect. You're perfect." He kissed my forehead and then took our bowls to the small table near the wall that separated the kitchen from the hall.

Just when I got up the courage to speak, Travis beat me to it.

"Damn, this is so nice. Coming home to you, a hot meal, just sitting here enjoying each other with no drama to talk about. This is how it should be."

I nodded, taking a bite. There was no way I was dropping a bomb on him after that.

We finished our bowls, and then Travis got up for seconds, grabbing another beer on the way back to the table. We talked about the weird things he came across in Mrs. Pennington's garage, the stupid text Brandon sent him about coming in to fill out paperwork, anything else that got on Travis's nerves, and our classes.

"Damn, I feel like I've been talking your ear off. Sorry. I told you, I've missed you like crazy today! This is why people take honeymoons. It's not right to get married and then have to go back to classes and jobs and normal life. All I want to do is be around you all day. What did you do after class?"

"Oh, you know, that essay, housework. I stopped by Finch's." As soon as I said it, I wanted to bang my head on the table.

"How's he doing? He's got a new man, doesn't he?"

"He's fabulous as always, and yes," I said, grateful he didn't ask more.

"Welp, I'm disgusting. I'm going to hop in the shower. Want to watch a movie after I get out?"

"I do."

He smiled and winked at me. "God, I love this. I don't know what all these guys bitching about married life are talking about, it's fucking amazing. Hey, leave the dishes, I'll get 'em."

I smiled at him as I watched him rinse out his bowl, put it in the dishwasher and then leave me for the bathroom.

The water whined as it gushed through the pipes and the metal rings grated against the shower rod. Travis hummed a tune that I couldn't quite make out while I rinsed my own bowl and set it in the sink.

As I settled onto my spot on the couch, my body felt heavy. I was an asshole. Travis was going to be livid when he found out I'd had coffee with Parker. I wondered how I would react if Travis told me he'd had coffee with Megan.

I could make all the excuses in the world, like he'd slept with her, but I hadn't slept with Parker. Or that my intensions were pure, but I wasn't sure that justification would satisfy my husband. And I couldn't blame him.

My nerves were getting the better of me and waiting to tell him seem impossible.

The bathroom door opened and then he padded to the bedroom, returning to the living room shortly after in a fresh T-shirt and shorts. He crawled onto the couch and lay on my lap looking up and smiling.

"Jesus Christ, this is Heaven."

"What do you want to watch?" I asked.

"There's a new Ryan Reynolds movie on Netflix. What do you think?"

"I think … we need to talk."

He sat up, and I sighed. "God, you're having such a good day, I don't want to ruin it."

CHAPTER *Eleven*

IN THE WRONG

Travis

I HESITATED. “RUIN IT HOW?”

She swallowed, staring at the dark television screen.

“Please don’t tell me you’re in love with Tommy.”

She chuckled but worry still flickered in her eyes. “Trav ... I love you. I love you so much, I do stupid things. So, please, please remember that when I tell you what I’m about to tell you.”

I frowned. “Just tell me.”

“I …” she sighed. “God, I’m just going to say it. I’m just going to say it. I … I asked Parker for a favor today.”

“*Parker*?” I seethed, already feeling my temper flare.

“Yes, but,” she closed her eyes. “It was for you. I’m worried about you.”

"What does that have to do with Parker?"

"Just ... please hear me out," she said.

I clenched my teeth and nodded.

She continued, "Remember the guys from The Red? The ones you and Shep beat the shit out of? They're not cops, Trav, they're from the college paper. They've been asking questions about you. The people who go to The Circle, they won't talk to the cops. But I'm afraid they'll ... what if those wanna-be reporters get someone to admit you were there?"

I waited a full minute to calm down before I spoke, breathing through my nose, trying to get my hand stop shaking. "You," I began, feeling that old but familiar rage bubbling to the surface. "You come to *me* about our shit, Abby." My face twisted. "You don't go to Parker fucking Hayes. He is the *last* person you should …" I sighed, feeling my eye twitch. It had been a long day, and I'd rather take an elbow to the face than hear from my wife that she was talking to Parker.

Her eyes filled with tears. "I know. You're right. I don't know what the hell I was thinking. I acted impulsively in a moment of desperation. He was there, and ... he agreed to help me if I had coffee with him."

I closed my eyes. "Abby." I took a deep breath. "Tell me you didn't."

I looked at her, my stare probably more severe than I'd wanted it to be toward my wife. Tears toppled over her lower lashes and streamed down her face. Every muscle in my body tensed as I waited for her answer, on edge about her news and that she was upset.

She shook her head. "I'm sorry."

I let out a sigh. "Goddamn it, Pidge."

"I didn't go because I wanted to. I don't want to be anywhere near him."

"Then *why*?" I yelled. She winced, and I stood, pissed that I wasn't handling the situation better. "I'm sorry. I don't mean to yell, but damn it, Pidge." I began to pace, my hands perched on my hips. "Do you know how satisfying it must've been for that piece of shit? That you agreed to spend any time with him alone at all?"

"I know. I'm sorry, Travis. I did go, but I left. I left before the coffee was even on the table, the second I got a better idea."

I stopped to look at her. "You met him there, right?" My heart felt like it was about to blow right outta my chest. "You didn't get in his car with him."

Her face paled. "He drove."

I looked away, trying not to lash out. "That's just fucking great. Parker Hayes on a lunch date with *my wife*!"

"I ubered back to campus when I realized I didn't need him."

"Why in the fuck would you need him, Abby? You don't *need* him!"

She held up her hands, attempting to calm me down. "I *know*. I know that now. I was considering borrowing money for a bribe, but …"

I turned to her, feeling my anger about to boil over. "I don't want my wife owing Parker Hayes anything! Do you hear me?"

"I know. I know, and I'm so sorry, but I was desperate, Travis! I can't lose you!" she cried.

We were both breathing hard. Her cheeks were soaked with tears. I'd never seen her so frantic. She was screaming that she loved me and needed me and all I could think about was my damn ego. My shoulders sagged. "But you left?"

"I'm so sorry," she said, wiping both cheeks with her wrists. "I feel terrible. I would never intentionally embarrass or hurt you. It was what I thought I had to do at the time, but I should've thought it through. I was wrong, and stupid, and I wish I could take it back."

I blinked a few times, realizing this was the first time she'd fucked up. She was the one in trouble for once. I sat next to her and frowned, trying my best to look stern. "It better not happen again, Pidge. I mean it."

She shook her head. "It won't."

"I can't believe you did that," I said, my voice thick with disappointment. Her bottom lip quivered, and she burst into tears again.

I couldn't take it anymore. "It's okay," I said, sitting next to her. "It's okay, Pigeon, I'm not that mad."

Her entire body shook as she sobbed. "I know you're disappointed. I'm disappointed in myself."

I cupped her cheeks in my hand, forcing her to look at me. "Don't you know?"

She sniffed, shaking her head. "I hate disappointing you."

"There is nothing you could ever do to make me think less of you. You think I don't know what's at stake if the Feds find out the truth? We're not in the clear, yet. How can I blame you for doing whatever it takes to keep me home?"

She turned, kissing my palm. "I was so stupid, Travis."

"You are many things, Pigeon, but never stupid." I leaned in to press my lips to hers, and she pulled me closer.

I could feel her hot tears smear on my cheeks, her soft tongue caressing mine. For the first time, I realized Parker was a pointless source of contention. He was no more a threat than her ex, Jesse. She felt the same for me as I did her, and that kind of crazy love led to irrational behavior at best. But she didn't want him. It was me and her, and no one else. A switch flipped in me, and it took that moment to finally realize all the jealousy I'd felt was pointless.

I was going to ignore that Parker tried to take advantage ... for now.

"You came up with another plan?"

"I did. It's risky, but the benefit outweighs any risk. Parker let it slip that Justin and Ricky are in major debt. They show up to the Sig Tau poker nights."

My brows pulled together. "Those games get insane, especially when the rich kids like Parker are at the table."

"Yes, but I'll win. They're going to owe me, Travis, and then we don't have to pay them anything."

"What do you mean? I thought you said you were done?"

"This is important. If you're okay with it, I think it's the best option."

I thought for minute, wondering if keeping me out of the local school paper was worth Abby going against the one thing she'd promised herself she'd never do again. "I don't know, Pigeon. You said ..."

"I know what I said!" she yelled, covering her eyes with one hand. Her next words were quieter. "I know what I said." She put her hand on my knee. "But if I can do it for my loser father, I can do it for you. Please, Travis. Don't argue with me. I feel helpless and it's making me crazy. Just ... let me do this."

I glared at the television, and then looked at my wife. "You're sure?"

She nodded.

"Okay."

"Really?" She sniffed.

I wiped her cheeks with my thumbs. "Just you and me against the world, right, Pidge?"

She managed a small, tired smile. "You bet your ass it is."

I planted a kiss on her mouth, her cheeks still wet from her tears. She pulled away, and then crawled into my lap. I held her tight, her head fitting perfectly between my neck and shoulder.

"Do you forgive me?" she whispered.

"That's what marriage is, right? Love, patience, and infinite second chances."

CHAPTER *twelve*

CAKE

Abby

I GLANCED OVER THE CONTENTS inside the glass casing. As my mouth watered, I wondered which cake Travis would like best.

After almost an hour, I had finally narrowed my choices to just three: yellow cake with chocolate frosting, Neapolitan cake, also with chocolate frosting, or wedding cake.

Travis had made a fuss over the tiny cake at our wedding in Vegas, so I knew he liked white on white, too.

"Jesus Christ, Abby, pick one already," America said, bored. She pulled a string of pink gum from her mouth and wrapped it around her finger. "I hate to think how long it took you to choose a wedding cake if it's taking you this long to pick one for a casual birthday party for Travis."

I didn't take my eyes off the contents of the case, which included tiered cakes, cupcakes, round cakes, and rectangles, all decorated as differently as any personality one could imagine. "A wedding cake is for guests. This is for Travis. It has to be right."

"You didn't have guests," she said, rolling her eyes. "So, yeah, if you had no guests, I see how it would be an easy choice. Ya know—if you'd bothered to invite anyone who wanted to be there, anyone who expected to be included in the biggest day of your life. Like your best friend."

I wrinkled my nose. "What the hell, Mare? Why are you so cranky?"

She put her gum back in her mouth and then crossed her arms. "They're not going for it."

"Who isn't going for what?"

"My parents. They said if Shep and I move in together, they won't pay for my college."

I was stunned.

America's parents weren't exactly pushovers, but they'd always made a point to support whatever truly made their daughter happy.

If America wanted to continue to attend college, I couldn't imagine what the difference was. America spent the night with Shepley almost every night.

"I'm ... I'm sorry. I didn't know."

She shrugged. "How could you?"

"I'm surprised, actually."

"Well … your wedding scared them. They think if we move in together, we'll run off and get married. I'm not saying it's your fault, it's just the truth."

I hugged her. “I’m sorry. I really am, Mare.”

“It’s just that … I’m going back to Wichita for summer break. Shep’s freaking out a little. I am, too ... and I know how that sounds, okay? I’m not the type to care if I spend three months away from a guy. Normally it would be a breath of fresh air. But I don’t want to miss him. Ever since we broke up ... it’s just different, you know? I really, really love him, Abby.”

I gave her a squeeze and then held her far enough away to look into her eyes. “Stay with us, Mare. You do, anyway.” I smiled. “It will be fun.”

She shook her head. “They won’t let me.”

“Why?” I asked, frustrated.

“I told you, they’re scared. Dad said he doesn’t want us getting too serious too fast. I understand their concern, but it just sucks.”

“You could still do it, you know. Get a job, and we’ll move your things.”

America’s eyes glossed over. “Easy for you to say. You have a scholarship or five. They pay for my tuition. If I want that to continue, I have to follow their rules.”

“Fair enough. But you can come visit on the weekends, right? They’ll at least let you come see me.”

“Yeah. Yeah, of course.” She released me, wiping her nose. She smiled and shook her head. “God. This is stupid. There are much worse things happening in the world.”

“Not to you, and not right now. It’s okay to be upset about being apart from Shep for three months. You’re right. It does suck.”

She smirked. "Thanks."

"For what?"

"Not making me feel like an asshole."

I made a face. "That wasn't intentional. You're still an asshole."

America playfully elbowed me as a woman behind the counter stepped in front of us with a smile.

I pressed my index finger against the glass, pointing to the white cake. "It should say, *Happy 20th Birthday, Travis.*"

"Actually," America said. "Can you make it say *Happy 20th Fucking Birthday, Travis*?"

The woman smiled. "Sounds like a fun party."

I mirrored her expression. "It will be."

"Kegs. Ice. Cups. Music. Cake ..." I said, pointing at the various stations. "We're missing something. I feel like we're missing something."

America crossed her arms, nowhere near my level of stress. "If you're comparing with years past, I'd say you're missing at least two dozen sluts."

I shot her a look. "Funny."

America giggle-snorted, and then walked across the room, picking up a small balloon and touching it to her lips. Her cheeks bulged; her face turned red.

I looked at my watch. "Less than an hour." I glanced outside. "Why isn't anyone here, yet?"

"Spring training," America said.

I hissed the word *fuck* under my breath, and then froze when I heard a commotion just outside the door.

"I said no! Stop! Fucking stop, Travis!" Shepley said as he fell backward through the door and onto the living room floor.

Travis stood in the doorway, breathing hard, a wide, triumphant grin on his face. "Honey, I'm home!"

My mouth fell open, and in what felt like slow motion, I scream the word *No!*

"Why is he here?" America asked her boyfriend, accusation in her voice.

Shepley stood up and brushed himself off, red-faced and annoyed. "The second I tried to get him to go anywhere but home, he knew, okay? I did my best!"

Travis smirked, but his expression fell away when he saw mine.

"You couldn't have just pretended? You had to force your way in here to ruin *all* my plans?" I whined. I wasn't going to try to pretend. It was unfair.

"Baby," Travis said, shoving Shepley to the side as he walked toward me, arms out.

"No," I said, pushing him away. "Don't touch me. Don't!" I said, sulking. "Do you know how long I've been planning this? I didn't run around trying to ruin my surprise party!"

"No," Travis said, encapsulating me in his thick, inked arms. "Parker ruined it."

I frowned, pushing him away. "I was still surprised! You still pulled it off. Get off me!"

Travis leaned in to kiss my cheek. "I wanted to come home and see my wife, who I knew was working hard to make my birthday special."

"And then you ruined it!" I snarled, still shoving him. I didn't bother trying too hard. Travis didn't budge.

America hugged Shepley, and then kissed his cheek. "Do you ever get tired of him getting you in trouble?"

Shepley smoothed his hair, his brow furrowed. "He would have stolen my car and left me in the parking lot had I not jumped in the passenger side."

"Aw!" America said, unable to stop from giggling.

Shepley's arms were crossed, and he tried to pull away from his girlfriend—also, not very hard.

Travis grabbed my jaw and forced me to look at him. Once our eyes met, I stopped struggling.

"Thank you, baby," he said, smooching my already protruding lips. He let me go, and I felt a bit disorientated from the kiss and my futile struggle.

Someone knocked on the door, and a second later, Jason Brazil opened it and walked through, abruptly stopping when he saw Travis standing amid the half-decorated apartment. "Oh. Damn. Are we late?"

"Yeah," I said, throwing a balloon at Travis. "And he's in trouble."

"I am not," Travis said, half playful, half annoyed.

"Is the, um," Brazil stuttered, "the, uh ... the party still on?"

"Yes. I can't exactly cancel ten minutes before forty people are supposed to be here," I grumbled.

"Forty?" Travis said. "Is that all?"

"Minus the sluts," America explained, straight-faced.

Travis wasn't amused.

A couple of girls walked in behind Brazil, overly fake-baked, layers upon layers of makeup, and double D implants bulging from their tight V-neck Ts.

"April Fools'!" America said. "The sluts have arrived."

"Uh … this is Alexis," Brazil said, pointing to one. "Tabitha, Meg, and Bonnie."

"Of course," America said.

"Easy, babe," Shepley said.

The carbon copy sorority sisters wrinkled their noses at America but, after that, paid her little attention. They followed Brazil as he hunted for the keg tap, and then laughed when he held it high in the air.

"Found it!" he said, waving it around like a toddler with a toy on the playground.

Brazil and his friends helped finish decorating by blowing up balloons and stringing streamers.

More people arrived and joined in. The more Travis helped, the more disappointed I became. Not in him—but in myself.

I had a famous poker face. I could hustle Vegas veterans for tens of thousands but couldn't pull off a small surprise birthday party for my husband.

As the sun set, the last of the guests arrived. Trenton limped in with Camille on his good arm. She moved slowly, still sore from the accident. She'd suffered a concussion, bearing black stitches along her hairline. I was surprised she was there at all.

Trenton helped remove her coat, slowly and gently.

His lime green cast was covered in black ink, some signatures, but mostly drawings.

"Want some help?" Travis asked.

"I got it," Trenton said, winking at Camille. "I always take care of my girl."

"Even one-handed, still does it better than anyone else," she said, kissing his cheek once he was finished. "Thank you."

Trenton turned to hug his little brother. "Happy birthday, ass hat!"

"Hey," Camille said, hugging me. "Looks great."

"You didn't have to come. You were just in the hospital for a major car accident. I know you're not feeling the best and you're still healing."

"Yeah, we've both got a long way to go. But we wouldn't miss it. And it's kind of nice to get out of the house."

"Trenton said you've been getting migraines."

"The meds help. But to be honest, I probably won't be able to stay long. We're just stopping by for a sec. I know it's probably … awkward for everyone."

I gave her the nicest smile I could manage—which was dry at best—and then watched Travis hug her gently.

"Looking good, Cami! Glad you made it," he said. He turned to Trenton. "And that has to be the coolest fucking cast I've ever seen."

Trenton held up his arm, turning it back and forth to show off the artwork. "Yeah, I got bored."

"You did that?" I asked, surprised. "That's incredible."

He shrugged. “It was kind of fun. Like starting all over. It’s itchy as fuck under there, though. Driving me insane.”

Travis hooked his arm around his brother’s neck. “I really appreciate you guys being here. Love you, brother.” He kissed Trenton’s head and then grabbed my hand. “Can I talk to you a minute?”

“Is everything okay?” I asked as he pulled me into the bathroom.

“Can you please—for me—be nice to Cami?”

My eyebrows shot up. I felt instantly defensive. “I didn’t say a damn thing to her, Trav. I was nice.”

“I know … you’re just … I mean this in the nicest way possible. You suck at faking it with Cami, which is weird considering your gift of indifference.”

“I’m *trying*. How do you do it? How can you act like she didn’t do what she did?”

“It was an accident, Pidge.”

“I’m not talking about the wreck, and you know it.”

Travis sighed. “Trenton loves her. She loves him, too. She makes him happy. C’mon. We’ve had our problems and she’s not a bitch to you.”

“I’m not being a bitch, and I didn’t fuck one of your brothers!” Once I said the words, I immediately regretted them.

Travis’s expression screwed into disgust. He wasn’t used to me behaving that way, and in truth, neither was I.

The Maddoxes were a broken but beautiful, tightly knit family. There were thousands of similar families in the world, but this one was special. They all loved each other fiercely from such a damaged place. Their sorrow fueled them, and their loyalty was unconditional.

Trenton had just proved it. That Camille would risk endangering what they'd built, over nearly two decades of tears and ashes, made me angry in a way I couldn't describe.

I covered my face. "I don't want to do this on your birthday. Please?"

"I didn't mean that you're being a bitch. I would never call you that. That's not what I meant, I'm sorry."

I touched his face. "Don't apologize. I know you're trying to keep the peace." I crossed my arms. "But I don't know if I can do what you're asking."

"Do you think she meant for any of that to happen? I could understand you hating her if she was maliciously fucking with their heads, but I don't think that was the case. She isn't Tommy's type. I know he loved her—"

"Looks like he still does."

He sighed. "She's not his. She's Trenton's. They're perfect for each other. Tommy knew they wouldn't work out, that's why he cut her loose."

"You don't *know* any of that."

His jaw clenched, but he waited a beat to answer. "I know my brother. I'm just asking that you give her a second chance. Let all that go and start fresh."

I shook my head, looking at the floor. "I don't know why I'm so angry. If I knew, maybe I could."

"Because you're protective of us. And believe me, Pidge, I love you so much for that. But Trenton's made his choice. Our only job is to support him."

I nodded. "Okay. Okay, I'll work on it."

He kissed my forehead. "That's all I ask."

We stepped out of the bathroom and I put my game face on, walking straight to Camille. "Can I get you a water or beer or anything?"

"I'm good for now, thanks," she said with an awkward smile.

I got the distinct feeling she knew we'd been talking about her.

"What?" she asked, her tone border-line defensive.

"Nothing," I said. My smile faded. "Travis came home early. I wanted it to be a surprise."

"Sounds like him," Camille said with a smirk. Travis joined us and she handed him a bottle of whiskey, a red ribbon tied around its neck. "Happy birthday, anyway."

Travis kissed her cheek. "Thanks!"

"Hey!" Trenton said, frowning and playfully pushing Travis's shoulder. "Get your fuckin' lips off my girl!"

Travis held up his hands. "All right, all right. Just showing my appreciation."

I grabbed Travis by the hand and brought him to the kitchen, where I sunk twenty candles into the icing of the cake, and then searched the kitchen for a lighter. After opening one drawer after another, I came up empty-handed.

"This is ridiculous," I seethed. "I'm married to a man who is trying to quit a pack-a-day habit and we have no lighters?"

Travis flicked his lighter and held the flame in front of my face.

I paused, and then snatched it from him and I smiled. “Thank you, my love,” I said quietly.

As I lit the wicks, America turned off the lights.

Travis stood at the breakfast bar over his cake, smiling at the words scrawled with icing on top. He slid his arms around my middle, nuzzling my neck while each new flame flickered.

“Nice cake,” he said, whispering the words on top.

Happy 20th Fucking Birthday, Travis

“Glad you like it. The swearing was America’s idea.”

Travis held up his hand, high-fiving America. “Well done.”

America simply nodded; her arms crossed just above her waist.

Shepley held her, and they swayed playfully as they watched the candles burn. Shepley had the sweetest smile on his face.

I wasn’t sure what he was thinking about, but I knew it involved America.

We sang *Happy Birthday*, and then Shepley turned up the music.

We danced and drank, ate cake and laughed. It was a perfect evening—even the neighbors left us alone for the most part. The police only showed up for a single noise complaint.

Half of the football team was present, as were most of his brothers from Sig Tau.

Jim, Thomas, Taylor, and Tyler all called at different times, but each time, Travis would go outside to chat with his family.

I kissed Travis every time he left, and all night I was reminded of my birthday, of how sweet he was that night, and how hard I tried not to fall in love with him.

Looking back, my stubbornness seemed like such a waste of time and effort. I was always meant to be Mrs. Maddox. Every turn I'd made, everything that had happened to me—good or bad—had led me to my husband.

At one point, Travis backed me into the hall and curled his fingers behind my neck, impatient to put his warm mouth on mine. He tasted like cheap beer and sugar, and I drew him deeper into my mouth.

Just when I thought he might lift me into his arms and carry me into our bedroom, the rhythm of his mouth slowed. He pulled away, kissed my cheek, and then whispered in my ear. "I'm surprised you haven't set up shots for me, yet."

"I didn't think you were hard up for money."

"I will be if I don't get that job."

I breathed out a laugh. "You've got the job. You just have to go in and accept it."

Travis glanced around the corner, and then returned his attention to me.

"What?" I asked.

"Just making sure they're not trashing the place."

"Aw. Listen to you. All grown up."

Travis frowned. "I've never had a party here."

I thought about it. He hadn't since we'd met. It

hadn't crossed my mind as to why, but it surprised me that he hadn't before.

I thought of the first time I'd seen his apartment and remembered thinking that it didn't smell like the usual college boy dwelling: dirty socks and stale beer. He and Shep kept it picked up and vacuumed.

I was married to the man and realized there were still things about him I didn't know, simply because I'd never asked.

"What's that face?" he asked.

"I was just thinking how much I've failed at getting to know you."

He kissed my forehead. "You know me better than anyone else."

"I didn't realize you didn't have any parties here. What other mundane things about your past did I fail to ask about?"

He shook his head. "I don't care to talk about my life before you, anyway. Everything changed when I met you. And, to answer your question, I didn't want to have to beat someone's ass for breaking anything."

I touched his cheek. "Strictly a love dungeon, huh?"

Travis's face twisted into disgust. "A what?"

I giggled. "Nothing."

"Oh, you got jokes," he said, playfully pinching my sides with his fingers.

I ran out into the living room, giggling and hiding behind America. Travis only chased me for a few seconds before a slow song came over the speakers. My favorite song; our song.

Travis pulled me into his arms. We swayed for a few moments before Travis squeeze me tighter against him.

"You sort of told me you loved me the last time we danced to this song at a birthday party," he said.

"What?" I said, pulling back to look into his eyes. "I don't remember that."

He chuckled.

I smiled. "I don't!"

"Yeah. You were wasted, but you said it. Well, kind of said it. You said that in another life, you could love me."

I smiled, gazing into his warm, russet irises. I recalled the first time I saw those eyes staring back at me—in the basement of a building on campus. He was sweaty and we were both spattered with blood, but from that moment on, those eyes were my home.

"What did you say to that?" I asked with a smile. "You didn't run screaming?"

He shook his head, his gaze growing more intense. "I said I might love you in this one."

"You did?" I asked, touched. That was almost six months ago, and he'd never told me. "I still said it first."

"No," he chuckled.

"I mean … I kind of said it first."

He narrowed his eyes.

"You just admitted it! I said it on my birthday."

"You kinda said it."

"According to you, you said you *might* love me in this one."

"We both know that was me being a hard ass. You saying you could love me in your next life doesn't count."

"Well," I said, lifting my chin and feeling victorious. "Welcome to our next life."

He stopped in the middle of the apartment. His shoulders fell, and his eyes poured over me with such love and adoration, my cheeks flushed.

"I'll be damned," he said, hugging me to him. He rested his chin in the crook of my neck, causing him to hunch over. "Got my birthday wish before I made it."

I pressed my cheek against his ear, listening to the words of our song, and taking in the moment. "How weird is it that it's your first birthday with me, and as my husband."

"Best birthday to date," he replied.

"What did you do for your nineteenth?"

"I don't remember, and even if I did, I know it wasn't this good. I'm sorry I ruined the surprise."

"You're forgiven," I said with a smile.

"Don't worry. You have the rest of our lives to try to surprise me."

"You're damn straight I do," I said, hugging him closer. "We have a thousand more surprises ahead of us."

I closed my eyes. All of them good, I hope.

CHAPTER *Thirteen*

WEAKNESS

Abby

"BABY," TRAVIS SAID, PULLING OFF his jacket and tossing it to the bed. "I said I was sorry."

"It's not your fault," I said, kicking off my heels.

"I'm not fighting in The Circle again, I told you that. But I'm not going to be disrespected, either."

"I know, Trav." I walked over and touched his cheek. He leaned into my palm. "It's not your fault."

He'd made so many strides to change. Yet, I couldn't help but feel frustrated for being asked to leave The Red for the second time in as many weeks. Travis was jealous enough when I was just his girlfriend. Now that I was his wife, men would try to buy me drinks right in front of him, make lewd comments on my body, or even—like that night—pat my ass. The level of restraint he'd shown was nothing short of miraculous, but every man had his limit.

"I should've just walked away," Travis said, clearly angry with himself. "Jorie keeps threatening to ban me. One of these days she's going to do it."

I unzipped the back of my dress. "Jorie saw it. That guy deserved you kicking his seat out from under him." He didn't respond. "They'll quit, Trav."

"Maybe we should lay low for a while."

I nodded.

Travis sighed and unbuttoned his shirt. We undressed in silence, took turns in the bathroom, and then Travis watched me climb into bed next to him.

I crawled beneath the sheets, snuggling up beside him as he stared at the ceiling. "It could be worse. We still have movie nights. Date nights. Mini golf. Rides on the Harley. It seems to only happen at The Red. That just means more alone time together."

My hands slid over the peaks and valleys of his middle and settled on the bulge below the waistline of his shorts. "We should take these off."

He didn't move.

I kissed his neck with small kisses, and when he didn't respond, I moved my hand and hugged him tight. For the first time, I felt like Travis might not want me.

His life was fun and freedom before me. Now it was mafia, fires, and the constant feeling of needing to protect me. Now, he couldn't go to his favorite bar.

Knots began to form in my stomach. "Trav?"

"Yeah, Pidge?"

"You promised you would love me forever."

He breathed like my words had knocked the wind

out of him, and then he covered his eyes with his arm. "It's not that, Pidge. Not even close." He turned onto his side and wrapped me in both of his arms, squeezing gently.

"Talk to me," I said against his chest.

"I know you didn't want this. Now we're having to stop going to places and you're going to feel even more trapped." He squeezed me tighter. "I don't want you to get tired of everything, of me, and leave."

I leaned back to look at the tears welling up in his eyes.

He looked down at me. "You're going to leave me. No matter how hard I try to get this right, you're going to get tired of my shit."

I laughed once, shocked.

He frowned, unhappy with my reaction.

"No … I didn't mean to laugh, I'm sorry, it's just that … I was just thinking the same thing. That before you met me, your life was easy. Now it's one thing after another. And not petty fights … like real, scary stuff and I was just worrying you were going to get sick of it."

"I would never leave you. No matter what happens, there is not one thing from before that I'd rather have than you. But you … you're not like me."

I sat up, and he sat up with me, his expression full of worry, like yet again he'd said the wrong thing and I might end it. It was my fault; the entire time we were together I was famous for that very thing.

I took his chin in my hand. "Look at me, Travis Carter. Of course, you're going to worry. I've left you before. More than once. But we weren't married then, and I wasn't sure which way was up. I made a decision, I made a promise, and I need you to believe me. You can't keep worrying about it, it's going to drive you insane. I will never, ever leave you. Do you hear me? You're my husband, and I'm your wife. That will never change, Travis. *Never*. No matter what happens, I'm in this, we're in this, for life."

"You made the decision," he said, still unconvinced. He looked away, the wheels in his head spinning, then he looked down. "But not because it's what you wanted."

"What are you talking about?"

"I saw you!" he said, loud enough to startle me. "I saw you." This time his words were quieter. He sounded broken. He stood up, his fingers interlaced on top of his head. The floor creaked beneath him as he paced. "I saw you on the floor of the casino, on the phone crying to someone."

As guilt buried me, I couldn't help but cry. "Oh, my God. Travis, no. It's not what you think at all."

Tears spilled over his cheeks, his bottom lip trembling. "And I let you do it. I let you marry me knowing you didn't want to, or at the very least weren't sure. What kind of piece of shit lets the girl he loves do that? I'm so sorry, Pidge, but I was desperate to keep you. I still am. It consumes every thought I have. Every decision I make. I've never been in love before, I don't know if this is normal or there's something wrong with me or … I'm doing the best I can, but I … I don't know what the fuck I'm doing. Pidge … I don't …"

I sat up on my knees, moving to the end of the bed, reaching for him. "Come here."

He didn't hesitate. He immediately crashed into me, holding me tight and burying his face into my neck.

"I swear … I swear to God … I wasn't crying because I didn't want to marry you. I was crying because of the fire. Because …" I shook my head, knowing I shouldn't say more.

He looked up at me. "Who were you talking to?"

"Trent and Cami. They were updating me," I said. I positioned myself in a way that would force him to look me in the eyes. "It wasn't because I was doing something I didn't want to do. I wanted to, more than I can ever explain to you. More than I can explain to me."

He nodded, wiping his eyes.

"You've thought that since Vegas? Why didn't you tell me?" I asked.

He shook his head, his eyes glossing over again. "Because I was afraid of what you'd say, Pidge. I couldn't get everything I wanted and then have it ripped away. I know that was a selfish, pussy thing to do, but"—he held his hands out to his sides and then let them fall—"I'm not man enough to tell you if you wanna go, go. Because I don't want that."

"I don't want it, either," I said, wiping my cheek. *Huh. I was wrong that he wouldn't have let me go through with the wedding if he knew the truth. Still, I couldn't have risked him saying no. He says that now, but would he have felt differently in the moment? It was a risk I couldn't take.* "Listen to me. I don't know what

I did before you, Travis. And I never want to remember. I don't."

He took a deep breath and exhaled. He looked down to the floor, his face crumbling, and then he looked back up at me from under his brow. "You crying on the floor was about the fire?"

I sniffed. "I know it looks bad, but I swear it was. Please, please believe me."

"And because you were afraid about what might happen when we got back."

"I *wanted* to marry you. I love you and I love being your wife."

He nodded but began to pace again.

"Hearing you talk like this breaks my heart for you," I said, my voice cracking. "It was earlier than I'd planned, Travis, we both know that, but everything changed when Keaton burned."

"You knew I'd need an alibi. Just say it, Abby."

I sighed. "It created an alibi for you, okay? That's a symptom, not the cause. I married you because I *love* you. I'll say it a million times if I have to. I was certain, about everything. That's why I asked you to marry me."

"Thank God," he breathed out. He walked over to me and held my face with both hands. His lips and hands were trembling, but he put his lips on mine. I opened my mouth, more than willing to feel his tongue against mine. Just ten minutes before I'd thought he was having second thoughts, but the way he was pulling at me, the relief made the usual butterflies I felt do full-fledged somersaults all over my body.

"Can we agree then that we're both afraid the other is going to leave, and we know now that we're both staying?"

He nodded again. "You're really mine," he said.

"I'm really yours."

His mouth pulled away long enough for him to trace a line with his lips down my neck to my collarbone, noticing the strap over my shoulder. He looked over me with longing, his eyes pouring over my black, flowing tank top and matching panties. At the same time, I was thankful that was all he'd have to remove to be inside me. He stared at my skin as he slid the narrow fabric of the tank's strap down, kissing the very spot he'd been focused on.

With one of his hands and in one motion, my torso was bare. He moved his mouth slowly and tenderly down my chest and stomach, pausing just long enough in all my favorite places to make my insides ache. He leaned me back against the mattress, and I relaxed, closing my eyes.

I had never felt so at home with not only someone else, but inside my own skin. Travis made me feel like the most beautiful woman he'd ever seen, and more loved than anyone had in my life.

He didn't just want me, he needed me. He worshipped every inch of my body.

I was his religion.

"I love you," I whispered.

"I know," he said, his voice muffled as he situated himself between my thighs.

He reached beneath me, yanked down my panties,

and then returned to the apex of my thighs as if he'd been starving for me all day.

My knees involuntarily quivered, and I moaned his name along with a few inappropriate religious references.

He kissed my thighs and then my stomach, gazing up at me with a proud smirk. He barely gave me a chance to recover before he was crawling up my body and staring into my eyes as he slowly sank himself inside of me.

Those were the times I was glad that he was unable to restrain himself. I'd only had an idea of what Travis had been like with other women, but with me, he didn't hold back. He'd let me peel away all his layers, to see every weakness—I was one of them, and it no longer felt like a bad thing.

Neither one of us knew before the day we'd met that we were both waiting for the other to come along, and in that moment, in the cafeteria of a tiny college, our lives began.

There was no *before* or *after*.

Travis knew from the beginning that we had always been, and we would always be. That truth was finally in his eyes, in the way looked at me, the way he was gazing at me in that moment as he hovered just inches from my face.

"Oh my fuck… Pidge," he breathed. He looked at me in awe, the exact expression that was on his face the first time he made love to me—and every time after—as if he were still surprised at how perfect and amazing I felt.

He worked agonizingly slow, paying attention to every part of my skin. Even after an hour had passed, Travis didn't skip a beat.

My muscles were trembling with fatigue and, although he refused to pick up the pace, I was unable to catch my breath. The longer we were tangled together, the more I needed him. I felt insatiable, easily seducing Travis over and over, from one climax to the next until we were both exhausted.

I lay on my stomach, peeking from my pillow at my husband who was doing the same. Our pinkies were crossed over one another, the sheet haphazardly draped over a small section of our backsides. My skin was glistening with sweat, my eyes heavy, and my hair tangled all around me.

Travis's free hand was above his head, twirling a caramel strand of my hair.

We didn't speak, we didn't need to. Everything each of us needed to hear had been said.

We were saturated with one another, the air filled with sex, love, and satisfaction, but more importantly, the confidence in the knowledge that no matter what obstacles were put in our path, we both knew the other would stay.

And there was no love deeper, more precious than that.

CHAPTER *Fourteen*

TWISTED

Travis

I SCREWED THE COLD METAL of my wedding ring around my finger as I stared into the Iron E gym from the parking lot. It was Monday, cold, and it was shit fucking weather.

Spring was making its presence known, the rain clouds above pissing all over my car, the raindrops bouncing off the pavement in a hundred thousand tiny splashes. And, if I wasn't in a bad enough mood, I had to act like I didn't want to murder Brandon Kyle just for breathing in my direction.

I turned off the ignition and grabbed the wheel, pressing my head against the headrest. I was nearly late. It had been a challenge for Abby and me to coordinate our schedules to get everywhere we needed to go with just one vehicle, especially on the days it was raining. Today, though, I had a bigger problem.

Perkins Plaza nearly surrounded me with boutiques, a golf equipment store, a small organic foods store, a nail salon, a coffee shop, and in the center, Iron E gym. Every building matched, painted white with each store's name in simple black letters.

It reminded me of the old generic groceries Dad would buy when I was a kid. Now it meant *modern*.

The thick, gray clouds outside made people walking around inside the gym under the fluorescent lights more visible. They were lifting, spotting, or running on one of the fifteen treadmills. Brandon was behind the front desk, nuzzling the receptionist's neck with his nose.

I clenched my teeth. To be honest, I didn't get the appeal.

Brandon stood just shy of six feet but had a thickness that made him look stubby. His body was ill proportioned, and although he worked out, it looked like the muscle he had was residual from a year ago or more.

His brown eyes always had too much white around them when he talked, making him look crazy, and his ridiculous hair, even crazier. He kept it too long, used too much gel to make it stand too far off his head. He looked like a washed-up Disney villain.

I was embarrassed. I didn't want to be seen with him, much less work for him.

Eakins had plenty of flexible jobs for college students. The problem was that it was nearing mid-April, and most of the jobs that were still somehow available were only meant to support a weekend partying habit, not a married couple.

I had scoured the classifieds. Three dozen people had held my application in their hands and had either told me to come back next year for the Christmas rush, or that they had already hired several college kids and didn't need more until the end of the semester. I wasn't stupid.

The summer break exodus meant there wouldn't be enough business to sustain more employees. The trick was to find something early in the fall semester, and timing just wasn't on my side. Jobs on campus paid nine dollars an hour or less—nothing that could pay rent and bills with the hours I could work around my classes.

Most of all, I was pissed that I'd wasted so much money on bullshit over the past two years. I didn't save anything left over after tuition, and worse, I'd spent it on booze, tattoos, furniture and motorcycle mods.

I had no idea I'd meet the love of my life and get married at the same time the fights ended, leaving our income landing just below the poverty line.

Working for Brandon and letting local cougars paw at me while they pretended to work out was the last thing I wanted to do, but the bills had to get paid somehow. Abby was on her second week of tutoring, but that barely covered the groceries and gas money.

I took a deep breath, pulled the keys out of the ignition, and slammed the door behind me, feeling the pooling rainwater slosh under my feet. I knocked on the glass door and waited. There was a code box outside, and each member had their own four-digit PIN.

A man whose neck was twice as big as his head set down his bar bell and, with the telltale stick-up-the-ass-and-arm-swing walk of a weightlifter, he opened the door and greeted me with a nod.

The man looked over his shoulder. "Brandon," the meat head called with a gruff voice. He smiled at me, and it lightened his entire expression. "I'm Chuck," he said, reaching his thick hand out to mine. "I was hoping you'd come in."

"Travis. Nice to meet you."

Brandon was mid-peck behind the receptionist's ear when he looked up. Chuck noticed it, too, and his smile vanished.

It was nice to know not everyone at the gym agreed with Brandon's antics.

"Maddox!" Brandon exclaimed, holding out his arms. "The fuck, man? What took you so long?"

He grabbed my right hand in a tight handshake and then pulled me in, tapping his shoulder to mine, patting my back with his free hand. The douche bags always went for the bro hug.

"You've met Chuck, he's the management for all three gyms. Are you here to fill out an app or what?"

I nodded.

Brandon turned, reaching out toward his receptionist and snapping his fingers. "An application, Tiffany. Now."

Tiffany turned her back to us and bent over, pulling open a filing cabinet and fingering every file.

Brandon back-handed my shoulder, chuckling and nodding toward Tiffany's ass like a twelve-year-old.

I didn't smile, or frown; I just concentrated on appearing indifferent.

Tiffany found what she was looking for and trotted over to Brandon with pen and the paper in hand.

"Found it," she said, waiting for praise from her boss.

"You're great," he said. "Isn't she great?"

If fucking a married man with a pregnant wife is an admirable accomplishment. "Yeah," I said, clearing my throat. "Filing is hard."

Tiffany dipped her chin a few times in dramatic nods, appreciative that I understood her plight.

"You wanna fill that out in my office?" Brandon asked.

"You got an office?" I said, only half joking.

Brandon puffed out his chest. "Right this way. Tiffany," he said, snapping at her again. "Water."

She nodded, rushing away.

"Chuck, Maddox is finally filling out an app. We need to start a list of clients for him."

Chuck nodded, then resumed his workout as if Brandon hadn't said anything at all.

As predicted, the walls of Brandon's office were covered in posters with ripped, half-naked fitness models.

I was hesitant to sit down in the chair opposite his desk, sure he'd jerked off there every night. A corner of my mouth turned up, remembering Abby's similar disgust over my old couch the first time she'd visited the apartment. I'd come a long, long way since that night.

Tiffany brought in two cold plastic bottles, and

then nodded when I thanked her. She kept her eye on Brandon as she turned around, as if he didn't already know she was dying to be bent over his desk. Again.

"Married," Brandon said, shaking his head, staring at Tiffany's ass until she closed the door behind her.

I sat down and placed the application on his desk, clicking one end of the pen with my thumb and filling out the information as quickly as possible.

"What made you do that?" he asked. "Can't just be that she's hot. You used to get two on a slow weekend, am I right?"

"No. How long have you owned this place now?" I asked without looking up. I didn't want to punch Brandon in the mouth for talking about my wife, so I chose to change the subject.

"Four years," he said. "Three of that was with Joan." His chair creaked as he leaned back and folded his hands behind his head. "She signed it over to me in the divorce. It's not what you know, it's who you know, am I right?"

"Oh, yeah. I forgot. You inherited it."

"Kids inherit things from their parents, Maddox. Joan opened this place with her ex-husband, but then I fucked her brains out and she gave me everything I wanted. This place was a shit hole, for old bags and fatties. I married that geriatric, made this place into what it is. Now, it's mine. I bring in triple what Joan ever did."

I scribbled down the little legitimate prior work history I had beside The Circle—landscaping in high school for my dad's old partner—and then signed my name, sliding the paper toward him.

Brandon looked it over. "You're missing something, aren't ya?"

"No."

"Didn't you make banks in those campus fights?"

"No clue what you mean," I said, straight-faced.

Brandon laughed. "Right. That fight ring was all about secrecy. I get it. No worries, I happen to know for a fact you KO'd everyone you've ever come across. Except that last dude. I guess the fire KO'd him."

I frowned, unable to maintain the indifference I was going for.

Brandon laughed it off, and then rambled on forever about the history of the gym, still having to deal with Joan, and how pissed she was that he'd gotten one of his girlfriends pregnant. Now, Becca was his wife, and Brandon made her—just two or so months away from delivering a baby—deal with Joan so he didn't have to.

He was an all-around piece of shit, and he was now my boss.

I gripped the arms of my chair and listened, trying to think of Abby, the wedding, our new life together, anything that reminded me that having to be in the same room with Brandon every day would be worth it. I glanced at my watch, feeling exhausted just by resisting the urge to snatch his tongue out of his bitch ass mouth.

Brandon had been describing how awesome he was for nearly two hours.

Tiffany knocked on the door and peeked in. "I've closed out. I'm going to head home."

Brandon waved her off. "I'm going to take Travis out for a drink."

"That sounds fun," Tiffany said with a hopeful smile.

I stood. "I hate to cut you off, man, but I've gotta get home."

"Oh right," Brandon said, his voice thick with condescension. "Married life. You know, you need to set boundaries and intentions from the beginning. If you let them stop you from carrying on business-as-usual, they'll always expect it."

"Isn't that the point of being married? To stop acting like you're single? There's nothing I'd rather do than hang out with her, anyway."

"Consider yourself lucky, then. Becca is boring as fuck."

"Pregnancy has a tendency to wear them out I hear."

"I guess," he said, his lip curling up in disgust. "They're literally built for that, though. No reason for my life to stop. When can you start? It won't take you long to build a clientele."

"Next week," I said. "Monday."

Brandon stood and held out his hand.

I took it, feeling like I'd just sold my soul to Satan.

"I'll start you off with the Betties," he said.

"The who?"

"Betty Rogan and Betty Lindor. They smell like moth balls and have more wrinkles than a starved elephant, but they pay double so they can work out together and ogle the guys. They'll love you. Start you off decent money-wise, too. They'll ask you to lunch your first day. Go with them. They'll pay your rent for May. Here," he said, holding out a small booklet and another piece of paper. "This is our policy handbook and the contract. The handbook talks about your pay and commission. Don't tell me about your tips. I don't want to know how much you make or how you get them. A perk of working at Iron E."

So that's how he keeps his employees. He's actually a fucking pimp.

"Thanks," I said, rolling the papers and stuffing them in my back pocket. "See you Monday."

I dodged Tiffany without acknowledging her and walked across the empty gym, pushing out of the glass door. The sky was dark, and small ponds had formed in the parking lot, reflecting the tall lights that peppered the plaza. The Camry sat in the center of one of the larger pools.

"Fuck," I said under my breath, pulling my keys out. I fished out my phone from the other pocket and looked at the display. I'd missed four calls. *"Fuck!"* I growled, dialing and holding the phone to my ear.

"Travis?!" Abby said, sounding panicked.

"I'm sorry, Pidge. Brandon talked forever and I couldn't find a good place to tell him to shut the fuck up, and—"

"Oh, my God. No, it's fine. I was just … nothing, it's fine."

"No, it's not fine. Feds are sniffing around, the weather is shit, you know I hate Brandon and I'm not answering. I could've been arrested, in a wreck, or fired before I got the job. I don't blame you, babe. I'm sorry."

"It's fine, just … come home. I miss you."

"On my way. I'll be there in a sec."

"Travis?"

"Yeah?"

"Be careful. I have a bad feeling."

"I will Pidge. I'll be there in less than ten minutes and I'll hold you the rest of the night."

She sighed. "Okay. See you soon."

CHAPTER *Fifteen*

NOT BAD FOR A GIRL

Abby

THUNDER ROLLED, SHAKING THE WINDOWS of the apartment. Shepley and America were on the couch, watching a cheesy rom com—America's choice, of course—and I was standing next to the kitchen sink, lost in thought, staring at the messages on my cellphone.

Travis was at the gym, and even though he knew about my plans, I'd purposefully kept him out of the details. He felt guilty enough that I was going to play poker again, this time to save his ass instead of Mick's.

"Mare?" I said, drying my hands.

"Yep," she said, groaning and stretching as she stood. She lazily walked over to me, peering out the window. "Ugh, I'm so over the rain. It's been gray for days." She yawned as she spoke her next thought, "It makes me feel exhausted."

"I need some advice."

"Sure," she said, crossing her arms and leaning her hip against the counter. "Whatcha got?"

"I also need some air," I said, gesturing for America to follow me outside.

I grabbed an umbrella, and America stayed snuggled up to me as we walked to the complex playground. "This is scaring me."

"Don't freak out. You know me, I'm just being overly cautious," I said.

"Are you seriously telling me right now that you really think your apartment is bugged?"

"I … I don't know. But what I do know is that journalists at *The Eastern Star* are investigating the fire. Justin and Ricky, the guys Travis went after at The Red."

America seemed confused. "What's *The Eastern Star*?"

"The campus newspaper."

"Eastern has a newspaper?"

"*Yes*, Mare. Focus."

"Okay, they're investigating the fire. Seems like it should be on their radar, happening on campus and being the largest tragedy in Eastern's history."

"Yeah, but …" I trailed off.

"Oh. Oh, you're right. Them asking questions, not good."

The fire had become something of an elephant in the room. We couldn't talk about it for Shepley and American's sake, but they knew we were there. Ironically, what they say about lies is the truth: one has to be built on another. Even the best lies ever told are never-ending, shaky bridges to the truth.

"What are you thinking?" she asked.

I looked at my phone. "I might have a solution. I did some digging, and Justin and Ricky apparently have a gambling problem."

"No way. Where did you hear that? That's too convenient."

I shrugged. "Parker. And he had no idea he was telling on them. It's as if the Universe is on our side."

"What are you going to do?"

"There's a poker game every Thursday night at the Sig Tau house. I'm going."

America's eyebrows shot up. "That's tonight."

I nodded.

"Travis is at work. You're going by yourself?"

I nodded. "Parker will be there."

America frowned.

"Travis is aware," I said quickly.

Her expression softened.

"I have two hundred dollars. I was wondering …"

"Yeah, yeah," she said, pulling me back to the apartment.

When we reached the door, America made a beeline for her purse.

"Thank you," I said.

"What's up?" Shepley asked from the couch.

America ignored Shepley and responded to me, "Of course, silly. I know I'll get it right back."

"You'll get what right back?" Shepley asked, watching her rummage through her wallet.

America nodded to me. "Cash. Do you have any? Give everything you have to Abby."

"Sure," Shepley said, reaching to the side table. He pulled out every bill in his wallet and handed it to America. "What's this for?"

"Poker night at Sig Tau." America walked the money over to me.

Shepley smiled. "Does that mean I'm getting it back with interest?"

"Of course," I said.

"Parker will be there," America said.

"And Bentley Rutherford never misses a game. He drops thousands. I wish you'd told me," Shepley said, chuckling. "I'd have gone to the ATM earlier and gotten more money."

I looked down at the stack in my hand. "This is plenty."

Shepley grabbed his phone and began texting.

"Travis already knows," I said.

Shepley didn't look away from his phone. "I'm not texting him. The more people with serious money at the table, the more I'll make. I'm starting a text tree like I used to do for the—"

"Shepley!" America and I yelled in unison.

"Be careful!" America continued, holding her index finger to her mouth. "You almost knocked over my wine."

Shepley had frozen, but he nodded.

"Sorry, baby, I forgot … it was there."

America gently popped my arm with her elbow. "Go get 'em, sis."

The windshield wipers kept a steady beat with whatever was playing on the car radio all the way to the Sig Tau house, and I was still weaving back and forth to my hype music while I sat parked at the curb.

Praying occurred to me, but I was more focused on strategy. I'd made tens of thousands from Vegas vets practically a few days ago, I could railroad a couple of frat boys.

I closed Sig Tau's front door behind me, the air inside chilling my wet skin. I followed deep voices and laughter until I reached a room that looked like it was for meetings.

There were three round tables that sat six a piece, and two games were already started. Shepley really came in clutch. There were plenty of trust fund babies in the room.

Justin and Ricky were sitting with Parker and a few other men I didn't recognize.

"There she is," Parker said, beaming. "Hey Abs, I saved you a seat."

Next to him. Of course.

I nodded and slid into my chair, exchanged money for chips, and without much chit chat, the game started. I was the only female in the room, a novelty. *Entertainment,* as Parker put it. They were going to be entertained, all right.

The first few rounds, I played soft. Scaring away money right from the start wasn't smart. I had to lure them into betting more while also challenging their manhood so they'd make stupid decisions.

Not an hour in, and both Ricky and Justin were

sweating.

"You're not bad for a girl," Parker said.

The way he looked at me reminded me of when we were in his car making out in front of Travis's apartment.

I inwardly cringed. It was bad enough that I'd been with him in that way at all, but the thought of it now made me hate myself.

After three hours, two of the tables were empty, and Parker, Justin, Ricky, Bentley, and the real star the night, Collin Vanderberg, filled the seats at mine.

I'd already fronted Justin and Ricky a thousand to stay in, but my objective wasn't to make money.

"I can't believe I didn't know this about you, Abs. I think I'm even more attracted to you than before, if that's even possible."

"Pay attention to your cards, Parker. You're down eight-fifty," I said.

"I'm getting ready to make it all back," he said, pushing in chips.

"Not this time," Ricky said. Ricky and Justin glanced at one another. Ricky seemed confident, but I'd figured out his tell within the first hour. He was bluffing.

"Fold," Justin said, frustrated.

The other two put in without hesitation. Bentley was bluffing, too, but Collin was a significantly better player than anyone else at the table—except for me, of course—and I caught myself wondering if he'd played in more serious circles.

Collin didn't need to win like I did, though. And

because of that, my four-of-a-kind easily beat his straight. Parker wasn't bluffing, but he was too much of an amateur to know his hand wasn't worth a damn.

"Fucking hell!" Parker said, throwing his cards to the table and standing.

Collin peered over at me. "Impressive. You should come to one of my games sometime."

"You put games together?" I asked.

"You're inviting her? She's just lucky," Bentley said.

Collin laughed once. "Do you really not know? That's incredible."

"What?" Bentley asked.

"She's Mick Abernathy's daughter. Don't you remember Lucky 13 in the papers a few years ago? She's a fucking poker legend and has been since before she got her first period."

I made a face at the reference. Parker's mouth dropped open at the information.

"That gambling addict in the papers that got mixed up with the mob, right?" Ricky asked, his eyes darting between Collin and me.

"Oh, yeah," Collin said. "You'd better pay up, asshole, she's got some scary friends."

Ricky swallowed.

"On that note," Collin said, "I'll be heading home. Bentley?" He pointed to him. "You're a fucking idiot." He looked to the rest of us. "Good night." He bowed his head a bit to me. "It's been a pleasure, Abernathy."

"Maddox," I said. "It's Maddox now."

Collin grinned and nodded. "Congratulations."

Parker rolled his eyes.

I gathered my winnings, cashed in my chips, and watched Justin and Ricky.

Ricky leaned back, feigning a calm demeanor. "We'll get it to you next week. Ask anyone, we're good for it."

Justin nodded.

I stood. "Why don't you boys walk me to my car? It's late, and dark, and you owe me."

"What are they going to do?" Parker asked, standing. "I'll walk you to your car, Abby." He pulled at the lapel of his jacket and puffed out his chest.

Ricky and Justin seemed relieved.

I stared at him for a moment, unable to hide my disdain. "I just took all of your money, Parker. What about that do you think screams *alpha male* to me?"

Parker blinked a few times. "How was I to know you were raised among thugs and miscreants? I've tried to make amends with you, but who knows why. You've proven over and over you're …"

"One of the peasants? Yes, Parker, we can't all be born and bred from fancy Olive Garden money."

"Fancy Olive …? You can't be serious. You're the one who came to me for help!"

I crossed my arms and smirked. "Yes, and now everything that was in your wallet is in mine. Thanks for the help. Not bad for a girl, right?"

Parker snarled. "There's a lot more where that came from. More than I can say for your gutter rat husband."

"Good. Meet me at Collin's next game and I'll take that, too."

Parker swallowed.

I flicked my index and middle fingers at him. "Run along. Mother is surely worried."

Parker buttoned his jacket and set out in a huff, red-faced and humiliated.

"Are you really going to Collin's game?" Ricky asked. He followed me out, closely tailed by Justin.

"No, and neither are you. You suck at poker."

"I'm telling you, Abby, we'll pay you. Five days, tops," Justin said, his tone nearly begging.

"I'm not a bank. I don't do loans."

Justin wrung his hands. "M-maybe we can come up with some kind of an arrangement? We have a lot of connections. We could get you concert tickets, jobs, whatever you want. And that's in addition to the money we owe you."

"I'm a newly married woman. I'm only interested in the cash. You have twelve hours. And you heard Collin. Where I come from, you play poker, you pay. If you don't, I'm making a phone call."

"Twelve hours to come up with four thousand dollars? C'mon, Abby! There must be something!" Ricky pleaded.

I reached my car and then turned on my heels. "Actually … maybe there is."

"Anything," Ricky said.

"I'll tell you what. You stop investigating the fire, and I won't have the Gambinos feed you what remain of your fingers."

"We won't … that's easy enough. So, that will satisfy our debt? In full?" Ricky asked. He was sweating, approaching panic.

"No more questions," I said. "To anyone."

They traded glances and then nodded.

"The story's dead," Justin said.

I made a face. "The campus paper not reporting on the fire? Don't be stupid. No, you write the story, acknowledge the rumor and that the police and Feds have been questioning whether Travis was there, and confirm that he wasn't."

"Absolutely," Ricky said. "It'll run on Monday."

I smiled, patting Ricky on the cheek. "Nice doing business with you."

I sat in the driver's seat and closed the door, watching Justin and Ricky walk away in the side mirror. My plan had worked, and I'd even made rent for the next month. I'd thought that bad feeling I'd had would go away, but it didn't.

Something else was looming over us, but I couldn't see it. That thought followed me all the way home.

CHAPTER *Sixteen*

FIRST

Abby

STARING AT THE BLANK CORKBOARD outside of Mr. Mott's office, we were all in the same boat. The top two scores would automatically become Mr. Mott's Teacher's Assistant for the fall semester. For an aspiring mathematics professor, scoring that position would look amazing on my resume, as it would for the other fifty or so students standing with me.

The hangnail poking out from the side of my thumb was surrounded by red, angry skin from me biting at it for the last half hour. My deodorant was struggling, my neck and jaw were tense, and my back began to complain from standing in wedged booties on unforgiving tile. I shifted my weight from one leg to the other, trying to ignore it.

If the other students standing with me weren't suffering from nervous energy, too, I might have looked insane. We silently supported one another, even though we'd also been silently competing all semester.

We were minutes away from summer break, and miraculously, the Feds hadn't been back to our apartment. Well, not a true miracle, everything had gone quiet since *The Eastern Star* had printed a front-page article with quotes from dozens of students, who denied Travis's attendance at the Keaton Hall fight, that had all but exonerated Travis.

I was hoping my luck would hold out for somewhat less important matters, like an assistant position.

Mr. Mott's statistics final was one of the last scheduled on Eastern State's campus, evident because we were the few remaining students still on grounds. We could have waited for the grades to come out online, but Mr. Mott was old school, and he liked to post grades on printed paper before inputting them into the system. So, those of us who cared, waited.

I missed the days when Travis would wait with me, but he was at work.

He was making a killing off the fifty and sixty-year-old women in Eakins. Not as much as he made from the fights in The Circle, but as a personal trainer at Iron E Gym, he was paying the rent and most of the bills.

With my winnings from Sig Tau's poker night, we were ahead. Travis definitely made more than I did from tutoring, though. Especially during the summer, my income would all but cease until fall semester. I tried not to feel guilty. Travis preferred to pay the bills, and except for hating his boss, he pretty much had the best job ever.

Travis worked out while the ladies he worked with pretended they weren't watching. Basically, Travis was getting paid to do what he would be doing every day, anyway. He was getting thicker, and his already impressive muscles were more defined—only prompting more clients to sign up with him. He was making the most of any trainer at Iron E.

I refused to worry about the day Travis signed on to train women our age. It would probably happen, but I trusted him.

Mr. Mott's door opened, and Trina, his current Teacher's Assistant, slipped through. She held the paper with the list of grades in her hand, backward. I know. I checked.

Trina stretched her neck to make her small, squeaky voice travel farther. "Please email Mr. Mott with any questions about your grade. He won't be taking any appointments today."

With that, Trina flattened the paper against the cork, used a red push pin to secure it, and turned on her heels, navigating through the quickly tightening crowd.

I was being bounced back and forth like a pinball, reminding me of the first underground fight I'd attended.

Travis had pushed people away from me. He'd always protected me, since day one.

"Hey! Back up! Back the fuck up!" Travis said from behind me. He hooked one arm around my middle, using his other hand and arm to push the men away and gesturing to the women.

My stomach filled with fluttering wings of a hundred butterflies just at the sight of him, but a repeat of the night we first met—a night I'd just been recalling—was enough to make me want to pull him into the nearest empty lab and rip his clothes off.

"You came!" I said, pressing my cheek into his chest.

He held me with one arm, holding people back with the other. "Martha told me to cut out early. I was telling her how nervous you were about your grade. I also might have mentioned how shitty it was that I couldn't be here for you."

Sounds of disappointment snapped me back to the present, and I turned, searching for my student ID. I started from the bottom, my eyes moving up until I reached the top. "Holy shit," I said. I turned to my husband. "I'm first."

Travis leaned forward to touch my grade with his index finger. "This is you?"

"That's me," I said, in disbelief. "I got it."

Travis's grin spread across his face. "You got it?"

I clapped my hands together and held my fingers to my lips. "I got it!"

Travis threw his arms around me and lifted me off my feet, twirling me around. "That's my girl! Woo!" he yelled.

Mr. Mott poked his head out from behind his door, searching for the source of commotion.

I tapped on Travis's shoulder, and he lowered me to the tiled floor.

Mr. Mott offered a small smile for our celebration, I nodded, and he disappeared behind his door again.

Travis mouthed, *You're a bad ass!*

I grabbed his hand and pulled him down the hall.

When we burst from the glass double doors of the Nagle Building for Math & Sciences, Travis continued whooping and hollering. "My wife's a fucking genius!" He pulled me to his side and planted a quick peck on my cheek.

"Thank you for coming, Trav. You didn't have to, but I'm so glad you did."

He beamed. "I wouldn't miss it, Pidge. We should celebrate. Dinner?"

I paused. "Maybe we should cook?"

His mouth pulled to the side in a half-grin, half smart-ass expression. He reached into his pocket and pulled out a small stack of one-hundred-dollar bills.

My mouth fell open. "What the hell is that?"

"Mrs. Throckmorton said congratulations on making it through my sophomore year of college."

"She just gave you …" I looked down. "Five hundred dollars?"

"Yep," he rolled up the bills and stuffed them back in his pocket. "So where am I taking you tonight?"

"We should probably save that for …"

"Pigeon. Let me be a man and take my wife out to celebrate, please?"

I pressed my lips together, trying not to smile. "Somewhere I can wear a dress and not look ridiculous."

The other students began spilling out of the double

doors and down the steps, parting once they reached Travis and me.

He only thought for a few seconds before his brows pulled together. There was only one nice restaurant in town: Biasetti's.

Immediately, regret washed over me.

Travis made a face. "You thinking Biasetti's? Parker's parents' place?"

Travis was still raw from my coffee not-date before the poker game. I knew better than to make such a stupid mistake.

I shook my head. "You're right. I wasn't thinking. We don't have to go there."

He stared at me a moment, and I could almost see the wheels spinning behind his eyes. His shoulders relaxed, and he smiled. "It is the nicest place in town, and I'm dyin' to see you in a dress. It's about time we make our own memories there, don't you think?"

"It's okay, Trav. We can drive to Chicago and spend the night. Go somewhere so fancy we can't pronounce the food."

"Pidge, that's over an hour away." He narrowed his eyes at me, and then smiled. "You wanna wear a dress and eat fancy pasta? Then you're gonna wear a dress and eat fancy pasta. Mrs. Maddox gets whatever she wants."

He lifted me up and threw me over his shoulder. I protested, but he ignored me, tromping down the steps, taking the path toward the parking lot. "Because why?"

I squealed. "Put me down!"

"Say it!" he said, playfully smacking my backside.

I squealed again, so overcome with laughter I could barely speak. "Because you're the best husband ever."

"Louder!" he said, twirling.

I screamed. "You're the best husband ever!"

He stopped abruptly and lowered me to my feet.

I giggled, out of breath from the struggle.

He watched me for a while and then grabbed my hand, leading me to the car. He sniffed, standing tall. "Damn right, I am."

My seatbelt clicked, and Travis reached over to give it a tug—a small habit he'd picked up since Trenton's accident. We drove in the direction of Trenton and Camille's apartment—another new part of our daily routine.

Travis drove our Camry to the far side of town, parking at the last building of the Highland Ridge apartments, a property that was mostly full of young professionals and newlyweds instead of rowdy college kids.

I followed Travis upstairs, waiting only long enough for him to knock and walk in. I stopped wondering why none of the Maddoxes waited for someone to answer. Travis insisted if he wasn't supposed to walk in to one of his brothers' residences, the door would be locked.

Trenton was lying on the couch with his casted arm perched atop a pillow on his lap. He held the remote in the other hand.

"What the fuck are you watching?" Travis asked, his nose wrinkled.

"Dr. Phil," Trenton said. "It's so fucked up. These

people are bat shit crazy and that bald fucker exploits the hell out of them, all for free therapy. They promised this chick her ex wouldn't be there. Well guess what? He's fuckin' there and she repeats their agreement and that son-of-a-bitch yells at her and tells her to leave if she doesn't like it, that it's his show. I would've left. What a piece of shit."

Travis and I traded glances, and then we sat on the couch next to Trenton.

"Cami's at work?" Travis asked.

"Yep," Trenton said. "I'm glad you stopped by. I'm driving her nuts, calling twenty times a day. I can't work, so I clean and do laundry as best I can until she gets home. Watch Days of Our Lives and Dr. Phil. That Sami Brady is hot. I'd bag her."

"No, you wouldn't," Travis said, ripping the remote from Trenton's hand. He turned off the TV and then tossed it to the recliner. It bounced but didn't fall.

"Hey," Trenton said with a frown.

"You should come workout with me at Iron E between clients," Travis said.

"Yeah? How's that going?"

"Brandon Kyle is a dick," Travis grumbled.

Trenton nodded to me. "Is he?"

"I wouldn't know. Travis doesn't think it's a good idea that I meet his boss."

"Oh. Can't keep his mouth shut, huh?" Trenton teased. "Does he still say his catch phrase all the time? *It's not what you know, but who you know*?"

"Incessantly." Travis looked to me. "It's better for everyone if you don't. That imbecile has no desire to live, apparently." His eyes fell to the floor, but he snapped out of it quickly. "How's Cami?"

"Good," Trenton nodded. "She's good. Apologizes every ten minutes. She still feels bad."

"She should," I grumbled, louder than I'd meant to.

"We were hit by a drunk driver, Abby," Trenton said, defensive. "Yeah, she was driving upset, but she couldn't have helped that. We had the right-of-way. Be nice, even if I know you're just saying that because you love me."

"Not really," I teased, leaning over Travis to nudge Trenton's pillow.

"Ow! Hey!" Trenton said with a smile.

Travis smirked. "You carried Cami for two miles with that arm. Now you can't handle Pidge poking at you? What a vag."

I chuckled. I loved nothing more than to sit back and watch the brothers interact. I could do it all day, every day.

They were either fighting, hugging, wrestling, defending, or insulting one another. It was adorable.

I had the family I'd always wanted.

Trenton ignored Travis's jab, looking to me. "She really likes you, Abby. She wants you to like her."

"I do," I lied.

In truth, I didn't care for Camille and never had, even when she was just Travis's favorite bartender at The Red. I could never put my finger on what it was that rubbed me the wrong way, but even if she hadn't been behind the wheel when my brother-in-law was hurt, she'd been dating Thomas and Trenton at the same time. That would have been the nail in the coffin for me had Travis not forced me to talk it out at his birthday party.

"She's been through a lot. You can understand that. Cut her some slack," Trenton said.

"I know," I said. "I'm sorry, I'm trying. I really am, Trent. I know you love her and that's enough for me."

Travis reached over my lap and patted my outer thigh. His hand slapped against my skin, and he rubbed the spot he'd slapped, just in case it was too hard. He was a big guy and getting bigger every time he went to work. He acted like every time he touched me he might hurt me.

I chuckled.

"What?" Travis asked.

"I won't break, no matter how big your muscles get."

"I was going to say! Damn, son!" Trenton took a handful of Travis's bicep and squeezed. "You're getting fat!"

"Fat," Travis repeated. "That's all muscle, ball sack. You jealous?" he asked, flexing his arm. His upper arm grew so big and so tight, Trenton couldn't keep his grip. It wasn't until that moment, I realized exactly how much bigger Travis had gotten in just a few weeks.

"Pussy," Trenton grumbled, leaning back.

"On that note," I stood, adjusting my shorts. "We should go. Do you need anything Trent? Is Cami bringing dinner or …?"

"I've got dinner," he said, waving us away. "Actually, she made me some frozen meals. I'm not sure I can eat it all. Poor thing. She's dotes on me like I'm an invalid."

"You kind of are," Travis teased.

"Seriously, no one has ever taken care of me like she does. She's already researching the best physical therapy methods, takes me to all my doc appointments and sits there soaking up every word the guy says. Asks questions, cooks me three meals a day and all while she's healing, too."

He looked so proud, and so desperate for me to approve, I allowed a small smile. "That's really sweet." I leaned over to kiss him on the forehead, and then I followed Travis out the door and down the steps.

Once we climbed inside the car, Travis jammed the keys in the ignition, twisting until the car rumbled to life. He sat back and sighed, tapping his fingers on the steering wheel.

"You miss riding your bike everywhere, don't you? We can take it. I don't mind. I miss it, too."

He made a face. "I just wish you'd forget about the whole Cami driving upset thing, and the Tommy thing, and let her start over."

I was taken aback. I wasn't used to being on the wrong end of things, and this was twice in as many months. I also wasn't used to Travis not trusting my intuition, but he was right. Camille was family. That aggravated me even more.

"You've always liked her," I said, watching the young couple waiting as their Yorkie took a crap next to Trenton's steps. "I just … haven't."

"She's going to be your sister-in-law one of these

days. You've got to iron out whatever it is. Trenton's in love with her. You've gotta talk to her."

"I don't want to. I don't think she's going to be around that long."

"Really?" Travis asked. "What makes you say that?"

"I think she'll either move to California, or she'll find someone else. She's the type."

Travis shook his head. "Don't say that, Pidge. It'd break Trenton's heart. And Tommy wouldn't take her back, anyway. He loves Trent too much."

"Not enough to stay away from her in the first place. Make no mistake. I'm pissed at him, too."

"It's none of our business, Pidge."

I craned my neck at him. "Seriously? You're so far up Trent's ass you can see out his belly button. Brandon, too. You're all up everyone else's shit, but I have to mind my own business?" I touched my chest.

Travis chuckled and leaned in. I leaned away, still pouting, but that only made him laugh harder.

"What's so funny?" I hissed.

"You're just so damn hot when you're mad. It's ridiculous how much I need to touch you when you're all red-faced and flustered."

"I'm not red-faced." I pouted.

"Oh my God, come here," he said, reaching for me. He tried to kiss me, but I leaned away. As hard as I tried, he was just too strong, and that was somehow erotic.

"Quit!" I protested, but I didn't fight too hard to keep him from planting his soft, warm lips on mine. It was times like this when it hit me that he belonged to me. It wasn't a dream, a fantasy, or a chick flick. Travis Maddox was real, and I was married to him. I touched his cheeks and opened my mouth, allowing his tongue to slip inside.

A knock on the window prompted Travis to look up.

I sighed, raking my fingers through my hair as Travis pressed the button to roll down my window. "Oh. Hey, Cami."

"Here for a visit?" she asked in a chipper voice.

She was too nice. Trying too hard. She knew I didn't like her—not that I tried to keep it a secret.

"We, uh … we just left. We were on our way home," Travis said.

"Oh," Camille said, deflated.

"We can stay if you want," Travis said. I pinched his side and he grunted, grabbing my hand. "For a few minutes. It's date night."

"Aw, that's fun. I'll be glad when Trent starts feeling better. It's been a while since we've been on a date."

"Well," Travis began. I begged him with my eyes not to say it. "You guys can come with us if you want."

Camille glanced at me and then shrugged. "Thanks, Trav, but we're saving money right now. Another time, though. That sounds fun."

We both waved to Camille. She crossed her arms over her middle as she walked up the stairs, only releasing them to open her door. Just before she walked inside, her eyes brightened and she smiled. I knew the feeling. I felt it every time I saw Travis, no matter how much time we'd spent apart.

"Okay. Okay, you're right," I said. "I hold grudges, and I need to let this go."

Travis lifted my hand to his mouth and pressed his lips against my skin. The air conditioner was on full blast, but his hand was still a little sweaty from the few minutes we sat in the car without it. He appreciated my words, but he was a man of action. I'd have to show him.

I sighed and pulled my cell phone from my purse, looking for Camille's number in my contacts folder. I pressed her name and held the phone to my ear.

"Hello?" she said, sounding surprised.

"Hey, Cami. It's Abby."

"I know," she said, amused.

I tried not to assume she was making fun of me, but that was the first place my thoughts went.

"I, um … we should have drinks or coffee some time. I'm out of school, now. If you have a morning or evening off, let me know."

"Oh." She paused. "I'd really, really like that, Abby. I have tomorrow morning off for our follow-up appointments. They're first thing in the morning, so we should be out by nine-thirty. I can drop off Trenton and can be somewhere by ten. Should we meet for coffee?"

"The Daily Grind?" I asked.

"Good. I mean, yes. That's great. Can't wait," she said, stumbling over her words. "Okay. See you then."

Before I hung up, I heard her speak to Trenton. "She wants to have coffee!"

"That's great, baby," Trenton said.

I pressed End before she realized I could hear her, and then gently dropped my phone into the cup holder. "She's excited."

Travis chuckled. "I heard. I think you made her whole year."

I leaned back, looking up. "I want to get along. I do. But I can't shake this feeling—like I should keep my guard up with her."

"Whatever it is, I'm confident you'll find out tomorrow."

"But tonight," I said, looking over at him with a smile, "you owe me dinner at Biasetti's."

CHAPTER *Seventeen*

WHATEVER SHE WANTS

Travis

WALKING INTO PLACES WITH MY wife and watching people stare never got old. I swept the door open for her and both of the hostesses' eyes lit up. They were college girls like Abby, but my wife was perfection, her baby pink-colored dress set off her tan from her days by the pool with America and whatever the hell she did to make her skin glow.

Abby didn't believe it, but she looked like a super model, and it was as amusing as it was irritating to watch men seated at tables with their own wives or girlfriends notice her, then look at me, and then quickly back at their date. Even the women couldn't keep from staring.

As the hostess seated us at a four-top, Abby settled into her chair and put her purse on the seat next to her. Her loose curls bounced, the golden ends falling past her shoulders. She called it a midi dress, whatever that was, the ribbed fabric of the cotton-ish fabric stopping at her shin. It looked like a cotton tank top on top with thicker straps, then BAM! Curve-hugging perfection. It reminded me of something a celebrity would wear, and as curious as the other patrons were, I couldn't take my eyes off her.

"What?" she asked, smiling at me from the across the square table.

"I just can't get over how beautiful you look tonight."

She scoffed. "You're just used to me looking homeless."

I shrugged as I opened the menu. "That's how you looked the first time you came to my apartment, and I still fell for you."

She nodded once, unable to stop grinning. "True."

As soon as the waiter took our drink order, a woman approached the table. She was middle-aged, sophisticated, and dripping in gaudy jewelry. Although she seemed familiar, I couldn't place her.

"Abby! It's so nice to see you, darling." The woman was smiling, but her tone was anything but genuine. Abby seemed to notice, too, and was instantly uncomfortable, although the woman probably didn't see it.

"Vivienne," Abby said, tucking her hair behind her ear. "Good to see you, too. This is my husband, Travis Maddox. Travis, this is Vivienne Hayes."

Fanfuckingtastic. Parker's mom.

I outstretched my hand, forcing myself to be polite and pretend I didn't want to murder her son. The last thing I wanted was to get kicked out of Biasetti's.

She forced a smile like I did, but just stared at my hand.

I looked down at it. "I washed it. No peasant residue."

Her forced smile faded. "I doubt that." The outer corners of her over-filled lips turned up as she looked at Abby again. "Try to enjoy your night, dear. And your life."

"Excuse me?" Abby said, only able to utter the words after Vivienne walked away. She closed her eyes.

"I'm sorry, Pidge, I couldn't stop myself."

"Try harder," she said, opening her eyes and trying to stifle a grin.

Oh, thank God. She isn't mad.

"Your French 75, and for the gentleman, our famous Old Fashioned. Any apps tonight?" The waiter might've been a college student, but I hadn't seen him before. His baby face was clean shaven, his round blue eyes paying far more attention to me than to Abby. He was happier than before when he took our drink order.

"What do you think about the Carpaccio and the Caprese?" Abby asked.

The waiter looked to me.

"Whatever she wants," I said.

The waiter leaned in. "Apps are on me, tonight. Mrs. Hayes is in the back, angrier than I've ever seen her, and it's glorious. Thanks for that," he said, standing upright. "Wonderful choices. I'll get those right in for you."

Abby seemed confused. "Did he say what I think he said?"

"He sure the fuck did," I said, beaming.

She shushed me, giggling at the same time.

I had never felt on the right side of anything, played the bad guy to a fucking T. But, even after being responsible for hundreds of lost lives and punching our small town's golden boy, people saw me differently when I was with my wife. I somehow found myself being seen as a hero, the way Abby saw me. I gazed across the table into her eyes.

"You're looking at me like you just fell in love with me all over again," she said.

"I did."

"I don't know what I'm doing tonight, but I clearly need to do more of it."

"I just … I like this," I said, gesturing to the space between us. "You and me, out, dressed up, just enjoying each other's company. Like we're …"

"Adults?" she asked with a knowing grin.

"Yeah. Crazy, isn't it? I was in high school two years ago and now I'm your husband. It's like I slipped into my own dream life. Except I'm living it. Do you feel like that? Is it just me?"

She slid her left hand across the table and intertwined her fingers between mine. "It's not just you."

I rubbed her wedding band with my thumb. "Best thing I ever did."

"Me, too," she said. I stared at her ring, and she must've seen something in my expression because she squeezed my fingers. "What else is going on in that head of yours?"

I tried to relax my brows. I hadn't realized I was frowning. "It's nothing. I don't want to ruin our night by having this conversation again."

"Baby, look at me," she said, her voice soft. "I'll reassure you as many times as you need. I miss you when you're gone, and when you come home from work, I still get butterflies in my stomach. Not a day goes by that I'm not ridiculously happy that I'm your wife."

I squeezed her hand back. "I fucking love you."

"So," the waiter said, stepping up to our table. "Unfortunately, we're out of the Caprese, but we do have an amazing Bruschetta that I know you'll love." He leaned in and whispered his next words, "Also, don't look but there are two men back there who look like they haven't been laid in years eyeballing your table since they were seated."

"Oh?" Abby said. "Weird."

He kept his voice low. "I wasn't going to say anything, but they only ordered waters." His eyebrows bounced up once. "At Biasetti's? Sketch as hell. And we're not really out of Caprese. I just wanted to give you a head's up."

"Thank you," I said. "Go ahead and send the Bruschetta instead to make it look legit."

"Done," the waiter said, winking before walking away.

"We're going to keep talking normally for a minute, and then I'm going to take a look," Abby said.

She didn't wait a full minute. She nonchalantly

raked her fingers through her hair, and barely adjusted enough to see behind me.

If I didn't know better, I wouldn't have realized that's what she was trying to do.

"Pretty slick, slick," I said.

She giggled, then reached across for my hands again. That allowed her lean in closer. "It's not the same men who came to the apartment."

"You think they're Feds? You think they're going to arrest me?" I said, my throat feeling tight.

Abby's smile didn't fade. "If they wanted to do that, they would've done it already. They're watching."

"Why?" I asked.

"Not sure. To rattle you, maybe? Hope you'll make a mistake? Let's just have a good night like we planned and go home."

I nodded, but I was acutely aware that the Feds were behind me because through appetizers, another round of drinks, dinner, and dessert Abby pulled off *unbothered* perfectly. It pissed me off that it was a relief to pay the bill and finally step outside. Once we got into the car, I sighed.

"Not yet, baby," she said. "Wait 'til we get home."

I knew exactly what she meant. No conversations in the car. I found a parking lot to pull into, and slammed the gear into park, jogging around to open her door. We held hands while we walked far enough away that she was comfortable to talk.

"I was going to tell you at dinner, but I have news," Abby said.

"What?" My mind came up with a hundred different scenarios before she could even answer.

"Adam made bail. We need to find a way to talk to him. Discreetly."

"When?"

She blushed. "A few hours ago. I've sort of been checking obsessively."

I thought for a moment, trying to process what that meant and what to do next. "That's why they were there tonight. Adam made bail, and they're hoping I'd go straight to him. What if he doesn't want to go anywhere near me? Or, worse, what if he made a deal with them?"

Abby nodded, and then hugged me. "We need a plan. We have to do this right and we need to know whose side he's on. We have to know what he knows, what questions they've asked him. What they know about you." She looked up, her eyes meeting mine. "But you're right. They'll be watching all of us, and they expect you to connect with him eventually."

I nodded, kissing her forehead. "Let's go home. I just want to crawl into bed and hold you."

"Sounds like a perfect end to a perfect date."

I grinned. "Perfect, huh? Even with federal agents as chaperones?"

She laughed. "When this all goes away and we have normal days and normal dates and normal conversations, you might just get bored with me."

My eyebrows pulled together as I matched her gaze. "That would be like me getting bored of my eyes or my hands. You're part of me, Pidge."

She pushed up onto the balls of her feet and kissed

me.

I'd kissed that woman a thousand times, but that night, her lips tasted like forever.

CHAPTER *Eighteen*

SECRETS

Abby

CAMILLE WAS ALONE AT A table for two, a perfect wooden square that sat in the morning sun.

As I approached, I noticed my probably-soon-to-be sister-in-law twisting a napkin in her tattooed fingers. When I took the seat across from her, she was still so worked up from whatever she was thinking about her attempted smile was crooked and pained.

"Hi, Abby," she said, her voice sounding small.

"Everything okay?"

Her head bobbed up and down in a quick motion. "Thanks for meeting me."

"How did the doctor appointments go?"

She looked down at her hands and put down the napkin when she realized it was nearly shredded. "Everything is healing. Trent hasn't been sleeping well, though. Sweating at night. He just feels like crap all the time, but he keeps saying I'm overreacting. He's more concerned about the doctor saying he'll have physical therapy for a while. He's nervous he won't be able to tattoo anyone again."

"He didn't break his hand," I said.

"His wrist. A lot of his job is in the wrist."

I tried to offer a comforting smile. "He will. What about you? How's the head?"

She touched the still-pink scar that ran along her hairline. "I still get headaches. Blurred vision sometimes. It's okay, though."

"I'm glad you're both okay."

"I know," she began, hesitating. She picked up another napkin, wringing it like it was her enemy. "I know you blame me. I can't defend it, so I won't. I've thought about the accident a hundred times, and I would feel the same way you do. He's already been in a horrible wreck with a previous girlfriend, and he was anxious about getting in a car with anyone else. So, naturally, when he gets in the car with me, I don't stop. I don't slow down or pull over. I keep driving—bawling, upset, and not giving the road my full attention."

Her words caught me by surprise. It was like she'd read my mind, and that made me soften a bit. "Trent said no one could have avoided the asshole who ran into you."

"Trent says a lot of things," Camille mumbled. She was touching one of her many tattoos Trenton had drawn on her. "My point is, I tell myself all those things, but I can't take it back. I can't blame you for being angry with me, because I'm angry with myself.

But I can promise to be more careful and thoughtful, and to learn from my mistakes."

"And Thomas?"

Camille winced. "Wow, no wonder Travis married you. You don't pull any punches, either." I arched one eyebrow, and she wiggled like she was an ant under a magnifying glass on a hot day. "What do you want me to say, Abby?"

"Are you still in love with him?"

"Yes." A tiny gasp left her mouth, as if that wasn't what she'd intended to say. "Abby," she said, closing her eyes. "I love Trent. I'm in love with Trent, and I only want to be with Trent. Thomas and I are over."

"You're sure?"

She frowned. "What if … what if Travis died?"

I glared at her.

She held up her hand. "Just hear me out. What if Travis died and years later, you came across someone who made you feel things you never thought you'd feel for anyone else but Travis? Maybe even stronger?"

"Impossible."

"Right, but what if it wasn't? That's how I feel about Thomas and Trenton. Thomas is no longer in my life in that way, and he'll never be, but I will always love him. When Trenton came around, I couldn't *not* fall in love with him. Believe me. I tried."

"So, you don't want to be with Thomas?"

"No."

"What if Trenton hadn't come into the picture?" I asked, crossing my arms on the table.

"Thomas had already ended things. He knew we

wouldn't work. And it's irrelevant, anyway, because Trent happened, and it's permanent. I don't wish I was with Thomas. I'm truly happy right where I'm at."

A waitress approached our table and set down two waters. "Hi, I'm Shannon. Anything else to drink?"

"Coffee," Camille and I said in unison.

"Easy enough," Shannon said, turning for the kitchen.

"Camille, I want us to get along. I love Trenton, and he loves you, and that makes you family. I just …"

She looked disappointed, but not terribly surprised. "You don't trust me, and you can't put your finger on it."

"Correct."

"Well, maybe I'll grow on you."

"Perhaps. Thomas and Trenton both fell in love with you. There must be something amazing in there somewhere."

"Maybe I'm just spectacular in bed."

I wrinkled my nose and she snickered, sitting back when the waitress brought our coffee.

Shannon pulled out a pad and pen. "Breakfast?"

"Pancakes," I said, handing Shannon the menu. "Eggs over medium. No hash browns or toast."

Shannon nodded and then looked to Camille.

"Just bacon. Burned, please."

"Done," Shannon said, scribbling quickly before taking Camille's menu. She turned on her heels, leaving us once again for the kitchen.

Camille poured half and half and sugar into her mug and then stirred, taking a small sip while looking out the window. She didn't seem as upset as before. Not that we'd solved anything, but she obviously felt better talking about it.

"Here's the thing, Cami," I said. "If Travis did die—if I could fall in love again—the next man I fell in love with wouldn't be his brother."

"So, do you dislike me because I put Trent's life in danger, because I was with Thomas, or both?"

"Both," I said without hesitation.

Camille nodded. "Fair enough. But I can't fix either of those things, Abby. Can't you just be mad at me instead of disliking me?"

"I've tried," I said. "I've also tried thinking it was because you're the first Maddox girlfriend after me, and I'm just not going to like any of you."

Camille smiled. "Technically that was America."

"That's different."

"So, you don't like me, *and* I'm not special. You are a savage, Abby Abernathy."

"Maddox." I said with a smirk. My smile softened. "And so I've been told."

"You're right. You were first to marry into the family. But what if I'd been first? What if Trenton and I had eloped, and you had just started dating Travis? What if I didn't approve?"

I thought about her hypothetical question. My first inclination was to say I wouldn't care, but that wasn't true. I could ignore it, but not being liked by a brother's wife would always bother me.

"What if," she continued, "I held it against you for breaking his heart so many times, and for dating Parker when you knew Travis was in love with you—"

I pointed. "I didn't know he was in love with me."

"Bullshit. You're not stupid, so don't pretend."

"I thought I was a novelty. To be honest, I thought something was wrong with me. He actually told me once he didn't want to sleep with me because he liked me too much. I was sure I'd been friend-zoned."

Camille laughed. "I remember that. It came back to haunt him for months. But it all ended up perfect, right?"

I shrugged. "Pretty much." I picked at my nails, sorting through my feelings.

Camille made great points. She wasn't half bad to chat with, but something was still bothering me.

"Is there something you're not telling me? Maybe something you haven't told anyone. There is something that's not sitting right with me, and I can't shake it. If you're not being completely honest with me, spill it and we can start over."

Camille's eyes glossed over.

"Oh, shit," I said. "What is it?"

"How? Are you psychic or something?"

I narrowed my eyes. "What aren't you telling me? What aren't you telling Trent?"

She leaned across the table, took my napkin, and held it to her face as she cried. "I wasn't going to say anything."

"What the hell are you talking about?"

"I, um … I was … pregnant. The doctor said it was likely that I lost it during or just after the wreck. He gave me two choices: to wait for a natural miscarriage or have a D&C. I decided not to hurt Trent further, so I opted for the D&C. And … he doesn't know. He'll never know."

"What?" I asked, trying to process what she was saying. "You're pregnant?"

"I was."

I looked down at her stomach, unable to control the repulsed look on my face. I didn't have kids and was an only child. The whole pregnancy thing was foreign to me. She was the first person I knew who was close to my age that was pregnant—or had been.

"Cami, you can't keep this from him."

She shook her head. "I can't tell him, either. I can't hurt him again. Not after Thomas."

"But it wasn't your fault, Cami. You can grieve together."

"I'm"—her bottom lip trembled—"I'm not grieving. I'm relieved. We were in no position to have a baby." She looked down, ashamed. "Maybe that's what you're sensing about me? That I'm selfish."

I sat back in my seat. "You trying to carry this alone isn't selfish at all. But it's the wrong choice. You should tell him."

"There was an infection after." She shook her head. "There is a slim chance to none that I can ever get pregnant again. You want me to put all of that on him right now?" Camille dabbed her eyes with my napkin, my attempt at understanding making her emotional. "I don't want to see that kind of hurt in his eyes. You know how much he loves Olive. He will be such a good dad, and I know he really wants that someday. He won't leave me over it. It would devastate him if I left him over it. You tell me, what good would it do to tell him?"

"You're okay now? No pain?"

She shook her head.

"You're right. He wouldn't leave you over it and wouldn't want you to leave him. He loves you more than he wants kids. But he'd understand, Cami." I sighed. "I'm sorry, but I have to ask. Are you not telling him because of what he's been through, or because you're not sure if it was his?"

A single tear fell down Camille's cheek. "The last time Thomas and I were together like that was months before Trent. It wasn't Thomas's baby, Abby. Jesus."

I covered my face for a moment. "God, I'm sorry. I'm … bad at this. Do you want a … a hug or something?"

Camille rolled her eyes. "No."

I looked down at my hands, the guilt slowly settling in. She'd just told me she'd lost her and Trenton's baby—my niece or nephew—and I was chatting with her about it as if it were something else to judge her for.

"Camille … I don't think it's you that's the problem. I think you said it earlier. I've done a lot of shitty things to Travis. Maybe I don't want to be the only one. Maybe I need to focus on your failings so I can ignore my own." The moment I said it out loud, the cloud of anger I felt toward Camille lifted. "How far along were you?"

"Six weeks."

"Pancakes with eggs over medium," Shannon said,

startling me.

I sat back, realizing I'd been sitting so far forward my chest was touching the table.

Shannon sat my plate in front of me, and then Camille's. "Bacon … burned to a crisp."

"Thank you," Camille said, sniffing.

I carved my pancakes and then put a bite in my mouth.

Camille just picked at her crumbling bacon, touching tiny pieces on her finger to her tongue.

"You're right, you know," I offered. "He's been through a lot, but he can handle it. And he'll understand you more. Neither of you are going anywhere. Healing together is better than betraying his trust."

She thought about my words, then nodded. "You're right. I should tell him. But now he'll be pissed that I didn't right away."

"Do it anyway," I said. "Better to be late than not at all. And Cami … I really am sorry. I know you guys weren't ready, but that doesn't make it any less sad."

Camille took a bigger bite, staring at her plate while she chewed. "Thank you ... and … Abby? Can we … can we start over? Can we just agree that we both messed up and probably don't deserve the love we have, and that we'll work our asses off to reverse that?"

"Oh, we deserve it. They've messed up, too. At least, Travis did. Plenty of times."

Camille chuckled, taking another bite.

"Are you okay, though?" I asked. "I mean, really."

"I'm okay," she said with an appreciative grin.

"This is exactly what I needed."

I smiled back at her, for the first time feeling like we were on the same side. "Good. And," I paused, making sure I meant it before speaking it aloud, "if you need someone to talk to after breaking the news to Trent, you can call me."

"Really?" Camille said, her eyes glossing over again. She had friends, plenty more that she'd rather share this kind of thing with other than me, but I was sure the gesture was making her emotional more than anything.

I nodded. The moment she'd told me her secret, the suspicion I'd felt vanished. I knew she'd been hiding something. Now that she'd come clean, the feeling I couldn't shake before was gone.

Not many people would understand what it was like to be loved by a Maddox boy. We had to stick together. I shoveled another piece of pancake into my mouth and smiled at my sister. We had a long life ahead of us. This was just the first day.

When we were done, I stepped out, looking up and shielding my eyes from the warm sun. Just as I took a step forward, I bumped into what felt like Travis.

"Oh! God, I'm so sorry!" I said, squinting to focus.

"Hey," the man in front of me said. He flashed a grin that also reminded me of Travis, but something in his eyes damn near repelled me. That, and the fact that he'd left the house with the three top buttons of his Oxford shirt undone to show off his hideous gold chain. Coupled with all the gel in his hair, he looked like he came straight from Jersey Shore looking like the discount version of Pauly D.

"Excuse me," I said, trying to side-step him.

"You're Abby, right?"

I looked down at his outstretched hand, confused. "Abby Maddox, yes."

He shoved his hands in his jean pockets. "I'm Travis's boss, Brandon."

"*Oh*," I said, realizing too late the disdain in my voice.

He chuckled, looking down. Too soon, his eyes were right back on me. "I get it. I've earned the reputation I have. Owning a gym is kind of like working at Hooters. The better you flirt, the more money you make."

I shook my head. "I don't know anything about that."

"Congratulations, by the way. Talk about a whirlwind. Travis is a lucky man. I remember when Becca told me she was knocked up. I was over the moon, and crazy in love with her. I don't know, though, something changed along the way," he said, shifting his feet. "She just never seems happy anymore. I kill myself at work trying to keep her comfortable, get her whatever she wants. I dunno, I do what I can, but I guess I'm just a dumb guy. Maybe you can give me some pointers."

I crossed my arms across my middle. "Pregnancy isn't something I'm familiar with, either."

He laughed as if I'd said the funniest thing he'd heard all day.

"Well, Abby, it was very nice to meet you. Or should I call you Pidge?"

I shook my head emphatically. "That's something only Travis calls me. I … wouldn't."

He smirked. "I wondered what kind of woman could've tamed the famous Travis Maddox." He scanned me from head to toe. "Now I know."

"Uh, nice to meet you, too," I said, trying not to walk too fast to my car.

"I'll walk you," he said, jogging after me.

When we reached my door, he reached for my hand. "It was really nice to meet you." Then, to my horror, he brought my hand to his lips and kissed it.

I pulled my hand away. "You mentioned that. Have a good day, Brandon."

CHAPTER Nineteen

KARMA

Travis

THE HEELS OF MY BOOTS were planted against the hot asphalt at the main intersection in our tiny college town. The hum of my Harley's engine helped me relax. It was easy to forget while driving around town on my bike, even if my muscles were aching and exhausted from a full load of clients at Iron E.

Abby had been damn near euphoric since our date, but I couldn't help but feel like something was off. Parker Hayes's parents might have owned Biasetti's, and it might have been the place Parker had taken Abby for their first date, but the second we sat down, Abby was the giggling, witty, sarcastic, natural beauty I'd taken to the pizza parlor on our first non-date. It was like we were just college students again; no bills to worry about, no federal agents sniffing around our apartment.

Even so, we knew we were lucky. Adam was waiting for a pre-preliminary hearing, knowing his freedom was temporary. I was taking my wife on dates and pretending like the worst problem we had was Abby and Camille getting along.

The light turned green, so I picked up my feet the same time I twisted the throttle, clicking through each gear like the speed limit was for everyone else. Another workday was behind me, and so was my sophomore year of college. I had more time to hang out at home with my new wife; no papers to write, no juggling time with her with my new job and homework.

Work … home … Pigeon. Sounded like Heaven to me—if I didn't end up getting handcuffed and escorted out my front door by federal agents. That scenario was always in the back of my mind.

I tried to remember the summer after my freshman year of college, a lot of drinking and fucking—no worries about a life sentence locked away from Abby, or any worries at all. But looking back, it was one long waste of time. Not a single girl or night stood out.

Abby made every moment mean something. Realizing that I'd just met her eight months before made me have momentary freak outs that none of it was real.

We'd been through so much crazy shit in a small amount of time, and somehow ended up together and happy. Some days I felt like I was waiting for reality to kick me in the balls.

The gravel in Dad's drive crunched under the wheels of the Harley, and I pushed down on the kickstand as the engine cut off.

Dad stepped out onto the porch, greeting me like he did every time I visited, but this time Trenton stood with him, holding his once-casted arm with his free hand.

"Well, hey there," Dad said with a warm smile. His cheeks pushed up, narrowing his eyes. "Good to see you. Come in … come in."

I patted Dad on the shoulder as I passed, and then nodded to Trenton.

"Hey, pussy," I said.

Trenton just nodded.

I made my way down the short hall and turned into the living room, falling onto the couch.

It banged against the wall, but Dad didn't mention it. He just sat in his recliner and pushed back, letting himself rock while he waited for me to tell him whatever was on my mind.

Trenton sat beside me—carefully—seeming more fragile than I'd ever seen him.

I frowned. "You okay?"

"Yeah," he grunted. "I'll live."

"I'm serious. You look like shit. You're moving even slower than you were."

"Thanks, dick head," he grumbled.

I looked to Dad. "Is it just me?"

"No, I've told him," Dad said. "I was hoping you'd say something."

Trenton leaned back and groaned, letting his head fall against the couch cushions. "Fine. I'm dragging ass. I just haven't been feeling great. But on top of being a cripple, I'm not going to get sick. I refuse."

"Don't be a fuckin' idiot, Trent. Ignoring it is going to make it worse. Especially when your body is already working hard to heal," I said.

Dad and Trenton both stared at me.

"What the hell, Trav?" Trenton said. "You got married and turned into Dad."

Dad's belly bounced as he laughed, and I looked down, cracking a smile.

"Fuck you," Trenton said, still staring up at the ceiling.

"Well? How's the new job going?" Dad asked.

I sat back, trying to get comfortable on Dad's worn couch. It was lumpy and had lost half its stuffing, but Mom had picked out that couch before I was born. Dad had to let her go, so he chose to hold on to things he had a choice in keeping.

"It's okay. My boss is a dick, but I've learned to dodge him for the most part." I glanced at Trenton. Sweat was beginning to form along his hairline. "Trent. Have you taken your pain pill today?"

He shrugged with his good shoulder. "Took one this morning."

"Then what's your deal?"

"I don't know, man. I just don't feel good. Quit bustin' my balls."

"How did you get here?" I asked. Camille's car was totaled, so she'd been driving Trenton's dilapidated Dodge Intrepid since she'd been cleared to drive.

"Dad picked me up in the truck."

I glanced at Dad, who was watching Trenton with a concerned expression.

"He didn't sound good on the phone," Dad said.

"All right." I stood up and held out my hand. "Gimme me your keys, Dad. We're taking Trenton to Urgent Care."

"What? Fuck no," Trenton said.

"Get up," I demanded.

"Trav," Trenton said. He looked up at me, exhausted. "I can't afford it."

I watched him for a second, and then sighed. "I'll cover it. You're going."

"No. I can't ask you to do that," Trenton said, looking worse by the second.

"Get up, Trenton, or I'll toss your ass over my shoulder."

Trenton glared at the carpet, cussing me under his breath, and then stood. He wobbled, and I slung his good arm around my neck, carrying his weight as we walked to Dad's pickup.

I helped my big brother in, and then Dad. He tossed me the keys, and I walked around to the other side, making sure my bike was far enough out of the way.

I pulled my cell from my pocket and started to text my wife, but knew any way I explained would be alarming, so I decided to wait until we had some news to report. I slid in behind the wheel and stabbed the key in the ignition. Dad's truck whined, and then silenced.

"Don't pump the gas," Trenton said. "You'll flood the engine."

I turned it again, listening to it crank without catching. I looked at Trenton. He was the one always working on Dad's truck, but he'd been hurt and not feeling well, so there was no telling what was wrong. Dad's old Chevy was a constant patch job.

Dad pointed to the ignition, rolling his finger in a circle. "Okay, turn it one more time, let it sit, then turn it again, pressing the gas pedal all the way to the floor."

I did as he said, and when I pressed the gas to the floor, it cranked four times then caught. I pulled down the gear shift and backed out of the yard.

Trenton grunted when we bounced over the curb, and then again when I pulled away. The farther we drove, the worse he looked.

"Trav," he said, closing his eyes. "I'm not feeling so hot. Pull over."

I glanced over at him. His face was ashen, the sweat now beading and falling down his forehead.

"Fuck this, I'm taking you to the Emergency Room."

Trenton said a few words that didn't make sense, then passed out.

Dad held his head against his chest, staring ahead, clearly worried. "Travis," Dad said. His voice was calm, but it was tinged with fear.

"Two minutes."

Dad nodded, knowing I was driving as fast as I could.

We all bounced as I yanked the wheel and gunned the engine into the hospital entrance. The truck whined to a stop just inside the ambulance bay and I shoved the gear into park, running around to the passenger side. Dad was already stepping onto the cement.

I reached in, pulling Trenton out and lobbing him

over my shoulder like he weighed nothing.

As soon as the sliding door sensed our presence and opened, the receptionist took one look at us and called for nurses. Three women in brightly colored scrubs rushed out of double automatic doors pushing a gurney.

I lowered Trenton onto his back, and the three women were already taking his vitals as they moved him toward the double doors again.

Dad looked at Trenton, and then at me.

"Go ahead, Dad. I'll take care of it," I said.

Dad nodded and followed his unconscious son. The doors closed, and I cleared my throat, looking at the receptionist. She seemed unfazed, using her mouse to click a few times before readying her hands to type.

"Name?" she asked.

"His name? Trenton Allen Maddox."

She typed his name and nodded. "He's in the system … fairly recently looks like."

I nodded.

"Oh. He's the one who …" Her voice trailed off, and she stopped before divulging any more information.

"Carried his girlfriend two miles with a broken arm and then set it without making a peep so he could be conscious when she woke up? Yeah, that's him," I said.

Her eyes widened and then she continued typing. Once she was finished, she turned to a woman behind her who was probably my age or even younger, a brunette with a pixie cut and hot pink scrubs.

"Ashley, take Mr. Maddox back to see his brother,

please. They're in two."

Ashley stood, gesturing for me to meet her at the double doors.

We walked through triage, and then I followed her down the same white-washed hallway I'd walked down the night of Trenton's accident.

"Your brother is pretty famous around here," Ashley said. "People are still talking about him." She stopped and gestured for me to enter Exam Room Two.

"Thank you," I said, walking in. I brushed back the curtain to see Dad standing in the corner, watching the nurses just finishing up with an I.V.

Trenton was awake, but exhausted. "Hey," he croaked.

I ran my hand over the stubble on top of my head and sighed. "You scared the shit out of me."

"Hi," a woman in a white lab coat said, holding out her right hand. Her auburn curls framed her face, making her blue eyes look enormous.

"Travis, I'm his little brother," I said, shaking her hand.

"*Little* brother …" she said, smiling at the tablet in her hand.

"I'm Dr. Walsh. He's stable and came to pretty quickly. His heart rate isn't where I'd like it to be, but I think with fluids we'll get there. I'm going to get a few tests. Make sure we don't need a neuro or cardiac consult."

"What's wrong with him?" I asked.

She smiled, a red curl falling from a loose bun on top of her head. She pushed her black-framed glasses up the bridge of her nose. “We’ll know more soon.”

“His accident was almost two months ago,” I said. “Does this have anything to do with that?”

She kept smiling, staring at me as if she were waiting for something.

“What?” I asked.

She tapped her tablet a few times, and then looked up at a screen on the wall. It brightened with the images of Trenton’s first and last X-Rays. Her nose wrinkled. “Those are pretty gnarly breaks, Mr. Maddox. It’s amazing you didn’t need surgery.”

“He wouldn’t leave his girlfriend’s room long enough to have surgery,” I said.

“Right, she was in the wreck, too. He carried her with that arm, didn’t he?” Dr. Walsh asked. She was still smiling, and the possibility as to why finally struck. The hospital staff were probably still romanticizing the story. We were a novelty to them.

“Yeah. Is he going to be okay?” I asked, annoyed.

Dr. Walsh reached down to touch my hand, and I frowned at her. She pulled me closer to the door, glanced over her shoulder at my dad and brother, and then leaned in, keeping her voice barely above a whisper. “My little sister goes to Eastern. You probably don’t remember her.”

My stomach knotted. *Did I bag this doctor’s sister and she’s going to bring it up here? Now?*

She smiled. “She liked this boy. She’s hopeless,” she said, shaking her head. “Once she falls for a guy, she follows him everywhere. She followed him to Keaton Hall the night of your last fight.”

I swallowed.

Her smile changed, and her eyes lost focus. "Once the fire broke out, he left her. He bolted. She wasn't familiar with the building. There was a lot of smoke. She got turned around. She ran straight into you." Dr. Walsh's gaze met mine.

I grimaced, confused.

"Do you remember?" she asked. "She was terrified. She thought she was going to die. You pushed her toward the guy who ran the fights … Adam? You pushed her toward him because you knew he knew the way out, and you told him to help her. And you know what? He did. He helped her and sixteen more people to safety when all he wanted to do was run. It was just a few seconds, but you, Travis Mad Dog Maddox, saved my baby sister's life."

I glanced back at my dad. "I …"

"The cops and federal agents have already spoken to my sister." The doctor's smile returned. "She never saw you. Adam said you never showed. The sixteen students Adam saved said the same, and your brother's hospital stay is on the house."

She grabbed the handle on the door and opened it.

"W-what?" I asked, stunned.

"I can't tell everyone what you did like you deserve, so I'm going to thank you in my own way." She closed the door behind her, and I looked at Dad, trying to keep the tears from my eyes.

"Am I gonna die?" Trenton asked.

I chuckled and looked down, pulling my cell phone from my pocket to text Abby. "No, circle jerk. You're gonna live."

"Did she say what it is?" Dad asked.

"They won't know until they do more tests, Dad, but he'll be fine."

I tapped out a short message to my wife, and then another to Camille. I cringed when I sent it, knowing they would both be blowing up my phone any second.

Trenton's pillow crackled when he leaned back against it. He sighed dramatically. "I'm gonna die."

A nurse pushed through the door, carrying a container with tape, gauze and other supplies. "Hi, I'm Lana. I'm going to be poking around on you for a second." She checked Trenton's wrist band, and then her small info sheet. "Can you tell me your name and date of birth?"

Just as Trenton began giving Lana his information, my phone buzzed. I held the receiver to my ear. "Hey, Pidge."

"Is he all right?" Abby asked.

"He's pretty sick. Passed out in Dad's truck on the way to the ER. They're running some tests. He'll live."

She sighed. "Oh, thank God."

I smiled, loving my wife for loving my family as much as I did.

The phone beeped. "Oh, hey, Pidge. Cami is calling."

"Okay. I'm halfway there."

I clicked over. "They're running tests. Taking his blood now."

"He's okay?" Camille said, panic in her voice.

"He's going to be okay, Cami," I said.

She sighed. "God. He hasn't been sleeping well. He's been exhausted and pale. I knew this morning I shouldn't have left him. I knew it."

Trenton held out his hand for the phone. "Let me talk to her."

I nodded.

"Hey, baby. I'm okay. Shhh … shhh. I'm okay. I know. I shoulda told the doctor at the appointment." He paused, and then frowned. "Cami, it's not your fault. Stop. Baby, stop. No. NO, don't drive here, damn it, I mean it. Cami, I said *no*." He looked to me. "Can Abby pick her up? She's upset."

I nodded.

Trenton resumed his conversation. "Abby's on her way to get you. It's gonna be okay, I promise."

Trenton handed me the phone, and I tapped out a text to Abby. She responded with a quick "K".

"Abby's picking her up. They'll be here soon."

Trenton sighed. "Damn it. I'm such an asshole."

"Get comfortable," Lana said, tagging all the vials with stickers. "They said you're staying."

Trenton's eyes widened. "What? No. No, I can't."

"Hey," I said, walking to his bedside. "It's covered."

"Trav," he said, the muscles of his jaw ticking. "It'll cost thousands."

Lana excused herself, and I waited until she was completely out of the room, and then looked to Dad.

"Can you grab him some ice chips, Dad? I bet he's dehydrated."

"Sure can," Dad said, standing. He hobbled from

the room and as soon as the door shut, I turned to my brother.

"I spoke to the doctor. It's covered," I said.

"What? How?"

"Her little sister was at the fire. I guess I helped her get out."

Trenton's brows pulled together. "Damn."

"You just rest easy. It won't cost a thing."

Dad returned with a cup with a plastic spoon poking out from the top. He handed it to me when I reached for it.

"Thanks, Dad," I said, spooning a few pieces of ice into my brother's mouth.

Trenton nodded and relaxed back, his breath slowing, allowing himself to feel the misery that was taking over his body. He closed his eyes and winced, his body curling inward from the pain.

Dad stood by the bed and ran his hand over the buzz of Trenton's brown hair. "Just rest, son."

Trenton leaned into Dad's touch, keeping his eyes closed.

Whatever it was, I had a feeling Trenton would be spending more than one night.

CHAPTER *twenty*

BETTER

Travis

I BLINKED MY EYES UNTIL they focused in the darkness of Trenton's hospital room.

Dad was lying still and breathing deep in a cot in the corner. I'd dozed off in a chair next to Trenton's bed, and Cami was hunched over, using Trenton's thigh as a pillow.

The IV pump seemed to suck in another breath, the PA system outside called for a nurse to come to the nurse's station, and—since I'd been there—someone had come in to take Trenton's blood twice, and a nurse had come in to take vitals and check his tubing every hour.

I wondered how anyone got any rest while recovering in a hospital. I wasn't even a patient, and I was starting to feel exhausted and sick.

My phone buzzed, and I noticed I had several

missed messages.

"Shit," I hissed, sitting up to check my phone. Only one message from Abby, telling me good night. I smiled, refraining from replying. God, I missed her.

It was the first night we'd spent apart since Vegas, and it sucked. A lot.

The other messages were from Thomas and the twins. I scanned them and answered back.

No new news.

He's stable.

I'll call if anything changes.

A light knock on the door sounded, and Raegan stepped in, looking like she'd just rolled out of bed. "She sounded exhausted on the phone last night. I thought I'd come get her. Let her get a few good hours of rest before her shift."

I nodded. "Good idea." I leaned over to touch her hand, whispering, "Cami?"

She stirred and then sat up, rubbing her eyes.

"Raegan's here. She's going to take you home to get some decent sleep before you have to go to work."

Cami looked back at Raegan, who waved sheepishly. She glanced around again, still a bit disoriented, then stood, watching Trenton for a moment before kissing him lightly on the forehead.

"Let me know if anything changes," she said. She grabbed her things, moving without a sound, and then made a point to walk out just as quietly.

We all knew if she woke Trenton, he wouldn't be able to rest as well without her there.

Raegan put her arm around her as they made the turn into the hall.

Moments later, Dr. Walsh slipped into the room, holding two Styrofoam cups of coffee with lids, looking like she'd just woken from nap. "Hey," she said in a hushed tone.

"Hey," I whispered back, rubbing my eyes.

She held out one cup to me.

"This is for me?" I asked.

She nodded, sipping her coffee, watching Trenton sleep. "His color's back. His vitals are good."

"How can you tell?"

She nodded toward the door. "Monitors at the nurses' station."

"You've been here keeping an eye on him?"

"On all my patients, but yes. Trenton in particular." Her answer worried me.

"Did any of the test results come back?"

Dr. Walsh scanned Trenton from head to feet. "Yes. His white blood cell count is significantly elevated at fifteen thousand. I'm keeping an eye on his band count. It varies with each lab, but ours considers less than ten percent to be within the normal range. Trenton's count is at nineteen percent."

I'd never heard of that before. "What are band cells? What does that mean?"

"Trenton's bone marrow is releasing too many white blood cells into his bloodstream. It's usually an indication that an infection or inflammation is present.

Elevated levels could mean any number of infections. The less likely but more concerning causes are autoimmune disease, cancer, or leukemia. But based on his recent accident and his additional lab results, I suspect it's a bone marrow infection that developed sometime during the healing process of his arm. We need to keep a close eye on it, but as of now the plan is to treat with intravenous antibiotics, and if all goes well, he should be good to go in two, maybe three days."

"Oh," I said, blinking. "Thank you."

She smiled, pushing back a stray curl and hooking it behind her ear. "He was pretty dehydrated. That could have contributed to his body's inability to fight off the infection. Does he have help at home?"

"Yeah. Yeah, his girlfriend is devoted. He's just stubborn."

"Where is she?"

"I . . ." I had to think for a second before answering. "I sent her home. She has to work in a few hours. She's the only income right now and—"

"Let her know it's time to be more stubborn than Trenton is."

"I will."

Dr. Walsh exited as quietly as she came in. The blinds were drawn, but the sunrise was beginning to pour through the cracks.

Dad's mouth was hanging open as if it had unhinged sometime in the night. His light, sort-of snore was straight out of my childhood, and I found it relaxing.

I vaguely remembered when he'd fall asleep next

to Mom in her at-home hospital bed, a tough memory that I had to hold on to because it was one of very few. I looked at Trenton in his bed, reminding myself that he was going to be okay.

A year ago, the alternative would've been impossible to wrap my head around, but after so many close calls, that fear had become too real.

Trenton had been restless earlier, like he was having a nightmare, but as the antibiotics worked through his system, he fell into a deeper sleep. His head had fallen to the side, his body sunken into the mattress.

I hoped this was the last time I'd ever see one of my brothers lying in a hospital bed. At least this time Trenton and Dad would wake up to promising news.

The twins and Thomas were on Mountain and Pacific time—one and two hours behind—so I'd give them a few more hours to sleep before calling.

A vibration from the small tray that sat next to Trenton's bed prompted me to put down my coffee and pick up my cell phone. Brandon's name lit up the display.

> **I need you to pick up four hours today. I have a couple of clients I need you to cover.**
>
> I tapped out a reply. **My brother's in the hospital. Ask Chuck.**
>
> **Chuck's sick.**
>
> **Then ask someone else.**

That reply was as diplomatic as I could be.

Knowing Brandon and considering the time, he was probably holed up in a hotel with some random chick so his wife wouldn't find out he was cheating … again.

I wasn't going to leave Trenton and Dad alone so he could get laid, but my job was finally paying all the bills. Keeping it meant walking a fine line with Brandon.

How about I ask your wife?

It took me five full minutes to cool down before even thinking of a reply.

Brandon learned early on talking about Abby was a sore spot for me, and he loved poking the bear. I needed the job almost as much as I needed to beat his ass. Brandon was the only person on earth who could mention Abby in any way other than respectful and get away with it. So far, he was residing just behind the line I'd mentally drawn for him.

How about I murder you in your sleep?

There. That was just direct enough that he'd think I was joking.

LOL. Fine. I'll ask Luke.

I put the phone down and covered my face with my hands, my elbows digging into Trenton's mattress.

"Hey," Trenton whispered, touching the top of my head. "What is it? Was the doc here?"

His worry created a deep line on his forehead. I took his hand into mine and held it on the mattress, patting once.

"Yeah. Your labs came back. You've got an infection in your blood stream, probably from the breaks in your arm, but you're gonna be okay and ready to roll in a couple of days."

Trenton looked up at the ceiling and sighed. "Thank Christ." After a few seconds, he punched the pillow with his good hand a few times until it supported his head enough for him to sit up.

"She'll be back in later and explain better than I can."

Trenton grinned, and then rubbed his face. "I don't care what it is. I just care that it's nothing serious. Fuck, I'm so relieved."

"Did you think you were gonna die, bitch?" I teased.

"I wasn't sure," Trenton said. His expression made my smile fade. "I've had some shit luck this year."

"At least the bill is covered," I said, sitting back and crossing my arms against my chest.

"No shit," Trenton said, raising his brows once. "So, if it's not me, what's wrong?"

"Oh, that was my boss on the phone wanting me to come in. He made a crack about Abby. I'm trying not to plan his disappearance."

Trenton's bed crackled as he moved to get comfortable. "Brandon's been rumored to have a death wish. You know he slept with John Brigham's wife last year?"

"The cop?"

"Yep. The one who was suspended for beating a cuffed dude. Brandon heard about it, then ran out and bagged his wife."

I frowned. "Abby I trust, but I need this job, and it wouldn't take much for me to attack that piece of shit."

"Just keep her away from him so he'll keep his hands off her. You're getting better at keeping your cool, but if he touches her … God help him."

I nodded. That was the plan. I'd have to explain better to Abby. This was one miscommunication I couldn't afford to have.

"Go home," Trenton said. "Get some rest. Take Dad with you."

I shook my head. "You know he won't leave until you do."

"I don't need both of you here. Get out, fuck nugget. No one wants you here, anyway."

I flipped him off, standing to grab my keys, wallet, and phone, and then leaned over to touch my cheek to his temple. I pecked his forehead, and then waved good-bye.

The drive home in the back of a cab was quiet and long. I was glad the driver was too tired for conversation, because I had plenty going on in my head.

My bike was still at Dad's but to hell with it. If I went straight home, I'd only get to crawl into bed with Abby for less than an hour before she would wake up to start her day.

As the sun peeked through the clouds, I directed the driver to park next to the Camry, and then I handed him a ten. Before he could bother to make change, I was already climbing up the steps to my front door, sliding the key into the bolt lock.

The apartment was dark, tiny nails tapping against the floor and the AC flowing through the vents were the only sounds. I leaned over to pet Toto, and then grabbed his leash, walking him back down the stairs to the patch of grass below. Toto sniffed every planter, every light pole and pedestal his leash would allow him to reach, and then finally, when he was satisfied, hiked his leg. He kicked back grass nowhere near where he'd just pissed like he'd just conquered a Viking army, and I scooped him up, jogging up the steps so I could lay down next to my wife.

I lowered Toto to his feet, unclipped his leash, and then reached back, pulling off my T-shirt as I made my way to the bedroom.

When I opened the door, it creaked, and I could see Abby's silhouette stir. I kicked off my boots, unbuttoned my jeans, and yanked them down over my hips, stepping out of them before crawling under the covers.

Abby hummed as I wrapped my arms around her, backing her ass up to my lap and moving her hips from side to side. I was hard within ten seconds, but that only made her rub up against me more.

"Did you finally decide to come home?" she asked.

I pulled her back against my torso, feeling her warm skin against mine. She smelled like citrus shampoo and her favorite lotion. I touched my forehead to the nape of her neck, and she froze.

"Is Trent okay?"

"Yes," I said, kissing her soft skin. "He's going to be fine. He'll stay another night or two and then they said he can go home."

She relaxed. "Good. Did they say what was wrong?"

"Probably a bone marrow infection," I said, burying my face in her back. My entire body ached for her.

She turned to face me. "A bone marrow infection? What is that?"

"I know, right? I'd never heard of it, either. Only Trent." I kissed her neck, making my way up to her ear.

"I have good news," she whispered. "Remember after date night we were trying to figure out how to make that recipe work?"

"Yeah?" I knew exactly what she meant. She'd found a way for me to meet up with Adam.

Her lips grazed my ear as she spoke almost inaudible words. "Finch had some ideas. He's going to help."

I leaned back, mouthing his name. *Finch?*

She nodded.

I thought about it for a moment, then nodded, too. She must've had a good plan. She wouldn't let me walk into a trap. I kissed her neck again, slowly making my way to the tender skin behind her ear.

She sighed. "I should take Toto out."

"Already done."

"Have I told you you're my favorite husband?" she asked, smiling as she stretched.

"That's because I'm your only husband," I said, pressing my lips against hers.

She turned over and sat up, then pressed me flat

against the mattress until I was looking up at the ceiling. Her mouth was on my neck, tasting, alternating between kisses and flicks with her tongue.

She hummed as she traced a line to my collar bone with her lips, and then she disappeared beneath the covers, tasting her way down my chest and abdomen until she reached into my boxer briefs with a single, soft hand.

"Holy God, Pidge," I moaned, reacting to the feeling of her hot, wet mouth around my dick. I covered my face with my hands, wondering what I'd done to deserve the woman I'd married.

Ten minutes before, I couldn't wait just to hold her. Now she was between my legs, gripping my hardness in her hand, showing me exactly how happy she was that I was home.

She peeled back the covers and looked up at me, her gray eyes sleepy and seductive.

I lifted my head to look down at her, running my thumb down her cheek, shaking my head in awe. Every day I thought I couldn't love her more, but I did. I always did.

Sometimes thinking about how strong my feelings would be a year in the future, or ten years, was scary as hell.

"Who's the best wife?" she asked, lowering her head while her gaze met mine.

"You are," I said, letting my head relax back. "You're better than best. No contest."

Her head dipped again. Her fingers were curled around my shaft, her mouth traveling agonizingly and wonderfully slow just behind them until she reached the base. Then back to the tip, just to repeat the movement again, but this time twisting her wrist to change her grip enough to send my every nerve into a frenzy.

My eyes rolled back in my head, forgetting everything else but her.

CHAPTER Twenty-One

HEATHENS

Abby

AMERICA SIGHED, HER OILED SKIN glistening in the early June sun. Her bikini had even less fabric than mine. The tiniest coral and white horizontal striped triangle top, and a matching cheeky bottom allowed for maximum surface area to brown.

The ice in her glass clinked together and popped as it melted—along with everything else in Eakins. Occasionally, a hint of a breeze would barely whisper through her hair, and she'd sigh.

We were happily baking our skin in the furthest corner of the fenced-in pool that was nestled in the center of my apartment complex.

Water splashed, and America snarled, raising her head to glare at the misfits we shared the space with.

"Mare," I warned.

"Just let me yell at them once. Just once."

"Then they'll make a game of it. Those are Marsha Becker's boys. She lets them run all over the property like heathens, and then yells at people for having the audacity to try to parent them. Just let it go. The water feels nice once in a while, anyway."

"Until you realize they've pissed in that water," she muttered, resituating her large, square sunglasses.

I chuckled, looking over at my best friend.

Her profile was flawless, her lip gloss glistening on her pouty lips, set just below her perfect pixie nose and above her divinely bestowed, softly defined jaw. She could have been a model or actress in L.A. had she not followed me to Eastern State. She could've been anything.

I looked over at her, wondering if she'd decided what that would be. So far, her answer had been, *Who knows*?

"So, Trent's going to be okay. That's a relief," she said. "I know Shep's parents went to visit him today. I think Jim was really worried."

"Yeah, he's good at hiding it."

"Must be why you get along with him so well," she said with smirk. "Congrats on the thing with that teacher, by the way. The internship or whatever. I'm so proud of you. You worked really hard for that."

I smiled, feeling uncharacteristically affectionate. "Mare, do you remember when we met?" I asked. "I mean the first day."

She pushed herself up onto her elbows and looked at me over her glasses. "How could I forget? You were this confident yet mousy, lost, sweet, jaded, and jilted thing. I loved you the moment I laid eyes on you. The first day of junior year."

I turned onto my stomach, smiling at her. "You didn't love me. It was just a crush."

"No, it was love. True love," she said, settling her head back against her lounger. "I purposely picked the seat next to yours and asked you to come hangout at my house within the first five minutes. You came to dinner and you never left. For the most part. I'm so glad we finally talked you into moving in. Even if it did take until the last three months of senior year."

"Your parents were awesome. My mom was …"

"A drunk." Her smiled faded. "Have you talked to her?"

I shook my head. "She wouldn't even know I'm married if it wasn't for Benny. I wouldn't know that she knew it wasn't for Jesse. How messed up is that?"

"Has he called?"

"Jesse?"

"Mick."

"No," I said, shaking my head. "Travis might kill him if he did, and you know Mick. Forever the coward."

America stared at the pool. "Travis will have to get in line. You know what I was wondering about the other day? You and Travis getting married in Vegas."

I tried to keep my face smooth, dreading the moment I'd have to remind her it was better if she didn't fully know the truth.

America knew we were at the fight, and knew we'd run off to Vegas, but she could still play dumb if questioned by the Feds, and I wanted to keep her as far away from our mess as possible.

"Did you happen to run into Jesse?" she asked.

Her question took me off guard. Jesse hadn't crossed my mind since he'd showed up with Benny's offer to help Travis. "What made you ask that?"

"I don't know. It just popped into my mind and I envisioned him seeing you in your wedding dress and throwing up."

"*Throwing up*?" I sat up on my knees.

I pulled my hair to the side, combing it through with my fingers before weaving it into a side braid. Even then, the ends hung past my breast. It was getting longer and lighter in the summer sun, a blonder version of my normally caramel strands. I wasn't model-esque like America, but I'd landed Travis Maddox. My looks clearly weren't vomit-inducing, especially not on my wedding day.

"I feel like I should be offended."

"No, stupid," she laughed. "Throw up as in him being sick over you marrying someone else. He was fully convinced, until the day you left Vegas, that you two were getting married. And by the text messages for almost a year after, I'd say he hung on to that for a while. Do you think that has anything to do with why … why he started working for Benny?"

"Nice titties," one of the Becker boys said, raising his eyebrows at me before running away and jumping into the pool. By the giggling and high fives, I imagined he'd been dared.

America opened her mouth, but I gestured for her

not to speak.

"Just don't," I said. "And I know what Jesse thought. But no, I didn't see him. And even if for some crazy reason he started working for Benny because he was heartbroken and thought being a made man would somehow prove himself, not my problem. He knows I would want the exact opposite of that."

"Yeah, maybe it's something else. It's probably something else. I'm surprised he let you stay to win back that money for Mick. I figured he would have hated you."

"He probably does."

America stretched, letting her head fall back. "Oh, well. Not like I would've gotten to see that drama unfold, anyway."

I craned my neck, glaring at her.

"What? He drove all the way to Wichita to see you. You didn't even let him down easy. Even my parents were appalled."

I closed my eyes, trying to keep the memory from forming in my mind. "Do we *have* to talk about it?"

"He just … I don't know, didn't look like himself. All that soft, sweetness in his eyes … gone."

I frowned, watching Marsha Becker's delinquents push unsuspecting little girls into the pool.

Jesse was in love with me, and I'd tried for a long time to be in love with him. Jesse was a safe place to fall when my mother was drunk, and Mick was on one of his benders. He was always kind and soft-spoken, thoughtful and affectionate.

It wasn't until I married Travis that I realized why

I'd found it impossible to love Jesse. I was meant to be Mrs. Maddox. And America was right, whatever had happened to him since high school, he wasn't the same person anymore.

"Do you wonder what Travis and Shep would be doing right now if we hadn't moved to Eakins?" I asked.

"I don't wonder, I know. Shepley would be at your apartment—except it would still be his apartment—and Travis would be in jail like Adam."

"Don't say that," I said, disgusted.

"He would have gone to that fight. Keaton Hall would have caught on fire …"

"Adam was trying to keep a low profile because the fight had already been rolled once. They used the lanterns to not draw attention because the cops showed up at the last one. The cops came because a fight broke out, the fight broke out because that douche attacked me. If we hadn't come, maybe the fire would have never happened."

America arched an eyebrow. "Abby, if they weren't conducting illegal fights in old buildings with too many people and just a few exits, no one would have been there to start the fire. No one would have been there to die. We all make our choices. And don't let Travis hear you talking like that. He feels guilty enough without you blaming yourself."

"I'm not talking to Travis about it. That's why I'm talking to my best friend."

"And your best friend is telling you you're being a dumb bitch. Quit it. Anyway, we didn't meet here to talk about the fire or Jesse or throwing up. We're talking about your wedding."

"Hey blondie, wanna come sit on my lap?" a Becker boy yelled.

America lifted her fist and proudly displayed her middle finger.

"Mare!" I scolded.

She smiled with her fist still in the air, then put it down, satisfied.

I climbed onto my stomach again, trying not to slip from all the oil and sweat. "Please, no wedding talk today."

"We've already talked about everything else, school, plans, my date with Shep, Lexi's pregnancy scare, and your in-depth conversation with Travis about his boss and how it would be best for everyone if you avoided him. Now, we can talk about the wedding."

"I told you we could do it. But this is for you. I don't want another wedding, remember?"

America pulled a notebook and pen out of her pool bag. "So, I was thinking St. Thomas. Why, you ask? Because we don't need passports, it's beautiful, not your average destination wedding, and the Ritz-Carlton has a beautiful venue with a wedding package."

"Sounds great," I said.

America made a check next to her scribbles and then dropped the pen on her mid-section, clapping. "I was hoping you'd say yes! It's going to be perfect! Okay. Second question. Colors. I was thinking aqua, coral, pink, sea foam, and cream. Or we can go a little bolder and do purple and orange, but I prefer the first swatch."

"First swatch it is."

"Really? Because the orange and purple with the sand and ocean …"

"That's fine."

She clapped again. "Obviously, I'm the maid of honor. I would suggest Finch, but his dad's birthday is the same day, you know."

"Kara … Cami …"

"Excuse me?" America said, her face screwing into disgust. "Cami I get but … Kara?"

"She went through a lot when we were roommates. And she sent me a card. It was sweet. We had lunch; it was nice."

America looked like she'd smelled something rancid.

"Kara," I said, pointing to her notebook. "Put her down."

"*Ugh*, fine."

"I'd tap that," a Becker boy yelled. "Twice."

America sucked in a breath through her nose, desperately trying to ignore them.

"Now, for the reception. The Ritz has a great outdoor restaurant called Sails. There are these huge tarps they pull out that function as a ceiling. And because it's the Caribbean it tends to rain, so they can roll down the sides like a tent enclosure to protect us from any passing showers. We could also move the wedding ceremony there if needed."

"Great."

She squealed. "I know you're not into this, Abby, but it's going to be beautiful, we'll all get to be there, and I'm going to be a gorgeous maid of honor."

"Yes, you will."

"One last thing," she said, serious. "The date."

"I assume you have one chosen."

"Well, it just made sense to me to do it on your first anniversary. It falls on spring break next year, but it's on a Sunday so we'd miss at least the first day back to classes after break."

I tried not to smile but failed. Our first anniversary had seemed so far away until that very second. I would be married to Travis Maddox for an entire year, and then we'd start on our second.

"What? You're making a weird face."

I laughed once, looking down. "I just … love him."

"March twenty-first, then?" she asked, putting the notebook away.

"March twenty-first."

One of the bigger Becker boys jumped into the pool holding his knees to his chest, sending a wall of water over America and me. We both gasped, sitting up with our mouths open.

"Mare!" I said too late.

She stood, beach bag in hand, dripping wet while she slid her bare feet into her shoes. "You little shits! The best parts of you ran down your momma's leg!"

Everyone in the pool froze, staring at us.

"Oh, hell," I said, gathering my things and sliding on my cut-off jean shorts. "Let's go before Marsha hears about what you said."

"I hope she hears it!" America screeched. "Someone needs to tell her! Her kids are little beasts! You're vile!" she yelled, stomping out of the gate toward my apartment. "Tell your mom the community pool is not a fucking babysitter!" She pointed at one. "And you need a haircut!" She pointed at another. "And you need braces! Jesus Christ, I would be embarrassed if I had this herd of obnoxious brats for children! You know why your mother's not here with you? Because she's sitting at home, hiding from society, humiliated at the horrible job she's done!"

"Oh my fuck, America, you've lost your mind. Walk. Walk!" I commanded.

The Becker boys cackled, overjoyed at America's reaction.

"I will have daughters and they will be well-mannered!" she said, pointing in all directions. She looked insane.

"You just jinxed yourself," I said, walking with her to my apartment. "Now you're destined to have a bunch of rowdy, repugnant boys."

"No, I won't. Twin girls in pristine white dresses, who will slap the shit out of boys like the Beckers."

Finch stepped out from between buildings, wearing all-white that practically glowed in the hot summer sun. "Ladies, you're looking … sweaty. And flushed."

America opened her arms wide. "You look like you need a hug."

He lowered his sunglasses to look her up and down, unimpressed. "This is Gucci. Don't you dare." He replaced his glasses. "Abby, can I see you in my office?"

He gestured to where he'd walked from. "Alone?"

I could tell America was trying very hard not to be offended, but her expression gave her away.

"It's uh … something you shouldn't hear."

"So Finch can know but I can't?"

"He doesn't know anything. I just had him talk to Adam for Travis."

"So why am I being dismissed? You know I would never repeat anything."

I glanced around. "It's not about that, Mare. I'm trying to protect you."

"But not Finch?" she asked, unconvinced.

"Like I said, he doesn't know anything, and it's better this way. Please trust me."

Her lips formed a hard line. "Fine. I'll wait for you at the apartment. But," she spoke softly and leaned in, lowering her sunglasses, "you were in the basement, Abby. And that terrifies me. Have you even talked to anyone about it? That had to have affected you."

"You know I can't."

"What about patient/doctor privilege?"

"If there's a crime committed, they have to report. I've talked to Travis, but I love you for caring about me," I said.

America replaced her glasses on the bridge of her nose and turned on her heels, walking toward my building. The farther away she walked, the guiltier I felt.

I followed Finch under a shade tree. Beads of sweat were already forming at his hairline.

"I love how we all act like we don't know what going on, but we all know what's going on and we pretend we don't all know that we all know what's going on," he said, nearly giddy.

"You don't know, Finch. Not really. What did Adam say?"

"It's all set. When and where you requested. He's on board."

"And how did he act about it? Nervous?"

"Very, but he did tell me to tell you something."

"What?"

"That he's got Mad Dog's back."

I thought about that. "Do you believe him?"

"I do," he said, standing tall. "He seemed kind of relieved."

I nodded. "And no one overheard you? No one was around? You left your cellphones out of ear shot?"

"Done, done, and done, baby. I was out there doing the Lord's work and wasn't about to fuck up. Now what?"

I kissed his cheek. "Nothing. You did good. Thank you so much."

"Really? That's it? But I'm so good at this!" he called to me as I walked away.

America was sitting on the bottom step when I arrived back at the apartment. She was picking her nails, her sunglasses hanging low on her nose.

"Please don't be mad. I know that was hurtful, I'm sorry. I really ..." I looked up to the apartment.

America held her finger to her lips briefly before speaking, "It's fine. Really. I understand, I promise. We don't need to talk about it."

"Thank you," I said.

We walked upstairs, and I unlocked the door and then closed it behind America. She sat on the couch, already engrossed in her phone while I put down my bag, sunglasses, and keys on the breakfast bar.

I kicked off my sandals and padded into the kitchen, wondering what to thaw for dinner. The house was clean, the laundry caught up. The only thing to do was cook. I looked at the clock hanging in the kitchen. Travis would be home in the next hour, and—

"Pigeon?" Travis called as he opened the door. He tossed his keys next to mine and nodded to America. When he saw me, he beamed. "Hey, Pidge."

"Hey," I said, grinning as he strode into the kitchen and wrapped his arms around me. His whiskers scuffed against my shoulder when he hugged me, but I didn't care. I just didn't want him to let go.

He stood taller, just enough to steal a few tiny kisses.

America groaned and stood. "That's my cue. Call me later. I'm driving to Wichita in the morning."

"No," I whined, walking over to her. "Can't you just stay here?"

"Mark and Pam are not that cool," she said, jutting out her lip. "Dad's still afraid if I spend too much time with Shep, I'll end up eloping."

"Can't imagine where they'd get that idea," Travis said, kissing my cheek before opening the freezer. He pulled out a package of chicken breasts and tossed them into the sink. "They should come up. See that Abby isn't miserable. She's actually pretty damn happy. I make sure of it."

He winked at me, and I tried to calm the butterflies exploding in my stomach. I thought that might've gone away after a while, but every time it happened, I prayed it never would.

"They still don't want me getting married before graduation. Neither do I, but Wichita sucks. And I'll miss Shep. And you guys, I guess."

I took the few steps over to her and pinched her side. She squealed and laughed out loud. I couldn't help but giggle.

Travis looked over at us and shook his head, amused.

"I'll come by before I head out." She hugged me, kissed my cheek, and then disappeared behind the door.

My phone went off seconds later, signaling a text from America.

"Some things never change," I said.

Proud of Travis. Didn't mention your bikini once.

"You weren't wearing that outside, were you?" Travis asked.

I giggled.

"What?" he asked.

I tossed him my phone, letting him read America's text.

He let his head fall back, hating being a forgone conclusion just as I did. "*Agh* … I can't help it. Look at you," he said, pointing all ten fingers at me. He wrapped me in his arms again, showering my face and neck with tiny kisses. "It's not easy having a wife this beautiful."

I'd never felt particularly attractive, especially being around America all afternoon in a bikini, looking like a super model. But Travis made me feel like I was not just the most beautiful woman in the world, but the only one.

"Get used to it."

"Yes, ma'am."

"How's Trent? Did you stop by?"

"No, he was discharged earlier this afternoon. I figured we'd stop by after dinner. He's staying with Dad while Cami's at work."

"Good plan," I said, opening the cabinet. I scanned the cans of vegetables, trying to decide between corn, peas, or green beans. "What are we doing with the chicken?"

"I was just going to grill it."

"So, corn and mashed potatoes, then?" I asked.

"Sounds good to me. Then Netflix and chill?"

I stared at him. "We are so boring."

"I like boring. Boring is good."

Someone pounded on the door, and I left Travis in the kitchen to answer. "Mare either forgot something, or it's Marsha Becker."

"Marsha Becker?" Travis asked, wrinkling his nose.

"If it's her, you'll figure out why real quick," I said before twisting the knob and pulling on the door. "Hi."

"Hi," the man in front of me said, his mouth pulling into a devilish half-grin. His muscles were trying to bulge out of his shirt like Travis's did, and he looked at me the way Travis used to look at everything with a vagina before he fell for me. "Is Travis around?"

"Brandon," Travis said, immediately tense. "What are you doing here?"

"Thought I'd stop by," he said, walking past me. He looked around, judging every corner of our apartment, then he scanned me from hair to toes. "To say hi again to the famous co-ed who tamed Travis Maddox."

I crossed my arms over my middle, feeling his eyes pour over my every curve. It didn't help that I was in a bikini top and cut-off shorts.

"Again?" Travis's jaw ticked, his hands balled into fists.

If Brandon looked at me one more time, I was afraid Travis would attack him.

"Baby," I said, walking around Travis until I was behind him. "We're about to eat dinner. I didn't realize your boss was coming over. It was nice to see you again, Brandon, but maybe another night?"

Brandon blinked, surprised by the rejection. "Uh … sure. Yeah, I apologize for the intrusion. I was just coming by to see a friend a few buildings over, and spur-of-the-moment decided to stop by."

"Have a good afternoon," I said with a forced smile.

"See you tomorrow, Trav." His gaze fell on me. "Hope to see you again soon, Abby."

Travis dipped his head once, watching Brandon leave like he was waiting for an assailant to make a move. The second the door closed, Travis turned to me asking, "*Again?*"

I shrugged, knowing if I told him in that moment, Travis would chase Brandon down in the parking lot. "We crossed paths after my meeting with Cami. Briefly. That's it."

His shoulders relaxed, and he exhaled. "Fuck me," he said, rubbing the back of his neck. "That was almost bad."

"What the hell was it?" I asked, walking over to twist the bolt lock.

"That was Brandon Kyle fucking with me."

"You make him a lot of money. Why would he do that?"

"I don't know," Travis said, returning to the sink. He stared out the window, watching Brandon walk across the parking lot to the next building. "I have a feeling we're going to find out."

CHAPTER twenty-two

DEEP

Travis

"GREAT JOB. ONE MORE SET, Betty," I said. "I mean, uh, Bett …" Two Bettys at the same time was confusing as fuck, so I started calling the white-haired one with the tight, short curls Bett. She nearly squealed every time I said her name, while the other—without fail—sighed with jealousy.

I crossed my arms and leaned back a bit to glance at Brandon.

He was a douchebag, doing douchebag things as he walked across his douchebag gym. He ogled a few women he knew were married, smacked a regular on the ass, because to anyone else it would be an acceptable *good game*. He finally ended up at reception, stepping behind Tiffany and wrapping both arms around her.

I could feel my heart rate pick up, and I began to

sweat even though it had been two hours since I'd gotten my work out in. I'd never liked Brandon, but after his unexpected visit, I knew he was up to something and whatever he had planned wasn't good. I tried not to assume it was to go after my wife.

Surely, he wasn't that stupid, but Brandon never thought about anything beyond what he wanted. That made him dangerous, and the thought of him even attempting to bag my wife made me feel murderous.

"You okay, Travis?" Bett asked, putting down her five-pound dumb bells.

"Yeah?" I said, snapping out of it.

"You're shaking, dearest. Do we need to take you for another meal? Are you not getting enough to eat?" the other Betty said with a smirk.

"That's so nice of you to offer, ladies, but my wife feeds me very well."

Bett frowned. "But you seem upset. Everything okay at home?"

"Everything is perfect at home." I looked at my watch. "Okay, that's it for today. See you Wednesday?"

"Wouldn't miss it," Bett said, glancing at my right bicep and then my groin before doing her best as a geriatric to walk seductively past me.

Brandon came up behind me and slapped my shoulder. "The old bats are shameless!" he said, chuckling. His expression turned serious. "When's your next client?"

"Uh, twenty minutes."

"Come to my office for a sec, would ya?"

I bristled. "Actually, I was going to run an errand

on my break. Is it important?"

"I was just going to apologize for coming over unannounced, and ask if you and the wife would like to do dinner one night?"

"The day you came over was my last early day for a while. I'm working late the rest of the …" I trailed off, realizing too late my mistake.

"Gotcha. No worries, brother. We'll figure it out." He looked around for anyone who might be listening. "Hey, so … that fight, on the news."

"What about it?"

"I hear you were there. I thought I should warn you. I was at poker night at Sig Tau and Parker was there. Losing. Drunk. Running his mouth to sound cool. You know how he is."

"Warn me? About what?"

He grew serious. "He said that report in the school paper was bullshit." After a few seconds he laughed once. "I mean, that's what he said. He didn't pull out any proof or anything. He said he was wishing someone would rat you out." He made a face. "He's too pussy to do it."

"I wasn't there, man. I don't know what he's talking about."

Brandon smirked. "I mean, if you were, there'd be a hundred witnesses. People had their phones out."

I glowered at him. "They can't have proof if I wasn't there."

He grinned. "Sure. But ya know, if you need to talk about it, I'm here for you."

I stared at him for a minute. "Yeah, I'll uh … I'll

talk to Abby about dinner."

"Yeah, yeah, you do that. Not sure if Becca can come, though, she's been exhausted. I've been steering clear of the house. Christ, she's been so damn whiny. I thought their bodies were built for that shit."

"By shit you mean carrying another human being in your body for the better part of a year? Vomiting? Exhaustion? Your body growing in ways that shouldn't be possible? That shit?"

"Yeah. Women have gotten soft. Back in the day, they pushed out their crotch fruit while running from saber tooth tigers."

"You saying you'd prefer a smelly cave woman, Brandon?" I asked.

He laughed so hard he bent over and grabbed his knees. Then he stood up, straight faced. "Nah, I like the college girls."

Before I could react, he walked off.

I tried to stare a hole into the back of his head before heading to the back to the line of tall, black employee lockers to grab my helmet. I reached for the lock, input the code and then pulled. Rage took over and I slammed it shut. It bounced open so I slammed it again, paused, and then rammed my fist into the metal, creating a dent. My face compressed.

This isn't me anymore. Why am I letting that stupid fuck get under my skin?

I touched my forehead to the locker, breathing hard, and pressed my damp palms against the black paint. I could feel beads of sweat forming on my hairline.

He's definitely up to something, but what?

I grabbed my helmet, shut the locker and made a beeline for the front door. As soon as I got to my bike, I pulled out my phone.

The sun was beating down on me, and I felt my shirt begin to dampen. I was already pissed, my skin on fire before I'd even left the locker room. Now I felt like I was about to overheat.

I put my phone away, put on my helmet and revved the Harley's engine, taking off down the street to the gas station on the next block. At least there'd be air conditioning and I could talk to Pidge without dying of heat stroke and anger.

I parked and went inside, buying a liter of cold bottled water and then slipped into the men's restroom to call my wife. The soles of my trainers stuck to the floor as I checked the stalls. Empty. I dialed her number, staring at myself in the mirror while it rang.

She took so long to answer I was expecting voicemail to pick up, but soon her soft, comforting voice was on the other end of the line. "Hi, baby."

"Hey," I said, exhaling. All of my muscles relaxed, and for the first time I could feel the relief of the air conditioning.

"Uh oh. What's wrong? Trent okay?"

"Trent's fine. Brandon just popped off and I'm trying not to kill him. He asked us to dinner and then said he liked college girls."

She thought for a second. "Well, we can make endless excuses for why we can't go."

"I might've let it slip that I work late every night this week. I wouldn't put it past him to stop by."

"I won't answer the door."

I smiled, looking down. "That's my girl. You always have a solution."

"He's a dick, but you don't have to worry about him, Travis. There is not one reason why I would ever be alone with him. He's not that stupid, anyway."

"I don't know. He said something else."

"Like what?"

"He was asking about the fire. He said he was playing poker with Parker, who mentioned the fire."

"And?"

"He said Parker was hoping I'd get ratted out because he's too big of a pussy to do it himself."

Abby grew quiet.

"They've already written that piece to clear you, complete with quotes from people saying you weren't there."

"You never said how that all went down," I said.

She was quiet again.

I closed my eyes tight, leaning my back against the wall. "Please tell me it has nothing to do with Parker."

"What? No! Hell no, Travis."

"So how did you get them to do all that with just owing you money?"

"Well …"

"What did you do, Pidge?"

"There was a guy there. Collin … something."

"Vanderberg. Parker's dad is basically the Wish version of Collin's dad. He runs a lot of shit in this state."

"Well, he recognized me, and knew who my dad

was. He's actually not bad at poker," she said, lost in thought.

I frowned.

"So," she continued, "I might've explained to Ricky and Justin who my dad was. You know, who he associates with. They owed me a *lot* of money, Trav. They know who I was raised around. Collin actually planted the seed. Which was kind of accidental genius on his part, but that's beside the point. They're too scared to say anything again."

"Abby," I sighed. "You can't keep sticking your neck out for me. You have to stop. You're getting in too deep, and if you're caught, you'll get arrested, too. If I go down for this, I can handle it. If you're arrested, Pigeon … I'll never forgive myself. You have to stay out of it."

"Travis …"

"No, damn it! I know you're scared, but you're done."

"I've already lied to the police and the Feds. If you go down, we *both* go. I'm not going to let it happen."

I scrunched my face. I felt helpless. I couldn't fix it. I just had to wait for us to get away with it … or not.

"We have to be careful, Travis. Whatever it is, he's one step ahead. I … I need to tell you something. And please know that I didn't tell you right away because I didn't want you to hate your job more than you already do."

The hairs on the back of my neck stood on end. "What the fuck did he do?"

"Remember when I ran into him in the parking

lot after my lunch with Cami? He was acting really weird."

"Weird how? Nervous or flirting?"

She hesitated. "He doesn't strike me as a man who gets nervous."

"So, he was flirting." I felt murderous. "You think he's trying to get me out of the way?"

"Surely not," she said with a sigh. "That's insane. Even for him. I made it very clear, as politely as I could, that he repulsed me."

"Did he touch you?"

"Babe …"

I closed my eyes. "Did he touch you?" I said, my voice firmer than I'd intended.

She paused before answering again. "He kissed my hand. I pulled it away. Travis, listen to me. Breathe. Do not go back there and confront him about it. It's probably what he wants. Travis?"

Every muscle in my body twitched uncontrollably. Rage welled up within me with such force, the only thing keeping me from sprinting out to my motorcycle and running it straight through Iron E's glass wall, and straight at him, was the sound of my wife's voice.

"You go after him and he'll press charges. You can't keep him away from me if you're in jail. Please? Travis? Answer me, damn it!"

I took a deep breath. "I'm coming home to you as soon as I'm done."

She exhaled. The next words she spoke sounded a hundred miles away. "You promise?"

"I promise, Pigeon."

"I need you home tonight. Do not break your promise to me, Travis Carter. I don't care what he says to goad you, you come home to me."

"I'll keep my promise. I love you. I'll be home around nine."

"It's going to be okay, I promise. We'll figure it out, and it's going to be okay."

I took a deep breath and nodded. "It will be."

"Trav," she warned.

"He'll get his. But not tonight."

"That's good enough for me. I love you," she said, emphasizing the last three words before ending the call.

I chugged the rest of my water, took a piss, and then stared at myself in the mirror while I washed my hands. I towel dried them, then checked my watch. I had a client in five minutes. I rushed out to my bike and headed back to the gym, but something caught my eye.

Brandon's truck was parked at the Pizza Shack near the back, and he was standing next to it with his arms crossed over his chest, in deep conversation with two men in dark suits. The same two men we'd seen at Biasetti's.

I raced to the gym and parked, shutting down the engine. *Why the fuck is Brandon talking to the Feds?* Especially after he'd asked me about the fire. He wasn't there, he didn't need immunity, so what did he have to gain? Was this how he planned to get rid of me to take a fair shot at my wife? Was he really that desperate?

My mind raced until I saw my next client get out of her car and walk to toward the Iron E.

"Hey, Travis!" Debbie said with a wide smile. "You ready?"

I mirrored her expression, but the last thing in the fucking world I wanted to do right then was smile. I was going to have fake it, maybe for a long time.

"Yep! It's leg day," I said. "Let's get in there and rock it out."

She gave me a high five, and we walked in together.

CHAPTER Twenty-Three

THAT SIDE OF LOVE

Abby

MY THUMBNAIL BENT AS I pressed it against my teeth, but I was careful not to bite it or break it with our first anniversary—and wedding—being a week away. We'd been lucky, celebrating our firsts as a married couple almost normally. My birthday was a stark contrast to the year before, intimate and relatively tame with just Kara, Finch, Shepley and America, Trenton and Camille in attendance. Our first Thanksgiving at Jim's was far better than the year before. It wasn't lost on us that the year before had been brutal, and we spent the day making everyone around us groan with disgust at our constant PDA. Christmas and New Year's came and went, and then America went into full wedding planner mode, finalizing all the details for St. Thomas.

The year had past almost as if federal agents weren't

still forcing us to having important conversations outside of our apartment. Travis and I went to class, went to work, paid our bills, and went on date nights like normal married couples, but there were still more than a few things we had to adjust to that I was sure no other newlyweds had to face, like carefully planning with Finch how to get Adam and Travis in a room alone together without anyone finding out.

Three times we'd thought we had our chance, but twice Adam chickened out, and a third time Travis came down with the flu. This time, though, was a now or never situation. Adam had a hearing coming up, and both sides were pressuring him for a plea bargain.

After almost a year of planning and stressing, Adam and Travis were finally meeting in the shed behind The Red Door, long after last call so they didn't chance being seen. I'd had a good feeling when he left that it was the right time and everything would go smoothly, but he'd been gone for hours.

Pacing the living room floor hadn't helped, so I resorted to sitting in the recliner and rocking back and forth only pretending to chew my nails.

The sun would be rising in less than two hours. In my mind, there were only two reasons why it was taking so long: they had a lot of information to go over, or they'd been caught and arrested.

Right when I thought I might go out of my mind, a key entered the lock and the door opened. My husband had just stepped into the entry and closed the door behind him, bracing himself as I threw my arms around his shoulders.

He held me at arm's length and held his index finger to his lips.

I nodded, and he led me outside by the hand, down the narrow walkway that ended at the complex's small playground.

Travis sat on a swing, and I joined him on the adjacent one. He rocked back and forth, keeping his feet on the ground.

"Tell me he didn't take a plea bargain and confirm you were there," I said, keeping my voice just above a whisper.

Travis shook his head. "He hasn't implicated me, but I found out why Brandon was talking to the Feds. He doesn't want to get me out of the way to get a chance at you—well, that may be part of it—but it goes deeper than that. I knew Adam made good money off those fights, but he was driving a Lambo for fuck's sake. He couldn't have made that much more than me. Now, it makes sense."

"What did he tell you?"

"Adam had a business partner."

I wrinkled my nose. "Since when?"

"Almost since the beginning. A guy who used to fight in The Circle back when my brothers did. When he graduated college and retired from the ring, he made a proposal to Adam so he could keep making money off the fights. But they weren't just taking bets in the basements. Adam set cameras up before every fight. They were streaming and taking bets from all over the world. Adam was clearing a million a year."

"What?" I said, louder than intended.

"He didn't tell me, so it didn't make a dent in his cut—he was already halving it with his partner."

My mouth fell open. "Brandon?"

Travis nodded.

"So … so, what? Brandon is in trouble, too, and he's wanting to take you down with him?"

Travis laughed once without humor. "He went to *them*. He thought it was only a matter of time before he got caught, so he went on the offense and told the Feds he could help them in return for immunity."

"And they agreed? Why would they do that if they could get you and him both?"

"Because they don't know about him yet. He hasn't told them about his involvement and won't until he can get what they need to take me down. Then he can get his immunity. If they go after both of us without proof, they could lose both cases. Or, they get proof from Brandon and have a solid case against me.

"The good news is, they haven't been able to find anything that'll stick. They know the wedding took place after the fire but we went so soon after, the investigation is reliant upon if they can place us at the airport or anywhere else prior to the flight. If we weren't on camera anywhere except for the airport—and they can't place us anywhere else—we can say we were anywhere we want prior to the airport. As long as there's no footage to say otherwise. Their case against me would be circumstantial. But with Brandon testifying against me, or if he could get a confession …"

I gripped the chains that held up my swing, feeling the metal dig into my skin. "We're going to nail him to the wall, Travis. I don't know how, but we're going to turn this around on him, and he's going to prison for a very long time."

Travis looked up at the stars. "I don't know how we're going to do that, either. Maybe it's time we called it."

"Called what?"

He turned to me with tears in his eyes. "This is bad. This is way bigger than we realized. Benny's wanting to get involved. You've already lied to the Feds and blackmailed reporters. It's bad enough that I'm going to be away from you for however many years, but I couldn't live with myself if you went, too. I'll go fucking crazy worrying about you in there, if you're being hurt, if you're sick, if you're sad … if you regret the day we crossed paths ..."

"Travis," I said, standing. I grabbed hold of the chains of his swing and slipped a leg on each side of his hips, straddling him. I wrapped my arms around his neck and kissed him. His lips were different, distant, stiff. I cupped his face. "We're going to be okay; do you hear me? I'll figure it out. I always do."

Travis shook his head, his gaze meeting mine. He looked heartbroken. "Not this time, Pidge."

I leaned back to get a better read on his expression. "What's going on in that head of yours?"

He stood up, bringing me with him and then setting me on my feet as if I weighed nothing. "You're moving out."

I laughed. "Shut up." He didn't smile. "Okay, where are we going? Mexico?"

"You're moving back to Mark and Pam's, and then you'll be back at the dorms for fall semester."

"Trav … what the fuck, our wedding is in a week!"

"Ssshhh," he said, holding out his hands to me and looking around. "You think I want to do this? This is the last resort. It's the only way I can protect you."

"So, you're saying you want a divorce?"

He winced and looked to the ground. He tried to speak, but the words caught in his throat for a moment before he cleared it. "We can get an annulment. Easily done for a Vegas wedding."

"No," I shook my head. "*No*, I won't agree to it."

Travis reached for me, and I became small in his arms, ducking my head and pressing my cheek against his shirt. My hands were together at my chest, my fingers intertwined.

"I love you more than anything, Pidge. More than my own life. When I go to prison, I'm going to lose you, anyway, so I need to do this. I have to save you."

"You don't mean it. Take it back."

"This is going to happen, and when it does, I don't want you anywhere near me. We'll say I came to you after the fight and asked you to marry me. We flew to Vegas and you had no idea. I lied to you about it all. I used you for an alibi."

"I've already told them I asked you to marry me, Travis!"

"Then I'll think of something else."

The finality in his tone gutted me. My bottom lip quivered. "Please don't."

He squeezed me to him. "You will always be

my wife. I will never love anyone but you. And who knows, by the time I get out"—he paused to clear his throat—"if you're not with anyone, and you don't still hate me for this"—his voice cracked—"maybe we can try again."

"You won't lose me. I'm not going anywhere." I looked up at him. "You're my husband. 'Til death do us part, remember? For better, for worse?"

"You think I wanna do this? I don't! It's fucking killing me to say or do anything to cause that hurt look on your face. I fucking *hate* this! But if I don't? You'll go to prison, too, and I can't live with that. I can't."

"And what if I go, anyway? What then?"

He ran his hand over his buzzed hair. "You won't. I lied to you. You told the Feds what you thought you knew. No one will know any different."

"The reporters will!"

"They're too scared to talk. Nothing changes who you are or who you know. I'll make sure they're reminded."

He let me go only to interweave his fingers with mine. "C'mon. We need to get you packed."

I slapped his hand away. "No! We're going to cancel our wedding and get an annulment instead? And you expect me to keep going to school here—everyone talking about how you went to prison but divorced me, first? You expect me to stick around when every fucking thing will remind me of you? *No!*"

"Pigeon …"

I held my middle, my eyes burning, my throat feeling tight. I was in a full-blown panic. All this time, and through everything, Travis had only fought for me. He'd never once walked away, until now.

"I've never loved anything as much as I love being your wife. You can't take that away from me, Travis Maddox. You can't make me fall in love with you, make me feel happier than I have in my *whole* life, and then take it away. Even if I have to spend some time behind bars, it won't be that long, and I know one of these days you'll be out, and we can pick up where we left off. But at least," my face crumbled, "I still get to be your wife."

A single tear welled up in his eyes and spilled over onto his cheek, quickly falling to his jawline and then staining his shirt. He reached out with one hand, touching his palm to my cheek. "I won't be able to bear the thought of you in there. The only way I can get through this is if I know you're free and happy."

I shook my head. "I won't be happy."

"But you'll be safe."

I couldn't hold in the tears any longer. I wept, my chest caving in with each sob, leaning my face against his hand. I was sure there were words I should be saying, but they were lost somewhere deep beneath the pain and betrayal I felt. I wiped my cheeks and then looked down, seeing the key fob sticking out of Travis's jeans pocket.

"You've made me promise over and over that I won't leave, just to kick me out and divorce me?"

"Don't say it like that."

"That's exactly what this is." Before Travis could react, I snatched the keys. "Pack it your fucking self."

"Pidge!" he called after me.

I made a beeline for the car, jogging the last ten steps or so, and locking the door as soon as I slid behind the wheel. I turned the key just as Travis arrived at my window.

He tapped on the glass with his palm in a panic. "You're upset, I don't want you driving."

I backed away from the curb, but Travis stayed at my door, banging on the glass.

"Pigeon, my bike keys are on that keychain. I can't … Pidge! God dammit!" He yelled as I pulled away.

From the rearview mirror, I could see him standing under the parking lot lights, his hands on his head.

I drove around for an hour, wiping my eyes so often the tender skin beneath them began to feel raw. America was out of town, so there was only one other person I could go to.

The blinker was the only sound in the car as I took the next exit and turned around, going back the way I came. Finch's apartment was halfway between where I was and home. I could be there in ten or fifteen minutes. I pressed the button on the steering wheel and then directed my phone to call Finch.

His phone rang over my speakers, and just when I thought he might not pick up, he answered. "Hey, betch."

"Are you home?" I said, sniffing.

"Oh, my *Gawd*! Yes! Yes, get your ass over here!"

He hung up on me, and I couldn't help but smile. He didn't even ask me what was wrong or where I was. He knew what I needed without knowing what I needed, like every best friend should.

I pulled into his apartment complex and parked.

Before I could get out, Finch stepped out onto his stoop, wearing only boxer briefs and an open robe. A cigarette hung from his lips as he waited for me, arms wide open. No matter how quickly my world was ending, it was difficult not to smile at the sight of him.

"Baby!" he said, hugging me as I reached the top of the stairs. He leaned back, taking a drag from his cigarette and then blowing the smoke to the side of me. His bottom lip jutted out. "Do not tell me what I think you're going to tell me."

Just then, a tall, tank of a man with shoulder-length hair arrived in the doorway.

"Oh! This is Felix. Felix, say hi."

Felix held out his large hand to shake mine.

"Nice to meet you," I said.

Felix's eyes were full of empathy. "I'm so sorry you're sad, Abby." He kissed Finch's cheek goodbye and then waved to me.

"Th-thank you," I said, watching him walk down the stairs to the parking lot. I looked to my friend, who was watching him, too, but with a smile. "Finch and Felix?" I asked.

Finch's smile disappeared, "Oh, shut the hell up and come cry on my couch. It's too late for Mimosas so I'm making pom-tinis."

I followed him in, closing the door behind me. Travis and I had helped him move in one Saturday, but I hadn't seen it since he put it all together. And it was … very Finch.

Clean and minimalist but with a touch of modern. Books stacked in single file up the wall next to the hallway door, plants in every space, large, cushy throw pillows on the couch begging me to cuddle them.

So, I did.

Finch busied himself in the kitchen, talking to me over the bar.

"So, fight with Travis. He had the … you know, the thing tonight. Was it about that?"

"Yes." I sniffed. "He wants a divorce."

"Ah, he's trying to spare you."

"I guess," I said, wiping my nose with my sleeve.

"Dear God, there are tissues right there, Abby. You're not a toddler, use them."

I leaned over to his white side table and pulled a few tissues from the box. "Felix seems nice."

"He *is* nice. The nicest man I've ever dated. He never gets jealous, or mad. Ever. He just … communicates. It's bizarre! I need a little drama. I mean, c'mon, it's me."

"Maybe you're just comfortable in the chaos. Maybe you need to realize that peace isn't boring. What I wouldn't give for a little peace." I dabbed my eyes.

Finch brought our drinks in martini glasses and placed them on the coffee table—atop coasters, of course—before sitting next to me. He stared at me for a minute and then gestured to the drinks. "Well? They're not going to drink themselves."

"Oh," I said, taking a sip, then a bigger one. "Oh. That's good. That's really good." I sat back and took a deep breath.

"Honey, Travis doesn't want a divorce. He's a wolf in a trap right now. He's lashing out."

I shook my head. "No, it wasn't like that. He was devastated. He was apologizing and crying and said that maybe one of these days, when he comes back and I don't hate him, we can try again."

Finch rested his elbow on the back of the couch, his jaw on his palm, narrowed his eyes and pursed his lips, deep in thought. "Travis Maddox was … crying? Okay, he thinks he's doing this for your own good, but he still doesn't want to."

"That isn't going to stop him, though. I begged him, assured him it was going to be okay, that we'd figure it out like we always do. Nothing worked. He's set on it." I felt my eyes burn with tears again.

"He's not set on it, sister. He loves you. Your wedding is next week, for fuck's sake. Which, by the way, thanks for scheduling it on my dad's 60th birthday. Brilliant."

"It's my anniversary."

"No excuse!" he said, pointing in the air.

"Was my anniversary," I said with a sigh.

Finch brought his hand back down, tapping his lip with his index finger. "You've never been broken up with before, have you?"

I sighed in frustration. "No, but this isn't a break-up, Finch, this is divorce. My husband is divorcing me. I have to figure out a way to fix this. You have to help me! How do I fix this?"

"You can't."

I blinked, not expecting his answer. "What?"

He placed his hand on top of mine. "You can't, honey."

"Really? That's what you're going to say to me right now?" I asked, heartbroken.

"You haven't known that side of love." He stared off across the room, but he wasn't looking at the books or walls or credenza. Finch was years away. "You give your heart to someone, hoping to Christ they take care of it, but you have no control. It doesn't matter how much you love them, how much reassurance you give them, or how many promises they make you. Six months from now or an hour from now, they can leave. They can betray you, stomp all over that fragile thing you handed over to them, as many times as you let them, and convince you to forgive them just to hurt you again. They can look you straight in the eyes and tell you they love you, knowing damn well what they're doing when you're not around is anything but love.

"Or, like Travis, they can walk away because they think it's best, and there's not a thing you can do about it … except cry. You just cry until it doesn't hurt anymore. That's love. You give your heart away over and over to be bruised and shattered until one day you find someone who finally—*finally*—protects it." He blinked and wiped a single tear from his cheek and then smiled. "Whew! Took me back!"

"I don't want to cry," I said, my bottom lip quivering.

Finch shrugged, empathy in his eyes. "No one does, baby."

I broke down again. "Travis said he'd always protect me."

Finch combed a few fallen strands of hair from my face. "Maybe that's exactly what he's doing."

I sobbed, and then wailed, and never once did Finch shush me. I cried until I was exhausted, and then I lay in his lap while he ran his fingers through my hair and gently rocked his body from side to side.

And still, as I felt myself give way to the exhaustion, I knew this was just the first of twenty-thousand four-hundred and forty days I would cry for him, because there would never come a day when losing him didn't hurt.

CHAPTER Twenty-Four

SAVIOR

Travis

I PACED THE FLOOR FOR an hour, checking my phone a hundred times, even though I knew it hadn't rung because I'd been holding it.

Letting Abby go was the right thing to do but causing the kind of pain I saw in her eyes felt anything but right. She'd been mad at me before, but when she looked at me through the Camry's window, it very closely resembled hate, and even though I'd prepared myself for it, Abby hating me forever terrified me.

Abby thought I'd been talking to Adam the whole time I was gone, but he'd been nervous so he said what he needed to say in thirty minutes and bounced. After that, I'd parked down the street from the apartment and sat there for hours, knowing I had a choice to make.

I thought about what prison would be like for her, that maybe she would end up hating me anyway and it would all be for nothing. Then I thought about letting her go, keeping her safe while I rotted in prison for a decade, hearing that she'd gotten married, had children, all but forgotten about us except for that one corner of her heart that couldn't forgive me.

Just the thought of Abby falling in love with someone else after I was carted off to prison made me feel insane with rage, and it took everything I had not to down the pint of whiskey in the cupboard and go pick a fight. In the state I was in, I'd most definitely kill someone. There was no one I could talk to because I couldn't tell anyone why I'd asked for a divorce.

Except for one person.

I said goodbye to Toto, grabbed my wallet and a jacket to stave off the rain, then locked the door behind me, hoping I'd either find Abby or she'd come home before me so I didn't have to call maintenance to let me back in.

Walking the eleven or so miles to Finch's apartment was going to take a few hours, so I zipped up my jacket and set out at a quick pace. Every mile or so I'd jogged to make up for lost time waiting at stop lights or dodging puddles and trucks splashing the sidewalk.

Two and a half hours in, I stopped at an all-night gas station for a bottle of water, chugged it, tossed it in the trash, then started again.

My conversation with Abby played over and over in my head as I walked. What I could've said different, better, but no matter how I changed it up, I knew it wouldn't hurt her any less. I did what I promised I'd never do. Even if, one day, she understood, she'd never forgive me.

Still, it was better than knowing she was locked up somewhere during the best years of life, dealing with God-knows-what. Prison would change her, that light in her eyes would extinguish just like it did when she sat at a poker table in Vegas.

She'd get stuck in survival mode, and no one would ever get to see the side of her that hopes, that lets her poker face slip, that laughs a little too hard and smiles in her sleep. Abby deserved to keep the part of her that Vegas couldn't touch, and the world deserved to experience it.

I sighed when I saw Finch's apartment complex, but when I saw the Camry, I broke out into a sprint before I knew what I was doing. My eyes saw that all the lights were out, my brain knew it was nearly dawn, but my fist pounded on the door anyway.

As soon as the deep booms echoed against the adjacent buildings, I regretted it. The noise was alarmingly loud when everything else was quiet. Even the birds. Not even a fucking dog barked.

The memory of me banging on Abby's dorm room door came flooding back and my eyes threatened to tear up for the tenth time that night. If I could make one wish, it would be to go back in time and not go to that fight. I might not have been married to Abby so soon, but at least I'd get to keep her.

To my surprise, it wasn't Finch who opened the door, but my wife. Her eyes were swollen, mascara smeared, her hair ratted, and her clothes wrinkled. I'd never seen her look more beautiful in my life.

I wanted so badly to hold her, so I reached out, but paused, realizing she may not want me to touch her.

She looked down at my hands. "You're soaked. You walked all the way here?"

I nodded.

"You didn't know I was here … so you came to talk to Finch? Because he's the only one you could talk to."

"Abby …"

"It's Abby now?" She nodded, indignant.

I winced. "I didn't think it was fair to … I'm just trying to make this easier on you."

"Well, you're not. You can't do this to me, Travis. You can't pursue me and make promises … make me fall in love with you just to leave me."

"Please don't hate me."

She stepped outside and closed the door behind her. "Hate you? I love you more than I've loved anyone in my life. *Ever.* I don't know that I've loved anyone except you, and I truly believe I'll never feel this way again with someone else. I don't want to. And after everything—the risks, the unknowns, the what ifs—I'm staying. I'm *staying*, Travis. *You're* leaving *me*. If you do this, I'll never give you the chance to hurt me like this again, do you understand that?"

"I …"

"I don't think you do. You can't. Because this isn't a college break up. We made vows to each other. This is a whole marriage you're ending."

"Because …"

"There is no because. There is no reason that's stronger than the promises we made."

"You'll be okay. I have to believe that. You'll be okay, out here."

"You don't get it. This feels like death. It will change me. I won't be the same person after this, and I'll blame you for it. Maybe I will hate you then, because it won't change me for the better. If you let me go now, you'll have to let me go forever because the woman you love won't exist anymore. I won't be her. She'll be gone."

It took me a long time to speak, and even then, I could barely get the words out above a whisper. "You don't know how sorry I am. I wish … I wish we could go back in time and somehow, some way not go to that fight. That's the only thing that could fix this."

"But we *can't*."

"I've tried to think of something, anything else, I swear to God. I hate myself for hurting you."

"Don't make me beg."

It was what she said the first time we made love, and we were both acutely aware of the reference. Now, she was saying it for a completely different reason. I'd once said I'd rather cut off my own arm than hurt her. I felt like a piece of shit, a liar, a coward … she was stronger than me. She was proving it. "Pidge …"

She fell against me, wrapped her arms around my middle, and squeezed. "Because I will," she cried. "I'll beg you every day."

On my long, wet walk, I'd imagined multiple scenarios for how Abby would react the next time I saw her. What was happening in that moment didn't even make the top one hundred.

I held her while she cried, trying not to break down myself. I owed it to her to be strong and not force her to console me after what I'd done. And still, I didn't know how else to protect her.

She said something, but it was too muffled for me to hear.

"What, Pidge?" I asked.

She looked up at me, the skin around her eyes red and wet. "I don't want to cry the rest of my life."

She looked like a little girl, innocent and lost. I couldn't maintain a strong front after that, instead cupping her face with my hands and kissing her over and over. The wetness on her cheeks smeared against mine. I wanted to keep kissing her until the pain went away, but I knew that was impossible.

I touched my forehead to hers. "I don't want you to, either. I want you to be happy, and free to live your life. I want you to be safe."

"Then fight with me. See this through."

"I can't live with myself knowing I let you go to prison, Pigeon. I don't want to do this, but letting you get sent to prison is so much worse."

"We'll do it together."

"It's too hard."

"So is this!" she screamed. "Being apart is hard! Not being in control is hard! Worrying about someone is hard! Watching someone you love move on with someone new is hard! Having to explain to everyone why we've made the mistakes and choices we have is hard! Facing your fears is *hard*! Choose your fucking hard!"

She wept, her body shaking with each of her next words. "And you better choose me, Travis Carter. You better fucking choose me."

Watching my wife fall apart in front of me, made any attempt at strength impossible. She was right. If the worst came, we could at least face it together.

I sucked in a breath. "Okay." It was all I could manage.

"Okay?" she asked, obviously hesitant to trust me. That broke my heart all over again.

I nodded, and relief washed over her face. She nodded, too, her face crumbling. I pulled her against my chest, wrapping her in my arms, and she held me tight, whispering, "Don't ever leave me again."

"Do you want me to leave?" Abby asked.

I was sitting on the private beach of our hotel, staring out into the water of St. Thomas. I'd just renewed my vows to my wife and been handed the bomb of the century.

"Never," I said, reaching out for her.

She sat next to me and held my hand, thankfully content to just sit in silence.

Shepley had been out there with me. Other than him, no one else had a clue that my world was crumbling. I hadn't been able to speak. Too much in my own head about the future to even pretend things were normal. When Abby joined us on the beach, he stayed close.

I closed my eyes. Shepley knew something was bothering me, but he probably thought we were fighting and was sticking around to keep the peace and mediate like he always did. It killed me to keep this from him almost as much as it did to lie to Abby. They were my best friends, and I couldn't tell them. I couldn't tell anyone.

I looked down the beach to where my brothers began filtering from the hotel, either from their rooms or from brunch.

Tyler waved, and then tossed a football to Ellie.

What a fucking mess. Even if I could tell Abby the truth, it was too crazy to believe. What? I was going to casually explain to her what Thomas and his partner-slash-girlfriend, Liis, had just dropped on me—that my older brother, who we all thought was a fucking ad exec, was actually an FBI agent? And not just any agent. *Oh no*, he was the one in charge of my case.

That sounded made up as hell. Maybe it was a good thing that part of their terms for immunity was to keep it a secret from my wife that I was now a federal snitch.

She'd lock me in a padded room.

I held Abby's hand to my mouth and kissed it.

She smiled at me. "We're okay, right?"

"Better than okay."

"You're not thinking about divorcing me again, are you?"

"It'll never happen again. No matter what. I panicked."

Even worse, I thought. If Abby hadn't spoken

sense into me, Thomas and Liis would be having this conversation with me back home. Abby would have moved out of the apartment and been in Wichita. We'd have started the annulment, and I'd have realized, after speaking with Thomas, that it'd been all for nothing.

My immunity extended to Abby, but if she hadn't helped me get my head out of my ass, she'd have been long gone and it would've been too late to get her back.

Out of everything, that bothered me the most.

"I know you did, but everything is okay now," she said, resting her head on my shoulder. "Just checking because you're not yourself. Wanna talk about it?"

I tried not to tense up, to keep my shoulders relaxed, because this was the first of many lies I would have to tell my wife.

"I've just been thinking about our future. About how bad I hurt you just a few days ago and how ashamed I am, because I know … I know everything's going to be okay. We're going to nail Brandon to the wall like you said, and we're both going to move on with our lives, together. I can't shake the horrible feeling it gives me to know I almost ruined it."

She pressed her lips to my skin. "I wasn't going to let you."

"Thank God."

"That wedding, though …" she said, her cheek against my shoulder.

"It was perfect. I'm glad we let America go a little crazy. It's the way it should've been."

"I wouldn't change any of it."

"Nothing?"

"Nope," she said, looking up at me. "We couldn't stop the fire, but here we are, a year later, more in love than ever … and, in paradise."

"That wedding night, though," I said with a grin.

"Think we can try that again?"

"What are you doing right now?"

Abby looked down the beach at our family, who were all in the middle of a friendly game of football. "Is it rude to leave them out here and not hang out?"

I frowned. "This is our honeymoon. They'll understand."

"Good point." She stood, holding out her hands for me to take. "Then what I'm doing right now is you."

I took her hands, stood, and looked up at the sky. "I love my wife!"

She led me by the hand back to our room, and I reminded her over and over—for hours—how much I loved her. That I meant to keep the promises I'd made, and that I'd never make her regret saving me. Not just the first time when we met, or the second time after the fire, but from myself when I almost made the worst mistake of my life by letting her go.

CHAPTER Twenty-Five

THE LAST BASTION

Abby

LIKE THE YEAR BEFORE, SHEPLEY was road tripping it to Wichita. But unlike last time, he was making the trip alone—in severe weather, no less—to spend the weekend with America and her parents the last precious days of spring break. We'd all just gotten back from St. Thomas, but America wanted to make the trip back with Shepley, and he was determined to see his girlfriend smile.

America grew up in Tornado Alley, so she wasn't nearly as nervous about gnarly clouds and thunder as I was. She knew what to do and would've passed on that knowledge to her boyfriend, so if something did happen, of all people, I should be the least worried about Shep. But still … there I sat, glued to my weather app.

Instead of calling Travis, I called America … again.

"Have you heard from him?"

America laughed. "It's light rain, Abby. The last time we talked, his windshield wipers were on low and they were squeaking over the glass. It's nothing. I promise, we're keeping an eye on it."

"But Mare … it's calling for hail."

"I think you have some PTSD from that tornado our senior year. It didn't even come close," she said, sounding distracted.

"But we … we saw it. It was huge." My mind traveled back to that day. It was nightmare fuel, standing on Mark and Pam's porch, watching a monster fall out of the sky. The funnel wasn't black like you see in the movies, it was white against the dark blue sky, moving slowly across the horizon, devouring everything in its path. That tornado was the most frightening thing I'd ever seen—until the fire in the basement of Keaton Hall. "There's a tornado watch in the exact area he's traveling, and it doesn't end until after he gets there."

"The tornado you saw didn't do much damage, though. It was outside of town, hit a few old barns. No fatalities. Plenty of warning. Listen to me. I promise. I promise he's paying attention. My parents are, too. No wall clouds, no bubble clouds, we're fine."

I smiled. "Doesn't your dad call those clouds cow balls?"

"Technically they'd be bull's balls, but I'm not going to correct my dad."

I laughed. "Yeah, don't do that. He's the guy who sits outside on a lawn chair and drinks beer to watch the weather come in."

"He does not!" America said. She tried to sound offended, but she was still laughing. "You're freaking out more than his own mother. Take a shot and lie down."

She was in a good mood, happy to see Shepley in a few hours.

Her parents were so worried a serious boyfriend would distract her, and, while they weren't wrong, Shepley was good for America. He kept her grounded, he truly cared about her and treated her like a queen. If Mark and Pam got even a glimpse of that, they'd probably ease off their daughter about her relationship, especially after Travis and I eloped. They were on high alert and driving her insane about how much time she was spending with Shepley. They almost didn't let him come, but it saved them the trip of taking her back to Eakins.

"I'm not doing this next summer," America said, determined. "We're making this trip together to visit my parents instead of visiting each other. Mark better mark my words."

"Okay, keep me updated and be safe," I said.

She hung up, and I sat on the sofa, petting Toto. He was sleeping in my lap, his rib cage moving up and down in a relaxing rhythm. I'd won the battle with the small-time journalists and then Travis, but something else was bothering me—even worse—I didn't know what it was. The not knowing was consuming my days, and I was finding other tangible things to worry about, like Shepley driving into a storm.

My fingers froze mid-stroke across Toto's wiry hair when a soft knock tapped on the door. I set him to the side, waking him. He walked with me, waiting at my feet while I looked out the peephole.

"Shit," I whispered.

Brandon knocked again. "Abby? Can we talk for a sec? It's important. It's about Travis."

"He's not home, Brandon. Call him."

He smiled and looked down. "I know he's not home. That's why I came by. I'm worried about him."

My heart began to race. I was almost certain he was there to get information, and I promised my husband I wouldn't let Brandon inside the apartment while alone. But if I didn't talk to him, would it make him do something worse?

I opened the door and stepped outside, closing it behind me.

Brandon looked absurd. His hair was gelled four inches off his head, and he was wearing a royal blue quilted blazer, a cheap-looking turquoise V-neck T-shirt, tight jeans that were rolled up at the bottom, no socks, and the best part: matching royal blue quilted loafers.

"Dear God," I said, taking a half-step back.

He tried his sexiest grin, and I tried not to throw up in my mouth. He obviously thought he looked irresistible.

"Hey."

I recoiled, but hearing Toto pawing at the door snapped me out of the nightmare I felt stuck in. "Fine. Let's get this over with. Worried about what, Brandon?"

He was trying to hide the triumph he felt and that made me want to punch him.

"He's been acting weird. I think he feels guilty about the fire."

He is wearing a fucking wire.

"Well," I began. "Sure, we all feel awful about it. We knew a lot of people who died in that basement."

"I'm worried he's going to do something stupid and get caught."

"Get caught? What do you mean?"

"Lying to the Feds. Lying to the cops. Everyone knows he was there, Abby. Your flight didn't leave until after the firetrucks got there."

I shook my head. "We didn't know about it until we got to the airport and saw the reports on the televisions. Are you insinuating he was there? Because he wasn't."

"Yes, he was, Abby. You both were. I get it, wanting to protect him. But everyone knows, the Feds know, and you shouldn't go down with him. Not when he's at the gym doing what he's doing."

I laughed once. "Here we go …"

Brandon sighed. "I wasn't going to say anything, but I can't watch you go down for this because you're trying to be loyal to him when he's … he's not loyal to you, Abby. Travis and Tiffany have been seeing each other on the side. He's with her at the gym right now. He's not working late. They were in my office talking and flirting when I left. She had her hands all over him. I'm going to talk to her. I'll make her tell you the truth. She will. She's a good girl, he's just … persuasive."

"Are you jealous?" I asked.

"Huh?"

I crossed my arms. "You're telling me Tiffany, the employee you're having an affair with, is also sleeping with my husband, and you walked away calmly to tell me?"

He seemed genuinely confused. "I don't know what you're talking about. Tiffany is my receptionist. We've always been pretty close but it's been going on with them pretty much since he started. You think I would've just watched that happen in my gym if I was having an affair with her? Listen… I know this is hard to hear. My ex-wife cheated on me and it sucks."

"That's not the way it happened according to the entire population of Eakins."

"People say a lot of things. Funny how no one asks me. All I'm saying is, I understand. I'm here for you if you need to talk to someone who's been there. I don't want you sitting here alone. Let's go someplace, have a drink, and I'll tell you everything I know."

I pulled my phone from my back pocket. "Watch how easy this is, Brandon. If Becca needs tips, have her call me."

"What are you doing?"

I held up my phone as it rang. "FaceTiming my husband."

Travis picked up on the first ring, smiling. "Hey, Pidge. Everything okay?"

"You still training?" I asked, noticing the background. He was in the main part of the gym. It was nearly empty.

He panned the camera over to his client. "Susan, say hi to my wife."

"Hi, Abby!" Susan said, waving. She was sweaty but smiling.

"Is Tiffany still there?" I asked.

He glanced around. "No, I'm locking up tonight. Do you remember when Tiffany left, Susan?"

"It wasn't long after I got here," Susan said off-camera.

"Why? Did something happen?"

"No, I'll tell you when you get home. I love you."

"What are you doing outside?" he asked, wary.

I went inside and locked the door. "Just taking out the trash. See you soon, baby. Love you."

He smiled, but he was still confused—and suspicious. "Okay, Pidge. I'll be on my way soon."

We hung up, and Brandon knocked on the door again. "Abby? I know she's still there. Susan and Travis are pretty tight. I'm not surprised at all that she's covering for him. And you heard him, he knows something's up. He was being defensive, asking questions. He wanted to know if you knew anything. I know it's hard to hear and you don't want to believe it, but it's true."

"Yeah … you need to leave."

He knocked again. "Just let me prove it to you. I'm sure he's told you all this bullshit about me to discredit me in case I ever told you." He laughed. "It's obvious if you think about it. You're going to get in trouble and realize too late it was all for someone who never loved you."

I looked down at my dog. "Toto, go to your bed," I said, smiling as he hesitated for just a moment, and then left me for the small cushy pillow he slept on in our room. "Good boy," I said quietly.

"Abby? I'm not trying to make this weird, but I need you to listen. I can't let you do this."

I sighed, then opened the door. "Let's get something straight. You will never *let* me do anything. You just made an ass of yourself on my doorstep, and you follow up with you're not going to *let* me? Let me what? Question your lies? Believe my husband when I just saw the truth for myself? I realize, Brandon, that you're used to dealing with teenage girls who don't think twice about being told what to do or what to think, but even if my husband didn't dominate you in every aspect of life, and couldn't reduce you to a puddle of your own blood, I would still be standing here, telling you to get the fuck off my porch."

"Abby—"

"GET THE FUCK OFF MY PORCH!"

He turned around and descended a few steps, hesitated, then kept going. Once he was at his truck, he opened the door and shook his head. "When it all finally goes down, don't come crying to me. I tried."

I slammed the door, adrenaline pouring through my veins. The bolt lock slowly clicked under the direction of my shaking fingers, but that was all I could manage besides making my way to the couch and whistling for Toto. He jumped into my lap, and with each stroke of his hair, my heartbeat slowed.

If I told Travis what had just happened—after what Brandon had already pulled at the gym—Travis would definitely be arrested within hours for assault. Keeping it from him wasn't an easier option.

I swore at Brandon, under my breath, for forcing that choice on me, and at the same time I already knew my decision. I couldn't lie to Travis, and I'd have to trust him not to lose his shit. And, I'd have to trust myself to be able to talk him into staying home.

"Daddy is going to have to quit his job," I said, glad I'd been frugal with my winnings from the Sig Tau poker game.

Mid-stroke through Toto's hair, a gentle knock came from the other side of the door.

I let my head fall back. I wasn't opening the door again. "Go away!"

The next set of knocking was just as timid as the first, and much lower than it would be if it were Brandon. I stood, my mind weighing scenarios of who it could be. What if it was a kid or someone else from the apartment complex who needed help? I peered through the peep hole and closed my eyes tight, letting my forehead thump against the door.

"You have got to be fucking kidding me," I whispered.

"Abby? I'm sorry it's late. I got lost, and then I went to the wrong apartment a few times." She knocked again, this time less patient. "I know you're in there, I just saw you verbally rip the balls off that meat head."

My hands wouldn't work. I just stood there, staring at the door, expressionless. Usually, I could figure out a solution or plan an escape, but there was nothing. Just … silence. Between worrying about America, dealing with Brandon, and now this, my system had decided to all but shut down. It was just too much for one day.

"Abigail Hope Abernathy! Open this door!"

I scrambled to twist the bolt lock open, and yanked on the knob, staring at the small, tired, worn, twenty-six years older version of myself.

"Sorry, Mom." I gestured to the living room. "Come in."

She smiled for a half a second before her face fell. She had aged at an exponential rate since I'd seen her. The caramel strands of her hair were frizzed and mixed with wiry grays. The lines on each side of her mouth were deep, her cheeks sagging, skin creped and yellowing, just like her hollow eyes.

She brushed past me.

I stared out at the parking lot before slamming the door behind her, wishing I was still dealing with Brandon instead. Even Mick at the door would've been better than my mother sitting on my couch, sipping straight vodka through the straw she'd put inside the worn, plastic water bottle she was using to conceal it.

I pointed at her. "Don't throw up."

She chuckled and settled back against the cushions. "I'm at least five more of these away from that."

"I've heard that before," I said, sitting on the recliner.

My mom wasn't always a bad mother, but she was never a good one. The house was never quite clean, the breakfast not always on the table before school. She didn't always come home at night, and she wasn't always sober.

As unpredictable as she was when Mick was winning, it was no secret that Bonnie Abernathy was always one drink away from falling off the map if her husband's luck ran out.

When I turned thirteen, it did.

Mom didn't stick around long after the money disappeared. Any small slice of normalcy I'd had until that point was replaced by late nights in smoky hotel rooms and mobsters' basements watching my father sweat over his shitty poker hands and then talk his way out of being pummeled or worse when he couldn't come up with cash.

The Mafia who ran Vegas were a particularly brutal bunch, but most of them had a soft spot for kids. So, I was Mick's human shield.

He'd say he was all I had left. That he was just trying to make ends meet, to put dinner on the table. That Bonnie had left in the middle of the night without warning, and he had to try to figure out a way to keep our tiny family off the street.

Those convincing pleas worked for years, but he lost more than just money when, without warning, Mom picked me up for school one day and drove through the night until we reached her new home in Wichita, Kansas.

Mick had lost his last bastion.

"How did you find me?" I asked.

The recliner squeaked when I shifted against its cushions, but Mom didn't seem to hear it over her instant annoyance at my question.

"That's an odd thing to ask your mother, don't you think?"

"Not if she left without as much as a note a few months before my high school graduation."

"Yeah, well," she said, pulling a cigarette box from her purse and fumbling with the flip-top lid.

"You can't smoke in here."

"I can't?" she asked, pulling a cigarette from the box and lighting it. She didn't lose eye contact with me as she took a puff and blew it into the air.

My lips pressed together in a thin line. I stood up, opened the door and waved my hands through the cloud of smoke. "*Why* are you here? If you need money, you're out of luck. We're doing good just to pay our bills."

Her eyes lost focus as she stared forward and took another drag. "Oh. I haven't had luck shine on me in a long time, Abby."

She'd had that same defeated look on her face when she'd stand in the doorway of the kitchen, watching Mick teach me how to play poker.

I'd always wondered what thoughts were behind her hopeless eyes. If she blamed me, too, for Mick's winning streak going as dry as the desert that surrounded our trailer home.

"So," she said, cupping her palm and ashing into it. "I hear you're a married woman, now."

"Better be careful, Mom, you're starting to sound like you actually care."

Mom narrowed her eyes at me, but she didn't break character. For the moment, she was cool, aloof, calm Bonnie. Five minutes later, she could be in tears, screaming, or laughing. It was hard to tell.

Regardless, it was surreal to have her sitting across from me after so much time had passed with no word. Not even a fucking birthday card.

"I heard about the fire," Mom said.

"What about it?"

"I'm glad you're okay. Mark and Pam said America was terrified that you'd be there."

I shrugged. "They didn't know that we'd eloped to Vegas."

Mom nodded. "I see. Interesting, that you'd pick Vegas. You couldn'ta went to the Justice of the Peace, or Reno, or—"

"You can get married in Vegas any time of day, and we didn't want to stress over the flights or itinerary."

"Sounds like you," she said, blowing more smoke into the air.

I stood, snatched the cigarette from her mouth and drench it in the sink before throwing it into the trash. The calendar on the wall worked well enough to waft the smoke out the door, but I knew Travis would still smell it when he got home.

"That was rude as hell," she said, watching me try to work the smoke outside.

"Not half as rude as you smoking in my apartment without permission. Now," I said, slamming the door shut. "You've seen for yourself that I'm okay. Anything else?"

"I just … I wanted to tell you I love you."

"You … what?"

"No girl—no matter what's happened—should go through life thinking her mother doesn't love her. I know I walked out on you. I know I was drunk more often than I was sober, I know I was a shit mother, but it wasn't because I didn't love you. It was because I didn't love me."

"What is this, some kind of twelve-step apology bullshit?"

Mom stood. "Nope. I'm still a drunk. I told you, I heard about the fire, and this was just something I felt like I needed to do. You can believe it or not, give me the finger, tell me to leave and never come back. Hell, I'm surprised you opened the door. But you did, and I'm here, and I said what I needed to say. I love you. I always have. Always will. You were the perfect child and you didn't deserve who you got stuck with as parents. I don't expect you to want to start spending holidays together—I have no expectations, really—I just wanted to say that. Probably hard to believe after dealing with Mick all these years, but that's all."

"I can believe it. You left the first time with just the clothes on your back. After that, you never asked for money, even after the news articles came out."

"I don't want anything from you, Abby."

"Not even a relationship," I said, feeling my eyes burn.

"Some people should never be mothers. Unfortunately for you, I'm one of them. But it wasn't because I didn't love you enough or because you weren't worth being better for. There is no better me." She gestured to herself with sweeping hands. "There's just this. That's all there is."

"Okay," I said, watching her get her things together. The ashes in her hand peppered the couch and the rug. "Thanks for, uh … thanks for coming by, I guess."

"Don't feel guilty, Abby. You don't have to love poison just because its name is Mom."

I sighed. "You're not poison. You're …"

"A drunk. And I'm sorry. I wish you'd been dealt a better hand."

"If I had, Mom … I wouldn't be here. I wouldn't be married to the love of my life. I wouldn't know the things I know or be able to read people the way I do. I wouldn't be so resilient."

"True, but don't you get tired? Of being resilient? I was."

"Not at all."

She nodded, then walked down the steps and across the wet parking lot into the dark.

I thought about following her, offering her enough money for a motel room for the night, maybe dinner, but I knew she wouldn't take it. I could see it in her eyes, she knew she'd taken enough. I chewed on my lip, watching the night swallow her without a sound.

A motorcycle growled in the distance, its headlight growing closer. Travis parked in his usual spot, shutting down his bike and walking toward me with curiosity in his eyes.

"Everything all right, Pidge?" he asked. He jogged up the stairs and kissed the corner of my mouth as I still stared into the night.

"Yeah, my, uh … my mom just left."

He turned to search the cars in the lot. "Your mom? Where is she?"

"Gone." I sighed. "Again."

He led me into the apartment by the hand and closed the door behind us before pulling gently, holding me against him. "You okay?"

"Strangely enough, yes." I pressed my cheek against his chest.

In truth I wasn't sure how I felt. I'd always thought my mom was a lost, sad, alcoholic, and then she strolled back into my apartment with two lifetimes worth of wisdom and understanding.

He sniffed a few times, looking around the apartment. "Did she ...?"

"Smoke in here? Yep. Until I took it."

"Is she coming back?" he asked.

I hugged him tighter. "Nope."

CHAPTER twenty-Six

ROADS TO FATE

Abby

"YOU SHOULD GO," I SAID, touching his arm.

"To which one?" he asked.

"You don't have a choice in going to California or not."

Travis frowned. Brandon had insisted he attend a health and fitness convention with him in San Diego, and we were both trying to hide how worried we were. Two solid days of quality time with Brandon wouldn't end well.

He hugged me. "I don't want to leave you."

"I know, but … You should go with me to Keaton's anniversary vigil tonight."

"What if it upsets people? What if it causes a scene?"

Someone knocked on the door, and Travis let go of me to answer it. Toto joined him, waiting patiently for who it might be.

"Mr. Maddox," a woman said.

I moved so that I could see past my husband.

The woman was wearing a gray fitted suit, a button-down shirt, and tall, black high heels that still didn't put her above 5'5". The man was dressed similarly, but with a tie. He was taller than her, stocky, his jaw squared and clean-shaven. They were Feds.

The woman flashed her identification at Travis. "I'm Agent Val Taber. This is Agent Joel Marks. Can we come inside and speak with you for a moment?"

I swallowed.

Travis turned to me, looking nervous. "Uh … sure. Come on in."

I watched them sit on the sofa, while Travis sat on the love seat with me.

We held hands. All of my fears bubbled to the surface. What if they were there to arrest him and last night was our last night together? We were so tired, we both practically passed out. We didn't cuddle much less anything else. More importantly, how could I stop it from happening?

Agent Taber smiled. "We've come to inform you, Mr. Maddox that we've concluded our investigation of the Keaton Hall fire, and there is insufficient evidence to pursue legal action."

Travis and I met eyes, then he looked back at the agents.

"Uh … thanks?" he said.

I breathed out a laugh. "Sorry, this is just a little strange. We're not sure how to react. We know we weren't there, so this is ... validating, I suppose?"

Agent Taber managed a dry smile.

"You came all the way here to inform us?" I asked.

"No," Agent Marks said, shifting in his seat. "The investigation of Adam Stockton is still ongoing. Are you aware of anyone else involved in this underground floating fight ring? Someone who sent out the texts or helped Adam with the money?"

Travis slowly shook his head.

I started to squeeze his hand, but the tiny movement garnered the attention of Agent Taber, so I relaxed.

"Anything you remember, or may have heard might be helpful," Marks said.

"I'm sorry, I've got nothin'. But if I hear of anything I'll let you know," Travis said. He stood. "Anything else? Would you like a water or something?"

The agents stood, too.

"We have somewhere else to be. Congratulations, Mr. Maddox," Taber said. "That's pretty incredible luck that you just happened to elope the same night as a big fight."

"Love'll do that to ya," Travis said, winking.

The agents saw themselves out, but I held my finger to my mouth, then looked to Toto. "Wanna go outside?" I asked him. He wagged his tiny tail, and I grabbed his leash, and then Travis's hand.

We didn't speak until we reached the street. Travis sighed as if he'd been holding his breath the whole time.

"Do you think they're telling the truth?" I asked. "What if they don't have evidence and they're hoping to pick something up in our conversations at the apartment? They could be thinking we'll get sloppy if we're not under a microscope."

"Which is exactly why I shouldn't go to the vigil tonight."

"Travis … something is up with you. I think it will help."

"Okay, okay, I'll go," he said, frowning.

"What else is bothering you?"

He paused, and I could tell he was thinking carefully about his words. "They just asked me if Adam had a partner. If anyone sent out texts to help organize the fight."

I blinked. "Shep? No. He wasn't there and has a solid alibi. He's good. If they can't connect him to the fire, they have no case."

Travis sighed and nodded. "I don't think we have to be careful at the apartment anymore."

"I disagree. We should wait until we know they're completely done with investigating everyone."

"You're right."

I smirked. "That is such a turn on, Mr. Maddox."

Travis scooped me up and carried me back toward the apartment. We laughed and I nuzzled Travis's neck while Toto happily trotted along.

"So, you'll go tonight?" I asked.

"I need to pack, Pidge."

"I'll help you this afternoon and we'll knock most of it out."

"Okay. It's going to be hard, but yeah, I'll go."

"Good, because I told America and Shepley we

would. And Trent and Cami are coming, too. I think it would be good for all of us."

Travis was packed, all but his toiletries.

We patted Toto's head goodbye and locked the apartment door behind us. We were both fidgeting and nervous, not speaking much, unable to find a good song to listen to on the radio. Travis kept wiping the palms of his hands on his jeans.

I checked Instagram, seeing that photos from the vigil were already in my feed. My stomach sank. It wasn't until then that I'd felt what Travis had earlier—we would have to remember that night, the fear, the desperation, the sadness and shock as they brought out lifeless bodies.

My most vivid memory after Travis and I escaped was of dozens of people calling out names—names that would never get answered to. Names that would be forever memorialized on funeral service handouts and headstones, and now could be found carved into each side the stone obelisk that served as the new Keaton Memorial.

Hundreds were gathered around the remains of Keaton. Where black and ash used to cover the ground, lush green sod had been laid, and tulips of every color crowded the base of the memorial. A dozen iron benches faced the stone, and we all stared at the bouquets of flowers, teddy bears, framed photos, and ribbons already laid at the monument's iron foundation. In delicate font, the iron was inscribed.

Keaton Hall Memorial
March 20, 2009

LET THOSE WHO COME AFTER SEE TO IT THAT THEIR NAMES ARE NOT FORGOTTEN

Travis wanted to crawl out of his skin the moment we arrived, panicked energy radiated off him.

This wasn't something he could fix or fight. Like the rest of us, he just had to live with it.

Someone near the front began passing out candles, and just as the sunset painted clouds began to darken, one by one, wicks began to glow. A few girls began singing.

I heard there was a secret chord, that David played, and it pleased the Lord ...

We all sang along, amid sniffles and tears, *Hallelujah.*

Travis's jaw worked beneath his skin, and he pulled his lips to the side in an attempt to not cry.

I wrapped my arms around his waist, and he rested his cheek on top of my hair.

"Hey," a man said from behind us, putting his hand on Travis's shoulder.

"Adam," Travis said, looking around.

"I know, I shouldn't be here."

"You should both be here," I said. "Everyone deserves to heal." I hugged him, and he squeezed me tight.

Once the song was over, people began hugging and chatting. Travis, Shepley, and Trenton embraced, holding one another for a long time. America hooked her arm in mine, and I took Cami's hand. And then, something we didn't expect happened.

"Travis?"

The girl's red, puffy eyes looked up at my husband, a ghost of a smile on her face.

I could see Travis bracing for the worst. "Yeah?"

"My name is Brittni." She glanced back at the obelisk. "I was there that night. I tripped and fell. Got turned around. It was so smoky I couldn't find the exit. Everyone was running over me, knocking me down every time I tried to get up, but you saw me, got me to my feet and pointed me to Adam," she said, looking at him. "And you got me out. You saved my life. Thank you both so much."

"Hi," another girl said. "You don't know me, but you're the guy who helped me out of the exit."

"I did?" Adam asked, touching his chest.

She nodded. "I'm Amy. Can I hug you?"

"Yeah," Adam said, a bit bewildered.

One by one, more people came, both men and women, to hug Adam and Travis and thank them for directing them out and saving their lives.

With each embrace, I saw the guilt that had weighed on Travis for the last year get a little lighter. When a line formed, tears began to spill over Travis's cheeks, and then Adam's. More people had something to say to Adam because Travis eventually left to find me, but it was heartening to witness Adam find comfort, too.

Back at the apartment, Travis came out of the bathroom with just a towel wrapped around his waist, water still dripping down his arms and chest. He fell to his back on the bed, emotionally exhausted.

I was already showered and in my PJs, waiting for him to join me.

I leaned down to kiss his forehead. "I knew it would be good for you to go, but I never expected that."

"Me, either. To be honest, Pidge, I was in survival mode. I don't remember all those people. I was on autopilot."

"Well, your autopilot is a hero, too."

"Not a hero," he said, his brows pulling in. "Not even close. If it wasn't for me, those people wouldn't have even been there."

"That's true. If you weren't so entertaining to watch, they wouldn't have been there to see it. If they hadn't wanted to pay, Adam wouldn't have kept organizing them. If we hadn't gotten busted the fight before, Adam wouldn't have used the lanterns. If it wasn't the final fight of the year, it wouldn't have been so packed. If they had other, better things to do, they would've been somewhere else.

"There were a dozen variables, Travis, and you controlled none of them. Those people, hugging you with tears in their eyes? They were there tonight because of you, too. Sometimes things come together perfectly for good, and sometimes for tragedy. It doesn't mean you deserve all the blame."

His brows furrowed. "I deserve some of it."

"Everyone who was there deserves some of it. That's my point."

He sighed. "I have to get up early. We should get some rest."

The sheets ruffled as we climbed beneath them and situated ourselves. I sat a little higher so Travis could lie against my chest and relax in my arms. Still, he was restless. Fidgeting.

"What is the itinerary for the conference?" I asked.

He stopped breathing long enough for me to sense subdued panic. "Uh, I'm not sure. After I get settled in the hotel room, I go downstairs and check in, and then I get some sort of schedule."

"That's … vague."

"I'm just supposed to learn about the latest in equipment, technique, stuff like that. Total waste of time. But at least … Oh, I forgot to tell you. Becca is having some kind of issues with her pregnancy. Brandon isn't going, so at least I won't get arrested for battery in California."

I shifted to look at him. "In what universe would Brandon not travel to be a decent human being?"

Travis didn't want to meet my eyes. "I don't know. Must be serious."

I kissed my husband goodnight and then settled back against my pillow, squeezing him one last time before he drifted off. I ran my fingers over his buzzed hair, lost in thought. My husband was lying to me.

CHAPTER Twenty-Seven

ADONIS

Travis

AFTER SECURITY CHECKS AT ALMOST every fucking door and floor, I finally stepped inside the office of Squad Five where—it was hard for me to wrap my mind around it, much less believe it—my big brother, Thomas, was boss. The office was full of busy people, typing, talking on the phone, rushing around with files in their hands.

I passed the first office, looking through the open door to see my brother's date to my wedding in St. Thomas.

She stood and walked toward me with a smile.

"Liis? That's a big office, do you run this place or does Tommy?"

She seemed irritated by something I'd said. "Well, make no mistake, no one runs this place but your brother. I'm the supervisor on this floor, yes. Come with me, his office is down the hall."

I passed by a maze of cubicles separated by short walls covered in gray fabric. I got brief glances from the other agents, some pausing mid-sentence to stare at me.

"Ignore them," Liis said. "It's like the Real Housewives of San Diego on this floor. They love to gossip, and they know you're the baby brother of the feared ASAC."

"What's an ASAC?"

"Your brother is the ASAC. Assistant Special Agent in Charge. Hello Constance," Liis greeted the woman at a desk separate from the others, her white-blond curls falling just past her shoulders. She looked more like an Alabama debutante than an employee for the FBI.

"Agent Lindy," she said with a southern twang.

Called it.

"Travis Maddox, this is Constance Ashley, the ASAC's assistant. Don't let the lashes fool you, there is a Ruger under her desk and she's the best shot in Squad Five."

Constance's blue eyes brightened, and she batted the long, black lashes Lindy had just mentioned. "Why, thank you, Agent Lindy. I've been telling Maddox that for years." She touched the earpiece in her ear and then nodded to us. "You can go in."

Liis led me through a thick wooden door into Thomas's corner office. Two walls were just windows, overlooking the Vista Sorrento Parkway, a vet clinic, and a self-storage yard. It wasn't a great view, but probably the best in the building.

Thomas stood up and opened his arms wide. "There's my baby brother."

"Not the welcome anyone else gets, but okay," Liis grumbled.

Thomas hugged me, and then noticed my unease. "Hey," he said, meeting my eyes with his. "Hard part's over. Those charges are behind you, and now you just have to be yourself. Have a seat."

I took one chair that sat in front of his desk, Liis took the other. She looked calm and collected. I felt like I wanted to jump through the windows and run until I was back in my apartment with Abby.

My brother was supposed to be an ad exec, but there he sat, in his federal suit and his federal tie, behind his huge federal desk. On the wall, awards I didn't know he'd won. On his desk, photos with important people I didn't know he knew.

"None of this is going to be easy, Tommy. Do you know how many fucking lies I had to tell my wife just to get here? How the hell am I going to pay my bills if I'm running around fetching intel for you?"

"Informants get paid. Well. And we've taken care of your back story for Abby. We're rerouting any calls to your hotel or the convention center. We've created content if she Googles the convention."

"How did you manage to get Brandon to go for it and have his wife fake a pregnancy complication to skip it?" I asked.

"The convention organizer, who happens to be our Agent Marks, stroked his ego and offered to sponsor him for the trip … and hookers."

"And Becca? Don't tell me you fed her bad food or something."

Thomas gestured to Liis.

She nodded once and turned to me. "Becca is fine. Brandon met who he thought was a college freshman, got extremely drunk, allegedly roofied, and robbed. Becca was an excuse. He didn't have an ID to fly."

"Thank God," I said, relaxing back into my chair.

"And," Thomas said, "you'll have an ongoing alibi until we wrap this thing up with Benny."

"When will that be?" I asked.

"Trav, I have to be upfront here. We began this investigation two years ago, and it just keeps getting deeper."

I shrugged. "What does that mean?"

"That means, be patient." Liis said. "When we have all the evidence we need, we'll make arrests. Your ties to Benny and Mick Abernathy will help us get there."

"And how am I going to do that?"

Thomas shifted in his seat, and I knew I was going to hate whatever would come out of his mouth next.

"Benny offered you help to get out of prosecution for the fire, yes?"

"How did you know that?"

Thomas smiled. "We're the FBI, Trav, we know everything. You're going to accept his help. He's going to get you off the hook you're already free of and agree to have you fight for him."

I sat forward. "No fuckin' way, Tommy. I promised Pidge …"

"Things are different now."

I sat back in my chair—hard—and crossed my arms. "You're really going to make me break every promise I ever made her? With a smile on your face? Fuck you." I looked at Liis. "And fuck you, too."

"Hey," Thomas said, bristling.

Liis raised her hand. "I don't blame you, Travis. It's a tough spot to be in. But this is the only way your brother could secure your immunity, and his plan is the quickest way to get you into Benny's inner circle."

Thomas leaned forward. "You accept your invitation, beat ass, slide into his security detail. You'll have access to everything. This is going to work, and better than any of us could have hoped." He was entirely too impressed with himself, and it was pissing me off.

Thomas's landline beeped and he pushed a button.

Constance didn't wait for him to answer. "Agents Marks, Taber, and Kostas, sir."

"Send them in," Thomas said. He spoke to her in a different tone than I'd ever heard. He didn't use that tone with Liis, either. It was authoritative, distant. It was jarring.

Three agents walked in, two I recognized—the man and woman who'd come to tell me I was off the hook—and a giant of a man I didn't.

My muscles had swelled since I started working at Iron E. This dude's arms were two times bigger than mine.

He was built like Lou Ferrigno in his Hulk days, but looked like a Roman statue, with blond hair and ice blue eyes.

"Travis, you've met Marks and Taber. They'll be your points of contact. Agent Kostas is taking over Iron E from Brandon."

I shot Thomas a dubious look. "Brandon isn't giving up that gym, Tommy."

"Yeah, he will," Marks said. "Kostas will help with your cover at home as well as serve as an extra eye on Abby while you're in Vegas."

I turned to look at Kostas, and then my brother. "You're assigning this Greek God-looking dude to my wife? You're out of your fucking mind." I glanced back at him.

"Well, he is Greek," Taber said with a wry smile.

"And Macedonian," Kostas added.

"Fuck no." I perched my elbow on the arm of the chair, touched my fingers to my lips and shook my head.

Thomas leaned forward. "You keep thinking you have a choice. This is already in motion, Travis. We're briefing you, not asking your permission."

I breathed out of my nose, trying to keep my cool.

"Kostas has experience as a trainer. Taber and Marks are going to take you downstairs and will direct you on surveillance, gun safety, and intel gathering."

"Real spy shit," Taber said, raising her eyebrows.

"How can I act as Benny's security and go to school and work and see my wife?" I asked, exasperated.

Thomas frowned. "Benny said before he'd work around your schedule if you fought for him, right?"

"Yeah, but … how did you know that?"

Thomas ignored my question. "Make him work

around it. Everything will be the same as you thought it was going to be when you were considering working for him before. Kostas is going to keep sending you to *conventions*," he said, using his fingers for quotes, "when you get extra time. Probably two weekends a month during school, more during breaks, and in the summer. You only have four semesters left before graduation. We'll all band together to make this work for you. We're not going to give you more than you can handle, or so much that Abby will begin to get suspicious."

"She's already suspicious! She's not stupid, Tommy!"

Liis held up her hand again. "We'll set her mind at ease, just like we did for this trip. It will all check out."

"So when do I go to Benny?" I asked, defeated.

"Tomorrow," Marks said.

"*Tomorrow?*" I stood and began pacing. Everything was happening too fast.

They'd obviously been planning this for a while, but it was my first day and it was all being dumped on me. I wasn't sure Abby would believe me. What if she asked questions I couldn't answer? I'd have to keep lying and there was no end in sight. If she ever found out, would she forgive me? Would I forgive me?

I was glad I wasn't going to jail, but I was surrounded by suits, a *Men's Fitness* model was going to babysit my wife every time I was out of town, and I didn't have a say in any of it.

On top of everything else, Thomas didn't seem bothered by my situation. He was my damn brother and he was sitting there, smug, and I wanted to choke him with his stupid tie.

Kostas watched me, amused.

"Quit smiling at me, you prick," I said. I stopped pacing and pointed at him. "And if you look at my wife too long, I'll gouge out those pretty blue eyes with a fucking fork."

"Travis," Thomas warned.

"Why a fork?" Taber asked.

"Listen," Thomas began.

"Why not a pencil, or a knife, or …" she continued.

"Damn it, Taber," Thomas boomed.

"Sorry, sir," she said, righting her posture and clasping her fingers in front of her.

"We're a team," Liis said. "And if we all work together, Travis is safe, Abby is safe, and we nail these assholes. Then, Travis, you go back to your life, back to your wife, and we get the warm and fuzzy ending for which we've all worked so hard. I know it's a lot to take in, but you've been around Benny. It will all be organic, believable, and most importantly, safe. Or, as safe as one can be in the company of bloodthirsty criminals."

"He can handle it," Marks said.

Thomas's phone beeped, and he tapped a button.

"Take me off speaker, sir," Constance said.

Thomas waited a beat as he looked around the room, and then picked up the phone. "What is it? Oh, shit." His eyes met mine. "They're sure?" He waited for a response, then sighed. "Get him a transport." Thomas rubbed his forehead before placing the phone on the receiver.

"What?" Liis asked.

"Change of plans," Thomas said. "Taber, you're escorting Travis. He's going to Vegas now."

"Now, sir?" Taber asked.

Our eyes locked, and I could see a glimpse of sympathy in my brother's eyes I was sure no one else noticed.

"Now."

CHAPTER *Twenty-Eight*

LEAVING LAS VEGAS

Abby

THE THIRD AND FINAL LOAD of laundry was in the dryer, mostly bikinis, cover ups and swim trunks. The last two weeks had been a rollercoaster I never wanted to ride again.

Of all the things we'd gone through in the past year and a half, Travis nearly leaving me was by far the worst.

It made sense, now, why he was so worried in Vegas after our wedding. He'd only tried to end things once and I couldn't help but question everything, even after we'd renewed our vows. I'd broken his heart a dozen times. I put my hands on the edge of the dryer and leaned over, ashamed.

No nineteen-year-old girl had it all figured out, and I'd tried not to be too hard on myself for being unsure when it came to Travis while we were dating. But after what I'd gone through when he tried to 'save' me by walking away, I wanted to beg for his forgiveness every time panic washed over me.

He'd left me for work the day before. The convention Brandon had sent him to was only two days. I thought Travis would be relieved not to be around his boss, but he still seemed agitated. He could barely look me in the eyes when he detailed his itinerary. Something was up, but I was still too nervous to question him.

Travis had promised to never leave me again, but he'd been in his head since the day after the wedding in St. Thomas, and I didn't want to push him, worried he'd try to 'save' me again. Being married wasn't a guarantee he'd stay with me, and I wasn't sure that was a fear I'd ever get over.

My phone buzzed, and I stood, took a deep breath and checked it, reading America's text.

My two o'clock class was canceled, I'm on my way.

My cheeks filled with air and I breathed out, pushing an escaped piece of my hair from my eyes. I hadn't told America about what had happened before the vow renewal and was unsure if I should.

She might hate him all over again, making Travis feel worse than he already did.

I was hoping St. Thomas would be a good way to start over, but Travis seemed to be in a dark place. My mind went over a thousand scenarios—if he didn't think he'd made the right decision to stay with me and a myriad of other things. I knew he loved me. I focused on that.

I'd just loaded the dishwasher when my best friend knocked on the door. I unlocked it and let her in, watching her stroll in and drop into the recliner, the same one I'd sat in the first time I came to this apartment.

The room looked a lot different now, and so did America with her freshly cut blonde bob and bangs. Her skin was golden brown from the Caribbean sun, and she looked relaxed and happy in a white crop top tank, light gray joggers and white high-top sneakers. It only took her a few seconds for her to notice my energy wasn't matching hers.

"Oh, God. What?" she bristled, sitting forward.

"I don't know," I said, sitting on the side of the couch closest to her. "Just a feeling, I guess."

"About what?"

"Not sure about that, either."

"Things seemed to have calmed down—if you know what I mean—right?"

I nodded. She was right. No more sightings of the Feds.

"Is it the Keaton Hall anniversary?"

I shook my head. "I don't think so."

"It was nice to see everyone come up to him."

I nodded again. I couldn't say it out loud for fear someone might be listening, but I'd never seen Travis so emotional.

We'd heard so many stories about Travis directing someone to safety or Adam leading them outside. I didn't know that Adam had gone back in several times to help as many as he could to get out.

With every grateful hug, Travis had struggled to

keep it together.

"He seemed more at peace after that … for a little while. There's something else."

"He's upset?"

"I'm not sure. Something's off."

"What do you think it is?" She looked around. "Or do you not want to talk about it."

"I don't know. I think I need some fresh air. I've been in a funk all day. I couldn't concentrate in my classes."

"Yes," she said standing. She held out her hand. "Let's walk."

I took her hand and grabbed Toto's leash and a jacket before locking up behind us.

I spoke as soon as I thought we were far enough from the apartment. "I'm going to tell you something, but you can't freak out." We'd both left our cellphones behind, accustomed to an abundance of caution.

"Is it that bad?"

I sighed, waiting as Toto sniffed a good spot to relieve himself. "A week before the wedding, Travis met with Adam. Brandon is involved, and Travis was sure he was going to turn him in, and Travis would go to prison."

"Brandon? How?"

"He's Adam's partner. They were streaming the fights online and making millions. Brandon was attempting to make a deal with the Feds for immunity."

"That motherfucker," she grumbled under her breath.

"Travis was even more afraid that he'd take me

down with him. So, he"—I almost couldn't say the words—"he tried to end it."

"What?" she yelled, immediately looking around. Her next words were quieter. "What the fuck did you just say to me? I know I did not hear you say Travis ended it before the damn wedding."

"He tried. I really thought he was going to. I barely talked him out of it."

"Why didn't you say anything?" she said, angry.

"He changed his mind. I didn't want to get into it before St. Thomas. I just wanted to enjoy it. I wanted everyone to enjoy it."

"Abby ..."

I closed my eyes, trying to keep from crying again. "He changed his mind, Mare. But there for a hot minute I really thought I was going to lose him."

She hugged me. "Oh, my God. Oh my God, Abby, I'm so sorry I wasn't here."

"It's not your fault. It's no one's fault. He was acting out of desperation. But now it's like he's not worried about it anymore. Since St. Thomas, he hasn't mentioned it. But ... there's something else. He's different. I don't know if he regrets not cutting me loose or he's upset that Brandon is going to make him start traveling for work. What I do know is, it's not prison. It's like he knows he's off the hook. Maybe he cut his own deal and he doesn't want to tell me? I'm not sure, but it's something."

We continued walking, and America took my free hand, holding it to her middle with both of hers. "I just can't believe he'd be willing to walk away from you.

Even for that."

"Well, he was. It was the scariest moment of my life, and I've had a couple of near-death experiences in the last year."

America was deep in thought. "Do you think it has to do with Benny? What if he agreed to take him up on his offer to help?"

I stopped. "You could be right. Let's get back. I want to call around and double check his story that he's in California and not Vegas right now."

We went back to the apartment, but both stopped short when we saw an unfamiliar black SUV parked in Travis's usual spot.

"Jesse, what the fuck?" America said, letting go of my hand to approach him.

He held up his hands. "It's not what you think, I swear."

I frowned. The smug expression on his face the last time he visited us was replaced by sadness. "What is it, then? Is it about Travis?"

He shook his head. "It's … it's your mom, Abby." He looked down and sighed. "Bonnie's gone."

I stared at him, trying to process the words.

"Gone? You mean missing?" I asked.

Jesse shook his head. "She passed away, Abby, I'm sorry."

"What?" America shrieked. "Are you sure? How do you know?"

"We've been over this. Benny. I had to tell you. I don't even know if you want to go back, but I already got you and Mare flights to Vegas."

"She's in Vegas?" I asked.

He shrugged and nodded. "She has been for a while. The flight leaves in two hours. I'm so sorry, Abby, I really am."

America covered her mouth and wrapped her arms around me. "Abby!"

Most people would cry in that situation, break down and sob, but all I felt was numb. "I guess ... I guess I should ask Cami and Trent if they can watch Toto."

"I'm going with you. I'm going, Abby, and I don't want to hear a word about it." She dialed someone's number and held her cell to her ear. After a minute she growled. "Travis didn't answer. I'm texting Shepley. We're going."

"You can't miss class, Mare, and your parents won't let you."

"I don't care! You just lost your mom! I'm fucking going! Come on, I'll help you pack."

I stared at the suitcase as America filled it up with undergarments, clothes and toiletries. She paused in front of my closet, grabbed two dresses and held them up. "They're the only black ones you have that aren't … clubby."

I walked over to her and touched the fabric. When I bought them, it was for job interviews. I had no idea I'd be wearing one of them to my mother's funeral. I took the one on the left, it had a higher neckline, and the fabric would be better able to breathe in the desert heat.

"Good choice," America said, choosing a pair of

black pumps.

After what seemed to be a short internal check list was completed, America zipped my suitcase and rolled it to the doorway. “Get your charger and purse. Make sure your ID is in it.”

“Oh, right,” I said, going over to the dresser. I confirmed I had what I needed.

America was typing on her phone. “Leave the key under the mat. Trent will pick up Toto after work and bring him to their place. He’s going to keep trying to get ahold of Travis.” She looked up. “And Trent wants you to call when you can. He feels terrible for you.”

Jesse loaded my luggage into his back seat, setting my roller bag on its side knowing he’d need more space for America’s belongings.

At her dorm, I sat in the SUV while Jesse helped America load her bags into the back, and then she climbed into the captain’s chair behind me.

“I’m surprised how fast you got all of that packed,” he said.

“I can be efficient when I need to be,” she said, buckling in.

Jesse set his GPS to the airport, and we rode there in total silence. No radio, no conversation. It crossed my mind that Travis wouldn’t be happy that I was traveling with Jesse, but he’d also understand my predicament. I couldn’t be picky about free tickets to get back to Vegas for my mother’s funeral.

Once we got to the airport, checking in and going through security was a blur. It wasn’t until America squeezed my hand while we waited to be called at the gate that I noticed how lost I felt.

"You haven't spoken in two hours, Abby. Do you need anything?" she asked.

I shook my head.

She squeezed my hand again. "Shepley will be on the next flight out. He'll meet us at the hotel in the morning."

I nodded, staring out the window.

Halfway into the flight, my mind began to focus on what it meant that I couldn't cry. I'd just seen my mom not long ago, for the first time in almost two years. She'd given me closure. I had to wonder if she knew she was dying. If that was goodbye.

I was seated in the middle of a three-seat row. Jesse was watching something on the screen in front of him, America was gazing out the window She left her ear buds out of her ear in case she was needed but kept herself distracted so I didn't feel like she was hovering.

Since Travis couldn't be with me, I was glad that she was. Besides my husband, only my best friend would understand exactly what I needed in that moment. Sometimes it felt like she knew before I did.

When the wheels touched the tarmac, the jolt snapped me to reality. I hadn't been able to speak to ask Jesse questions, as if I'd been on autopilot, too. The way my mom had died was still a mystery to me, and I'd known for hours that she was gone.

Jesse helped us check into a room at a hotel off the strip, scoring us a discount.

"Is that from an old connection at the Bellagio, or because you work for Benny?" America asked as we walked to the elevator.

"Both," he said with a smile. He pressed the button and we waited in silence.

America seemed to have gotten the same sense that I had, Jesse was obviously trying not to say something, and no one wanted him to ignore that feeling.

We walked up to our room and waited as Jesse used the key card to open the door. He waited quietly as America began unpacking our suitcases and organizing the bathroom as she always did.

"I, uh, I'll find out what we need to do." Jesse said finally. "I know her body still has to be claimed by family."

"Mick hasn't done it?" I choked out.

"Mick's been MIA. I'm not even sure he knows. They're expecting you. Call the funeral home and they'll do the rest; help you make arrangements and cover all the bases. We used the same one for both of my grandfathers."

"I remember," I said, focusing on a tree outside. It was similar to the one outside Travis's—our—bedroom window. That thought alone made me feel calmer, although, I wasn't sure what calmer than numb could be.

Jesse bent over the desk and scribbled something on the hotel stationary. He ripped it from the pad, started to hand it to me, then decided to offer it to America. "Here. The name of the funeral home we used and the address for where she … where she is."

"Thank you," America said.

"How did it happen?" I asked, looking back to the tree.

Jesse wrung his hands and fidgeted. "You know, Abby. She hasn't been doing well for a long time. She drinks more than any man I know."

"In the end, I mean."

Jesse winced. "You don't … you don't want to know. She's gone. Just leave it be."

"I do. I do want to know."

"She'd been in and out of the hospital for months. The last time I saw her she looked, I don't know, kind of bloated and uncomfortable. Her eyes were yellow. Her little body was just tired."

"Was she at home when it happened?" I asked.

"No, she was in her room at the hospital. She'd been there for a couple of days."

"Good," I said, nodding. "That's good. Was … was she alone?"

Jesse sighed. "No one's ever alone at the hospital."

"You know what I mean."

"She'd slipped into a coma the day she passed. She wouldn't have known if anyone had made it there to visit."

"You mean, if I had made it to visit."

"You didn't know. Hell, I didn't know until after," he said. "Abby, she was in a warm, comfortable bed right up to the end. You should take comfort in that."

"I guess so," I said, looking down at my hands.

"I should go. I left without telling anyone and I have to … I should go," Jesse said.

I stood and he hugged me, but I kept my arms at my sides.

"Call me, okay? I'm here for you." He waved, but

just as he reached for the knob, someone banged on the door. Jesse looked back at America and me, and then turned the bolt lock and the knob.

Travis was standing in the hall. He didn't seem surprised to see Jesse, but he was still unhappy to have to shoulder past him to get to me.

I was prepared for a jealousy-fueled lecture, but he took me into his arms and held me tight.

"I got here as quick as I could."

"That was … really quick," America said.

"I'm, uh …" Jesse said, pointing at the door.

"I appreciate you bringing her here," Travis said, his cheek still against my hair. "Still, fuck you, though."

Jesse nodded. "Fair enough."

He closed the door behind him, and Travis squeezed me tightly. "I'm so sorry, Pidge," he whispered.

I looked up at him. "How did you …?"

He frowned, the same way he did when he was telling me his itinerary before he left. "I came as soon as I heard. I had to move Heaven and Earth, but I'm here now."

"How? How are you here? Now?

Travis chuckled, nervous. "One of the organizers heard what happened, got me a private plane and then I was here."

I hugged him again, pressing my cheek against his chest. "I'm just glad you're here."

"Me, too."

"Okay," America said, tossing her phone to her bed and then sitting next to me. Her follow up was soft and comforting. "Once you identify her, the funeral home will step in. Then you'll have some decisions to make. Jesse sent me the address to her apartment. It's in Boulder City, about forty minutes from here." She looked at her watch. "But … I'm sorry Abby we have to go to the morgue now."

I shook my head.

"I'll be with you," Travis said.

America hugged us both. "You don't have to do this alone."

"I don't know that I can do this at all."

"Yes, you can," America said, meeting my gaze. "You have to. There's no one else."

I closed my eyes for a moment, to get my bearings while they kept their arms around me. America was right, I wasn't alone. I had my husband and my best friend with me, the two people in the world I was the safest with.

Again, the car was filled with silence. Travis had called us an Uber, and even the driver knew not to speak. It could've been Travis's natural ability to intimidate or the fact that our destination was a morgue—or both.

When we arrived, Travis and I stood in front of the building, three stories of nearly non-descript architectural features. Taupe brick, a few rectangular windows, double doors that perfectly matched the brick, and a sign that almost looked generic.

America took a few steps forward but stopped when she realized we weren't following. "You two okay?"

I looked up at Travis, who was staring at the building, a deep line formed between his brows.

"Oh my God. Oh my God, I didn't even think, Trav. You shouldn't have come," I said, covering my eyes.

He peeled my fingers back and then kissed them. "I want nothing more than to be here with you."

"But ..." I began.

He shook his head. "Is this hard for me? Yeah. I hate seeing you go through this because I can relate." He looked at the building. "But I'm glad I can hold your hand through it."

We walked in, and I let America handle the people at the desk. I gave them my ID, and then we waited.

And waited.

And waited.

... and waited.

Finally, a man in navy blue scrubs came to the door.

"Mrs. Maddox?" he called.

The three of us stood, and Travis steadied me as we walked forward.

The man asked me several questions as we walked to the back, and I answered, but moments later I wasn't sure what had been asked. We went through a swinging door, and then another, to a large sterile-looking room that smelled like a combination of a hospital and a deep freeze.

The man led us to a wall full of silver drawers with thin handles. He doubled checked the numbers and then pulled.

I saw my mother lying there lifeless, and again, I felt nothing. The numbness scared me more than what I was looking at.

Then, the tears came.

"I'm sorry, we need a verbal confirmation."

"It's her," I said, turning my back to her.

America and Travis never left my side.

Signing forms and making our way back outside was a blur. And between my panic that I was somehow broken for being unable to grieve at the sight of my lifeless mother and the pure rage I felt for Mick that he'd left me to handle everything—again—I was relieved that at least that part was over.

"I hate this town. I never want to come back here again," I said, trying to breathe through my tears.

"Just one meeting with the funeral director and we can go home," America said.

"Cremate her. Just have them cremate her and send her to me. Embalming and the makeup is for people to remember differently than what I just saw. I've already seen it. Just cremate her and send her to me. I'll … figure it out later."

America was surprised at first, but then nodded and began tapping on her phone. She held the receiver to her ear and walked away, chatting with whoever was on the line.

Travis ordered the Uber and put his phone away, holding me with both hands. "I'm so sorry you had to see that, Pidge. I'm sorry your piece-of-shit father is, yet again, letting you down and making you do the heavy lifting in the family."

"Well, I have you. He has no one."

"Whose fault is that?" America said, rejoining us. "They're going to email you some forms to sign and they'll take care of it. It's … it's going to be fifteen-hundred dollars, though."

"Okay," Travis said. "That's not a problem."

"Since when?" I said, stunned. My cheeks felt hot and wet, but Travis kissed one side anyway.

"I'll take care of it, Pigeon."

I took a deep breath and stared forward. "I just want to leave this place and go home. Pretend it was all a bad dream and that she's just … estranged, not dead."

America gently rubbed my back with her palm. "I'll run you a bath at the hotel. I've told Shepley to cancel his flight. We're flying back tomorrow."

I looked to Travis. "You can go back to the convention. Thank you for dropping everything and coming."

He frowned. "No way. Hell, no. I'm going home with you. I'm not leaving your side."

I leaned into him, relieved. Travis was my rock, my home base, the only safe haven I'd known. I wasn't even going to pretend I didn't desperately need him.

In the back of my mind, I worried that when the grief hit, there was no telling what those emotions might unleash. I was still on a rollercoaster with no way off. But it was bearable with my husband next to me, and America always at my side.

It seemed like a tragedy that my mother would have no funeral, no tombstone, no family to visit her viewing. But she chose to be alone, and I would never have to be.

"I'm so lucky to have you both in my life," I said. "I'm just glad tomorrow I'll be leaving Las Vegas, for good this time."

"You have a lot of good to look forward to, Abby.

Lots of distractions," America said.

I turned to her. "I need all the distractions. What do you have in mind?"

"Um," she said, thinking. "You want to talk about it now?"

"Anything else. Please," I said.

"Well, let's see. Um … Oh! The Spring Bash is coming up, and Boom Fest."

"Boom Fest? What is that?" I asked.

Travis spoke as he checked for the Uber's location again. "It's the annual campus music festival. They didn't have it last year because … well, the fire."

America offered a cautious smile. "Everyone's been talking about it. If you're up for it."

"It falls on my birthday this year," Travis said. "And it's my twenty-first. All my brothers will be there for it. But, if you're not up for it, I'm happy to sit at home with you and Netflix and cuddle with a big bowl of popcorn and Toto in our laps."

Just when he frowned, America spoke up, "Trent and Cami should be picking him up anytime now."

He nodded. "Good. Much better choice than Brazil." He kissed my hair. "You doing okay, Pidge? Uber is almost here."

"I'm ashamed to admit what's wrong," I said.

Travis and America positioned themselves to get a better look at my facial expression. I wasn't sure why; they both knew I'd never give anything away.

"I'm not sad," I blurted out. "What is wrong with me?"

"Abby," America said, holding my hand in both of

hers. "You just found out—hours ago—that she died. You barely know her but she's your mother. How are you supposed to feel?" America brushed my cheek with her thumb. "Feelings are never wrong. Whatever you feel, it's okay. If you're sad later, that's okay. If you never are, that's okay, too."

I took a deep breath, letting my body relax. "Lots to look forward to," I said to myself. "Distractions. And I'm leaving Las Vegas ... forever."

CHAPTER Twenty-Nine

MOSES

Travis

"YOU OKAY?" I ASKED ABBY.

She squeezed me with a side-hug. "Thank you. This is exactly what I needed"

Bonnie's ashes had been delivered to us the day before, and it took Abby a full hour to decide what to do with the urn. She didn't want to look at it every day, but she also didn't feel right storing it away in the closet. So, we decided on Shep's old room.

We popped over to the hardware store and I made a simple shelf. Abby set the urn in the center and decorated each side with small flower vases and seemed to feel okay with it. But I wasn't sure if she was ready for what we were about to walk into.

Boom Fest was Eastern State's lesser version of Coachella. The girls wore sparkling, skimpy outfits, wild makeup that usually included glitter or those little fake gems stuck to their faces. The guys had it easier, typically in Baha hats or fedoras and Hawaiian shirts.

Abby and America looked the part, America in some wild white ensemble: a white corset with wide straps that laced up the front and a pair of white *spanks*—she called them—but there was also a see-through white shirt she wore under the corset tank top thing, with sleeves that hung just above her elbows and then the rest of the fabric hung low over her shorts. Her hair was in a bunch of braids with white and silver ribbons and she was sporting some kind of white lace up leather combat boots. She even had silver metallic lashes and heart shaped goggles she was using as a head band or something.

Abby wasn't quite as flashy, but it still made me feel like my old self was bubbling just under the surface. I didn't say anything about the black bikini top that had a Route 66 patch on one triangle and a motorcycle embroidered on the other, or the black micro shorts she was wearing—but the old me would have.

For some reason, it was the shin-high lace up black leather boots she was wearing that made me the most uncomfortable, and I couldn't figure out why.

Abby adjusted the thick black choker on her neck and turned to search for Finch, one of her two French braids flipping over her shoulder. "You coming?" she called.

"I'm coming, betch! Patience," Finch called from thirty yards away. His boyfriend Felix was following close behind.

Abby rose up on the balls of her feet to kiss my

cheek, and then laughed as she wiped away the silver glitter than had apparently transferred from under her eyes to my face. "Oops, let me get that," she said with a smile.

"Leave it on there," I said, leaning back. I held her hand at bay and then pecked her lips when she didn't expect it, making her laugh even harder.

My brothers and their significant others were supposed to be waiting for us at the Ferris Wheel, but I didn't see them anywhere.

"That's weird," I said, looking at my watch. "We're ten minutes late."

"Sorry," America said.

"And none of them are here? Wasn't this the spot, Shep?" I asked.

"Didn't you see the group text?" Shepley said. "Thomas said he couldn't make it so everyone else kind of dropped out after that."

"No fucking way," I said, looking around. "They're not coming for my twenty-first birthday? I went to all of theirs! That's bullshi—"

"April Fools, motherfucker!" Trent said, tackling me from the back.

I turned to see all four of my brothers and their girls standing behind me, and all eight sets of their eyes lit up.

"Happy Birthday!" they said in unison.

Abby hugged Cami first.

America went straight for Falyn and Ellie.

The girls all took turns hugging each other, like my brothers did to me. When it was Thomas's turn, he hugged me tight.

"We wouldn't miss it, baby bro."

Seeing him felt awkward, and I didn't like that. He wasn't just my brother anymore, he was my boss, my warden, and I'd already seen him a second time in San Diego just since Abby's mom died to get in the rest of my training with Marks and Taber—and some other dude named Sawyer who showed up for no reason other than to watch. And no one else but Liis knew.

Liis nodded to me, and I was sure she could sense my sudden unease. "Happy birthday, Travis."

"Thanks, Lind … Liis."

From my peripheral, I saw Abby notice. She kept a relaxed smile on her face, but her eyes lingered on the awkward exchange for just a moment before she looked away to finish chatting with Ellie.

"Let's go," Finch said. "The bands are all the way on the other side."

We followed Finch and Felix, the girls chatting and side-hugging, the Maddox boys nudging and soft-punching.

The festival was packed, but the crowd parted like the Red Sea for us, seeing five different renowned fighters from The Circle approaching like a small army, with the loves of their lives in tow. We passed food trucks and various booths, and then we got into the area where there were carnival spectacles, fire breathers and acrobats, clowns and exotic animals. When we finally reached the back edge of the concert area, we kept going, easily making our way to the center.

The band began to play within minutes, easily

heard over the roaring cheers from the crowd. I stood behind Abby, wrapping my arms around her middle. She leaned back against my chest and we swayed, enjoying our first moment of real peace since the fire.

It made me want to believe Thomas that everything would be alright. That we'd get the intel they needed to make arrests and Abby and I could be happy in the meantime.

Ellie was suddenly on Tyler's shoulders, cheering for the band. And then America climbed onto Shepley's.

I looked down to Abby. "Want a better view?"

She nodded with enthusiasm, giving me an extra bump of adrenaline to pop her up with barely any effort. Soon, all the girls were sitting above the crowd—except for Liis, who wasn't interested—even though she was the tiniest of us.

The band played on, a third song, then a fourth, the lead singer telling stories and quipping to make us all laugh between songs.

It was a perfect day, the sun not too hot and with a gentle breeze once in a while to cool us off where we stood, shoulder to shoulder. As the sun began to set, fireworks were lit in the distance, and the crowd went insane.

One by one, the girls asked to be lowered to the ground, with Ellie being the last. They began dancing then—not Liis, of course—and my cousin, brothers and I watched with amusement.

Abby had her hands in the air, smiling and swaying to the music.

The music stopped and the lead singer thanked everyone for coming, and we all erupted.

Just as the crowd quieted down, Abby looked to me and smiled. A second later, a loud slap filled the air, and Abby jerked forward. Her eyes widened, she looked at me.

My gaze settled behind her, where Brandon stood.

"Damn, that was a good one! I've been wanting to do that for a while," he said, rubbing his hands together.

Abby rubbed her back side and turned to face him, quickly backing toward me.

The celebrating was over, then. The Maddox family was staring down a common enemy.

I started to charge him, but somehow stopped myself, breathing hard. The adrenaline running through my veins made me want to fight everyone in the crowd.

"Are you out of your fucking mind?" I said, seething.

"I mean," Brandon gestured to my wife. "Look at her. Look at that ass! It was right there, brother, I had to!"

Abby put her hand on my shoulder. "Don't. He's baiting you," she whispered.

"What?" Brandon asked, looking around. "You mad? Might want to ask your brother over there what it's like to throw with me. I beat his ass back then, and I'm better now."

"I was a pint and a half of whiskey in, you stupid fuck," Tyler quipped. He took a step forward, but I held my hand to his chest.

I looked to Thomas, waiting for him to stop me, but he was just glowering at Brandon, his fists at his side.

"I should've done it the other night," Brandon said, ogling my wife.

"Shut up, Brandon," Abby said, fuming. She was shaking. I hadn't seen her do that since the fire.

"What the fuck are you talking about?" I asked.

"I came over the other night." He winked at Abby. "Admit it. You were happy to see me."

"Is that what you thought when I screamed at you to get the fuck off my porch?"

Brandon laughed.

"Laugh at her again, bitch," America said.

"Hey," he said, shrugging. His eyes were wild, his adrenaline pumping, ready for a fight. "It's not my fault Travis's wife has wanted to suck my dick since we met."

"Don't fall for it, Trav. He's up to something," Abby said. She rubbed the back of her shorts again.

"Are you okay?" I asked her.

She hesitated.

"Pidge?" I said the words firmer than I'd meant to.

"It's going to leave a mark."

I clenched my jaw, leaning my head to the side. "I have to."

She looked at him, back to me, and then nodded. "Teach that asshole some manners."

I lunged at Brandon, and from my peripheral, I could see my brothers backing everyone up to provide me a perfect circle to beat ass in.

My throws had as much power behind them as they

did when I was attacking Benny's goons.

Brandon was strong as fuck, but he was slower than Trenton, not a smart as Thomas, and couldn't land a punch like the twins.

I railed on him, over and over. "Don't you ever! Look! At my wife! Again!" I yelled, hitting him with each word.

When the blood began to flow, I still didn't stop. After a solid fist to his jaw, Brandon flew up into the air, his feet above him, and then landed with a thud. The crowd reacted in a collective "*OH!*"

Brandon struggled to get back to his feet, and when he did, I held out my hands to my sides. "Still think you're better, you arrogant fuck?"

Brandon swung, knocking me sideways. I grabbed my knees, feeling the sting of his knuckles on my jaw, the vibration of the impact still in my head.

"Travis?" Abby called from behind me.

I stood, breathing hard, holding up my index finger. "That's your one."

The crowd detonated, and I went in for the kill, connecting my fist with his face, my boot with his stomach, knocking him to the ground. I jumped on him then, putting everything I had into each blow.

"Enough, Travis," Thomas yelled.

Seconds later, I was yanked up and away, but it wasn't my family, it was campus police. My brothers were about to step in, but Thomas stopped them.

I wiped blood from my mouth, then spit crimson onto the ground, staring down at Brandon.

He slowly crawled to his feet, breathing hard,

bleeding from his broken nose and busted mouth.

"Thank you," he said, laughing. "I knew you wouldn't let me down."

The campus police cuffed us both as the crowd dispersed.

"Travis?" Abby said.

I winked at her. "It's going to be okay. I'll see you soon."

She nodded as Trenton pulled her back and hugged her to his side. "We've got her. You just worry about you."

I nodded, and then a cop shoved me forward, following Brandon and his escort to the parking lot.

They were at least smart enough to place us in separate cruisers, and the ride to the station was short. I half expected Thomas and Liis to be waiting for us, but they weren't. Brandon and I were processed, and then put in neighboring holding cells.

After an officer slid my bars shut, I sat on the cold bench, glad I was alone. My body still shook with rage. If anyone had been there to fuck with me, I'd have beaten the shit out of them, too.

"Bars, chief? Really? You haven't updated this place since it's been built, huh?"

"Shut up, Maddox," the officer said, walking away.

"You've always been a dumb cunt," Brandon said from his side. I could tell he was leaning against the same wall.

"Yeah? Well I'm not the one who cheats on my pregnant wife, who bangs my receptionist or my clients, or who just got smashed in the face with karma about thirty-eight times."

Brandon laughed. "I hired you, antagonized you with your stupid, medium pretty wife, and set you up. And you fell for it."

"Set me up for what, Brandon? You think I don't know you were talking to the Feds? You think I don't know you were streaming those fights and collecting millions in illegal gambling? Not to mention not paying taxes on any of it and laundering it all through the gym. One step ahead of you, precious."

"None of that matters now."

I huffed a laugh. "It matters because you did it. And one way or another, you're going to get nailed for it."

"No. I'm not. They don't know any of that. And they'll never be able to trace it. I've made millions off your stupid ass and I'm going to get away with it. I've been doing that shit for six years and they've never even caught a whiff. I haven't made millions. I've made tens of millions and I'm going to keep making it while you're rotting away in some dank federal prison trading Little Debbie snacks for ass.

"And then you know what I'm going to do? Convince your wife you were shady all along and you're going to get letters from home about how good my dick is. I'll have the gym, I'll have the betting income, I'll have Becca kissing my ass, and your wife begging to be in my harem. And there's not a fucking thing you can do about it. What you don't know, *Trav,* is I have immunity. They don't know my involvement. They're focused on nailing you. They just needed a reason to arrest you and get you into custody, and I gave it to them. I'm going to be living my best life, and you—you broke ass overconfident puddle of shit—you're fucked."

"You got immunity, huh? You got that in writing?"

He was quiet for a moment. "What do you mean? We have a deal."

"You think the FBI runs on handshakes? Did you think, while you were doing all your wheeling and dealing, what we could offer them?"

He burst into laughter. "What the hell could you offer them? They can't trace my shit. You're too loyal to roll on Adam, and they have him by the balls, anyway. He was arrested at the scene and has no alibi."

"You ever heard of Lucky Thirteen?" I asked.

Brandon hesitated. "W-what?"

"Lucky Thirteen. A little girl, at thirteen years old, was a poker phenom. She was playing all the Vegas greats and winning. She learned from her dad and spent her childhood around Vegas mafia. Knows about their dealings, how they work, who they're in business with. Kind of a little bad ass if you ask me."

"Your story time is boring me to death, Maddox."

"Her father was Mick Abernathy."

"So?"

I smiled, wishing I could see the look on his face. "Her name was Abby."

He was quiet again. "What is your point?"

"My point is … my wife is Lucky Thirteen. She has ties to the Vegas mafia. When the FBI found that out, they went from trying to put me away to begging to be my best friend. Tell me Brandon, who has the better connections? You can give them me. I can give them organized crime bosses."

"You … you're full of shit, Maddox," Brandon said, a tinge of panic in his voice. "One of us is going to prison, and it ain't me."

A door opened, and two cops walked through, followed by Thomas and Liis. They were wearing their suits, looking serious.

Brandon scrambled to his feet, gripping a bar in each hand. "What's this about?" he asked.

One officer opened my cell, and I walked through.

"You're free to go," the officer said.

"What?" Brandon asked. "What do you mean he's free to go? I'm the one with immunity!"

He tried to yank on the bars, getting nowhere. His eyes danced from me, to Thomas, to Liis, who had her federal badge hanging from a long thin chain on her neck.

Thomas patted me on the back. "Well done. Got everything we needed."

"Wait. Your brother's a … Wait a second!" Brandon cried.

I stepped toward Brandon, leaning in with a smirk. "It's not what you know, it's who you know, am I right?" I winked at him, and then followed the officers to the exit.

Thomas and Liis stopped there, and my brother shoved his hands in the pockets of his slacks. "We can't go out there like this. They'll ask questions."

"Understood," I said.

Thomas nodded to me. "Get that eye looked at."

"Copy that," I said, pushing out the door. My wife and family were waiting for me, smiling widely as I walked toward them.

Abby didn't wait for me to reach them. She ran to me and jumped, wrapping her legs around my middle, pressing her lips hard against mine.

"Happy Birthday!" She kissed me over and over, and then threw her arms around my neck, squeezing. "Oh my God, I was so afraid I wouldn't get to tell you that in person today. You okay?" she asked, leaning back to look me in the eyes.

"Brandon was a bigger fish to fry. I got him to admit to everything, and now I've got immunity."

"Really?" she cried.

I sat her on her feet. "Really. We're home free."

She hugged me again, and then my brothers surrounded us with linked arms like a solid, steadfast Maddox fortress.

"I'm not sure what's going on," Trenton said, "but it seems like you're in the clear."

"I am," I said, trying to keep Abby from getting squished as they hugged us tighter.

Abby looked up at me with tears in her eyes, and then hugged me again, curling her body into me.

"Let's go home," I said.

"You're my home," she said softly.

Her words melted me. She was referring to what I'd said to her the time she'd tried to leave me. Not too long ago, I'd begged for her on my knees, in front of everyone who was staring at us from inside the campus cafeteria, not giving two shits what any of them thought. Nothing and no one was more important to me than the woman looking down at me, tears in her eyes, unsure if she could trust me. Then, it didn't feel right spending a day without Abby Abernathy. Now, there was nothing I was more certain of than knowing I couldn't survive without Abby Maddox.

I cupped her jaw with my hands, kissing her like it was the first time. I was married to the love of my life. And, as cliché as it sounded, my best friend. We had the rest of our lives together, and we could finally enjoy our happy ever after.

"I can't believe I almost ruined this," I said. "What a fucking idiot."

Abby shook her head. "You can't ruin this. I can't ruin this. Because this… this is forever."

I looked around at my brothers, each one with their arms around their girl. I nodded my head in the direction of the parking lot. "Let's get the fuck outta here."

Trenton flipped off the police station as he turned, simultaneously squeezing Camille and pressing his cheek against her hair as they walked. Abby handed me the keys, and the doors unlocked with a click of a button. I opened the door for my wife, then waited as she slid into her seat. She giggled as I stole a kiss before closing her door, then I wasted no time jogging around to my side.

She sighed as I started the engine, her shoulders relaxed.

I put my hand on her thigh. "We're gonna be all right. All that bullshit is behind us now."

She put her hand on mine. "I know," she breathed.

"It's finally over. It's almost hard to believe. And I'm so proud of us, for so many reasons. But you know what I'm the proudest of? Even on our worst days, we never stopped loving each other."

I shook my head. "That day will never come for me, Pigeon."

She smiled. "No one could ever convince me otherwise; not even you. I keep thinking about the beginning, wondering why I fought this so hard. I had to dig really deep, and while you were sitting in that jail, I realized it was because I once thought that to have real, lasting love it had to be perfect. But what makes love last is to be brave enough to push through the challenges and trust that you'll come out stronger on the other end. I knew that no matter what happened in there … I don't know. I just had this peace come over me. I knew that whatever happened, we'd get through it. Because the beauty of it is being almost perfect."

"We're almost beautiful?" I asked.

She nodded her head.

I kissed her hand, and then watched as she smiled at me with all the emotions I'd worked so hard to see on her face. Love, contentment and calm swirled inside those familiar, insanely gorgeous gray eyes. "You'll never convince me that being with you is anything less than perfect, Pidge."

She rested her head on my shoulder and hugged my arm. I pulled out of the parking lot, following my brothers' vehicles out into the street. No one was in a hurry. Everyone was glad to be going home, and I brought up the rear, the last in a line of a Maddox caravan. A bunch of motherless boys, seemingly never getting it right, clueless when it comes to relationships, and yet sitting next to the women we loved, almost perfect, almost beautiful, and never happier.

EPILOGUE

Abby

I WALKED INSIDE MY FATHER-IN-LAW'S home with my best friend to immediately hear cheers from our family, including Shepley's parents, Jack and Deanna, America's parents, Mark and Pam, the Maddox wives, and one more special guest attending our college graduation party: Trenton's god daughter, Olive.

Trenton held her in his arms between him and Camile, grinning from ear to ear. Everyone was happy.

This was the way life was supposed to be and we had earned it.

Travis stood in front of me holding up a beer, and his brothers, dad, and uncle followed his lead.

"To the most beautiful graduates to ever walk across Eastern State's stage!" he yelled. "And Shepley."

Everyone laughed and then applauded, shouting in agreement.

Over the last two years, Travis and I had settled into a routine. Once he graduated, Travis began to travel more and I stayed behind, finishing my accounting degree, interning for the Becken & Stall Accounting firm.

We missed each other like crazy when he wasn't home, but we made it work. Surrounded by my family, I was exactly where I was always meant to be.

Travis helped me remove my graduation hat and then hugged me to his side and kissed my temple. He was all smiles and had been since he came home the week before.

When all the brothers were home, though, it just felt right, like we were complete, and my husband was nearly euphoric.

Everyone chatted, Shepley, America, and I opened our gifts, and then we all sat down at the table—and the sofa and an extra card table—to eat a late lunch that Liis and Falyn had prepared.

Travis absent-mindedly reached down to touch my knee as he teased Trenton and talked to the twins about their insurance business in Colorado.

"So, Abby … how would you feel about a rematch tonight?" Taylor asked.

"Poker? No," I said, shaking my head.

The table burst into laughter.

"You wouldn't beat her, anyway," Thomas said.

I remembered the first time I played in Jim's home, at that very table, surrounded by smoke and smiles.

Thomas had figured out my secret, watching me with curious eyes that never really stopped observing his surroundings.

Liis was the same way, and over the years, I began to pick up even more things about them. How similar they were, how they sometimes left the room to have private conversations with my husband.

Thomas and Travis had grown closer, and Liis seemed to be in on it.

I'd been trying to figure it out, but they all guarded their friendship. Not in a way that made me uncomfortable, rather … curious.

"So, sis," Jim said, dabbing his mouth with his napkin. "What's next?"

"Well," I said with a sigh, "Becken & Stall has offered me a position."

The table erupted. Travis beamed.

"And?" Falyn asked with a smile.

"And … I'm thinking about it."

"The money isn't good?" Camille asked.

"No … No, it's good. Really good. I just need to figure a few things out first."

"Such as?" Thomas asked.

I shifted in my seat.

Olive leaned too far in her chair and fell backward, immediately crying out for Trenton. He rushed over to help her up and right her chair, examining her sore elbow.

"Is she okay?" Jim asked.

Trenton lifted her into his arms, placing a gentle hand on the back of her head as she cried over his shoulder. "She's okay, aren't you, Ew? You're tough." He took her elbow and kissed it.

She sniffed and nodded as he wiped the tears from her cheeks.

"See? All better!" Camille said with a smile.

"Are you finished, Jim?" Liis asked, standing up to take his plate. He nodded and she gathered a few more dishes before heading to the kitchen sink.

"I'll help," I said, standing.

"Nope, you're the guest of honor," Jim said.

"I can't just sit here. Liis cooked!"

"Does that mean I have to help?" Ellie asked, serious.

"No, please don't," America teased.

I took more dishes and followed Liis to the next room, leaving the laughter of my family echoing behind me.

"Thomas seems really happy," I said, turning on the faucet.

Liis smiled, scraping leftovers into the garbage. "I think so."

"It's nice to see him and Travis getting so close."

Liis's smile faded for half a second, and then her eyes brightened. "It's pretty cute."

"Cute?" I said with a wry smile.

"What?"

"I don't know. You don't really say *cute*."

She shrugged. "Well, I don't think another word would suffice."

Liis's phone beeped, and she checked it. The smallest flicker of concern shadowed her face, and then she stepped away from the sink to make eye contact with Thomas, who looked up from checking his phone.

Travis was staring down at his, a frown on his face.

Liis put her phone away and continued rinsing dishes, and I gathered courage for what I would say next.

"Travis doesn't quite have his poker face down—not like you and Thomas."

Liis paused, the water still running over her hands. "What?"

The counter dug into my hip as I leaned against it. I crossed my arms. "C'mon Liis. You don't believe I'm that clueless. Travis comes home from conferences with a busted eyebrow and lip. Fading bruises on his jaw and cheekbones. Cut and swollen knuckles."

"Really? That's odd," Liis said, trying to seem busy again.

"You know what's really odd?" I asked, crossing my hands across my middle. "Last month when Travis was in Philly and I got in that fender bender? Kostas came to help, and while we were waiting for the police to take the photos, he got a text message. From you."

"Who?"

"Kostas," I said, watching the wheels turn behind her eyes. "He's always … around. But not. Almost like he keeps an eye on me for Travis when he's gone."

Liis grinned. "That's kind of sweet. I can see Travis doing that."

"Strange how he swooped in and bought Iron E from Becca, and then decided Travis was his go-to for conventions. And … he never goes."

"You think so?"

"You know who else calls Kostas sometimes? Val Taber."

"You're saying these names like I should know them."

"Liis," I said, lowering my voice. "When you and Thomas visited last Christmas, you left your badge on your belt. It was hidden by your blazer, but when you leaned in to hug Jim, the lights glinted off the metal."

She looked at me and chuckled. "Badge? What kind of badge?"

"Your federal badge."

She burst into laughter. "Abby! You crack me up!"

I narrowed my eyes at her. "Travis was just let off the hook because they wanted Brandon instead? You don't really think I'm that stupid. I know everything there is to know about Mick and Benny and his associates. Why haven't you asked me to help? Why Travis?"

"Abby …"

"I want my husband home. And you're going to help me."

She glanced over my shoulder, and then met my gaze. "Help with what?"

"I'm going to get intel on my father, and in turn on Benny, and help you wrap this up so I get my husband back. Whatever agreement you have with him for immunity, him fighting for Benny, it's going to stop."

"You can't be serious."

I closed my eyes. "Just … stop," I said, trying to stay calm. "Stop lying to me. Travis is forced to every time he leaves town. You're going to help me do this, or I'm going to blow your cover."

Liis leaned in. I'd finally gotten her attention. "Abby, you don't understand how dangerous that is. You could get Travis killed."

I sighed, finally hearing the truth. "I don't mean with Benny." I pointed with my thumb behind me. "Those boys made a promise to their dad not to go into law enforcement. I know it's important to Thomas to keep up the façade. You help me help Travis, and we can all keep pretending for Jim."

"That is a *bad* idea."

As tiny as Liis was, she could be intimidating when she wanted to, I'd give her that. But I wasn't backing down. It had taken me this long to figure it out and now that I had confirmation, I was going to convince her to help.

"This day will end in one of two ways. Either you and I have an understanding, or Thomas will have a lot of explaining to do. And when they find out he's recruited Travis against his will and forced him to lie to me …"

"Okay," Liis snapped. She took a deep breath and relaxed her shoulders. "Okay. But it's going to be a long conversation, a lot of planning, and … Jesus, I could lose my job over this."

I shot her a dubious look. "For me trying to repair my relationship with my father? Good luck to anyone trying to prove otherwise."

Liis shook her head. "Abby, this is extremely dangerous. Travis wouldn't want you getting involved."

"You're talking to me like these people didn't pop

in and out of my entire childhood. I know them better than anyone, and I know how to navigate the dark side of Vegas. This is what I know. You should've asked me in the first place. Travis wouldn't be trading punches for a living … or whatever the hell else you have him doing."

Liis thought about that. "You make a good point. But we're still going to strategize, think of every possible scenario."

"Deal," I said. "Thank you."

She closed her eyes and shook her head, frustrated. "Don't thank me for this. This is … Just don't thank me."

We finished the dishes in silence, and then Jim called us into the living room. He held two bottles of champagne, walking around as he filled everyone's cups.

I held up my hand. "I'm good, Dad, but thank you."

"You're not going to drink to your graduation?" Travis asked.

"I'm stuffed, and champagne will make it worse."

"You want something else?"

I glanced at the liquor cabinet, then shook my head. "I have water. I'm fine, but thank you, baby."

Jim held up his glass. "To my favorite nephew, Shepley and our darling America, my favorite niece—"

"Your only niece," she teased.

"And still our favorite," Jim said. "Shepley, you have always been the peacekeeper. Without you, I don't know where Travis would be. You've always understood him in ways no one else did. You're loyal, caring, and steadfast. You are good to your girl, to your friends, and family. You have become an outstanding man, and we couldn't be prouder.

"And America, you are the apple of Shepley's eye, you light up every room you walk into. You are a fierce protector of those you love. We love you both, and we're more than just lucky that Shep's brought you into our family. We're better for it."

"You're damn right," Jack said, raising his glass higher.

We all took a sip, and Jim held up his whiskey glass again. "And Abby … the Maddox family's first daughter. Our little ray of sunshine. The woman who is the glue that keeps us all together, organizes our holidays, and makes sure her old dad takes his vitamins. We love you, Abby, we're proud of you, and if my sweetheart were here, Diane would say … congratulations, our darling. You've outdone yourself."

"Here, here!" Travis said, lifting his glass higher.

Everyone took a sip, and then I raised my glass. "Jim, your words, as always, are perfection. Please allow me to add a bonus toast to my best friend."

"Bonus toast!" Trenton yelled.

I looked to America. "You came with me to Eastern State to keep me on the straight and narrow, and you shoved me at one-hundred miles per hour into Travis Maddox."

Thomas choked out a laugh, making the rest of the family burst into laughter.

Travis frowned. "Hey …"

"We've studied together, walked to class together,

eaten lunches and dinners and brunches together, we've happy-houred together, cried together, and fell in love together, and these last four years with you, and this family, have been the best of my life thus far. You're sharp as a tack, you're undeniably loyal, and you're going to be one hell of a teacher. Congratulations, my sweet, sweet friend. The world is most definitely better that you're in it."

America's eyes were filled with tears, and then she led everyone in taking another sip.

"And," I began again, "you'll all have to forgive me. I borrowed this next toast from my husband."

Everyone groaned, again moderately offending Travis.

"Hey!" he said.

"Please forgive me for the language, but …" I held up my glass. "To douchebags! And to girls who break your heart." I pressed my palm to my chest, looking apologetically at Travis. I could tell he was worried where this was going, so I allowed the tiniest of smiles to soften my expression. "And to the absolute fucking horror—when you loathe being the center of attention—of announcing to your entire family … that we're having a baby."

The room was silent, and then all eyes were on Travis, who was standing with a confused look on his face.

"We're … You're …" he stuttered.

I nodded, beaming. "I'm pregnant."

"You're …" His mouth fell open and he looked at all the faces of our family.

America gasped, holding her hand over her mouth.

Travis looked to me, tears in his eyes. "Pigeon …" he choked out. "I'm going to be a dad?"

Jim paused, the realization just hitting him, and then he began to wipe his eyes with his thumb and index finger. "I'm gonna have a grandbaby?"

Jack hugged him to his side. "Congratulations!"

I nodded again, feeling tears burn my eyes. "Two. Two grandbabies."

Everyone looked at me with confusion.

"We're …" I sighed, in disbelief myself. "We're having twins."

The family exploded into squeals, yelps, and applause. America screamed through her fingers.

Jim was laughing through his tears, elated.

"Two?" Travis asked, holding up his fingers. I nodded, and his bottom lip trembled. Then, he slowly lowered to his knees, hugging me at the waist.

I cradled Travis's head until he leaned back and kissed my stomach.

"Hey, babies," he said softly.

My lips pressed into a hard line and my face crumbled. I had seen Travis rage, fall in love, fear for our lives, worry, and I'd seen him at peace. Watching him as he realized he was going to be a father was absolutely my favorite.

He stood and cupped my jaw, kissing me over and over. I wiped the tears from his cheeks, and then he wiped mine before turning to his dad. "You're going to be a grandpa!"

"Hell yes I am!" Jim exalted, hugging us both.

The family cheered again, then took turns congratulating us. We hugged, and hugged, and hugged some more.

My sisters were crying, and then my brothers began to shed happy tears, too.

That moment was what I'd dreamed of my entire childhood. The love I felt from everyone in that room was my highest hope, and because I fell in love with an unpredictable, hot-tempered, tattooed ladies' man who no one could have imagined would've ever settled down, my life was more beautiful than even the most perfect wish I could've made.

ABOUT THE AUTHOR

Jamie McGuire is the #1 New York Times, USA Today, and Wall Street Journal bestselling author of Walking Disaster, the Maddox Brothers series, the Providence trilogy, and the international bestseller Beautiful Disaster, which paved the way for the new-adult genre. She was the first independent author in history to strike a print deal with retail giant Walmart, and her work has been translated into fifty languages. She lives in Tulsa, Oklahoma, with her three children. To learn more about Jamie, visit www.jamiemcguire.com.

ACKNOWLEDGMENTS

Thank you to my mother who has supported me in so many ways this year. You're selfless, patient, and taught me to be the strong, independent woman I am, and that I can face any challenge and come out on the other side stronger and wiser. Thank you for always being there for me;

To Jessica Landers, for everything. You run my businesses, my day-to-day, and you've literally saved my life this year—one of the most difficult years of my life—more than once. You never tire of my late night, tearful calls, and aren't afraid to demand that I not give up. You're compassionate, yet know when to issue tough love. There is not enough thank you's in the world to honor the kind of friend you've been to me. I'm here today because of you, and that is no small act of kindness;

To my Wednesday night besties, our weekly story times have gotten me through many dark moments this last year. I had no idea when I started a subscription service to read chapters of my book once a week that I'd develop lifelong friendships. Your support has been invaluable to me. I appreciate your love and understanding, your encouragement and advice.;

To Mark, my business partner, dear friend, and brother. Your advice and encouragement have been invaluable, thank you for always having my back;

To Hailey, you are the best daughter a mother could ask for. You are everything I've ever wanted to be, you inspire me daily, and you've supported me and held me through some very long nights. I love you more than I could ever say.

Made in the USA
Middletown, DE
04 April 2023

28251377R00231